PRAISE FOR KRISTIN BILLERBECK

Praise for *The View from Above*:
"Billerbeck's stories whisk me away to another place and leave me with a smile." Denise Hunter, Bestselling Author of the Bluebell Inn Series

Praise for *Room at the Top*:
"Billerbeck's best novel yet—smart and witty with wise insights about sisterhood and family." Colleen Coble, *USA Today* Bestselling Author

She's All That:
"Christian Chick Lit star Billerbeck has moved on from her popular Ashley Stockingdale trilogy with an engaging new novel that features struggling fashion designer Lilly Jacobs and her two best friends, Morgan and Poppy...Snappy dialogue and lovable characters make this novel a winner." —*Publisher's Weekly*

Perfectly Dateless:
"Christy Award finalist Billerbeck turns her talent for witty dialog to the YA market...(a) hilarious novel." —*Library Journal*

With this Ring, I'm Confused:
"Kristin Billerbeck has an innate talent to keep readers guessing. With this Ring, I'm Confused is packed to capacity with startling, dazzling humor that soothes the edges of life. I recommend it to anyone with stress. For that matter, I recommend it to anyone breathing. So much fun, you don't even see

the message until it hits you between the eyes." —Hannah Alexander, Author of the Hallowed Halls of Medicine Series

THE VIEW FROM ABOVE

A PACIFIC AVENUE NOVEL
BOOK TWO

KRISTIN BILLERBECK

CAMPENNI PRESS

Author Note

Trigger warning: This book deals with the aftermath of narcissistic abuse. Sadly, Christians are not immune from this type of abuse. If you or someone you know is experiencing abuse (even if you aren't sure), please reach out to a local hotline or (for US residents) the National Domestic Violence Hotline at 800-799-7233 or text START to 88788.

CHAPTER 1

*W*entworth Manor was alight with twinkling bulbs hung from the heavy wooden ceiling. The live band echoed through the ballroom and closed out their set with the old tune, "Celebration." After six hours of playing, the musicians lost their spark and droned on like a junior high school orchestra.

Quinn, my only full sister, finally put an end to our misery as she grabbed the microphone and silenced the band with her hand. "Thank you to everyone who came and supported my sisters and our new ventures," she squealed with the enthusiasm of a pop star. I had to give her credit; she could turn it on when necessary.

The band packed up their instruments as if she'd said, *On your mark, get set, go!* while the partygoers groaned that another Wentworth Manor soiree had come to an end.

Quinn cleared her throat and continued, "The San Francisco police force is asking us to put an end to the music tonight for the good of all the Pacific Heights neighborhood." She paused for another audible groan.

"We're all here!" someone yelled from the dance floor. "Let's party!"

Quinn used her charming giggle and fashion-model looks to overcome his pleas with a cursory coquettish glance. "Be that as it may, the band is played out, but we are definitely planning another gala after the house remodel. The Wentworth sisters are committed to our community and the charities of our choosing tonight."

A final round of applause echoed through the mahogany-lined ballroom, and in the silence, to our relief, people began to slowly take their leave.

Outside the sheltered walls, San Francisco was a mess. Homeless camps everywhere, crime on the rise, but to Quinn's audience, none of those realities registered. Our guests were the privileged few and whether I liked it or not, I was one of them.

As the last guest straggled out, four of our five sisters communed in the floral room. This room had the distinction of being the only bright room in the mansion besides our individual bedrooms. The mansion's complete overhaul was scheduled for the following Monday—an event long overdue if we ever hoped to unload the mausoleum and get on with our lives.

I, for one, couldn't wait to escape back to SoCal to finish my education in finance. San Francisco only reminded me of my lost ballet career and my parents. Neither one of which seemed able to tolerate me. Wentworth Manor, the mansion we'd inherited after our grandfather's death, was symbolic of everything that was my life at home: *dark, foreboding and lonely.*

I was only back for the year, which was required in the will if we were to inherit his billions. Five sisters with three separate mothers and one randy father. Somehow, Grandfather expected us to make a family out of this mess and we were stuck here for a year.

I kicked off my shoes and tucked my feet under me on the sofa. I'd become very self-conscious about my feet, as a ballerina's toes are anything but elegant. No pedicure on the planet was capable of fixing the damage done. And in fact, I'd never subject any poor pedicurist to the task. "Well, thank goodness that's over," I said to my sisters.

"I think it went over phenomenally," Quinn, my only full-blooded sister and our natural leader, said. "Everyone had so much fun, I don't even think the scandal touched us tonight."

I couldn't take her enthusiasm at the moment. I untucked my feet and rose. "Excuse me a minute." I padded to the restroom in the main foyer and the door opened abruptly. A man I'd never seen before stepped out. I knew this because he wasn't the kind of specimen one forgot.

My eyes climbed to his crown of thick dark hair and rested upon his steely gray-green eyes. He was possibly the most attractive man I'd ever seen in person, and I lived in LA. Tall, with an aristocratic air, he wore his tuxedo as if it belonged to someone else. Clearly, he wasn't a man who dressed up often, and the stubble on his chin showed how little effort he'd taken to dress for the gala.

"Brinn." His voice was deeper than I expected, and it unnerved me.

"Who are you exactly?" I asked with my gaze narrowed. "How do you know my name?"

"I'm at your gala," he chuckled. "Why wouldn't I know who you are? As if the weekly society page hasn't told me my whole adult life what you're up to."

"You don't look like the type who reads the society page. Who are you here with?" I searched the room.

"My date." He looked around at the empty foyer. "I seem to have misplaced her."

"Well, do you have your keys?"

He reached into his pocket and produced a valet ticket. "I have my ticket."

"Your date appears to have left. You'd better get to your car before the valets leave for the night. I'd hate to have you out on the driveway all night."

He nodded, shoved the ticket back in his chest pocket and strode to the front doors. Security opened the door for him, but he looked back at me, the gray-green of his eyes as sultry from the distance as they were up close. "Lovely party, Brinn," he said as he exited. I stood outside the powder room, confused.

There were five of us Wentworth sisters. People rarely could tell us apart. Even though my sister Quinn looked nothing like me, we were both blonde and got called each other's name daily. Quinn was prettier . . . thinner, but strangers rarely noticed.

"Do you know who that was?" I asked the security guard at the door.

"No, miss."

"Is Joel here?" I asked him. Joel was my sister Sophia's boyfriend. Originally our bodyguard, despite a broken leg, he still managed the family security team.

"No, miss. He went with Miss Sophia to her grandparents'. I don't think they'll be back this evening."

"Please have your security detail run a check on all the rooms in the house. Make sure everyone is gone."

"Yes, miss."

"And don't forget the underground level."

The guard snapped his fingers and a few men spurred into action. "No, miss."

I walked back to the floral room, unnerved by my encounter, not because I felt frightened, but because it seemed like the guest with no name had stepped out of a time machine. He belonged in an era closer to when the mansion was built. Though his tuxedo didn't fit him, it did nothing to diminish his dignified appearance.

Quinn was still babbling when I entered the floral room. "Our charities have been announced and we successfully skirted the controversy that is my mother. I'd call that a successful night."

"If you say so." I plopped onto the sofa. "Sit down, Quinn, we're not your constituents, we're your sisters. You did an amazing job hosting, but it's over."

I didn't feel Quinn's triumph. Our mother was still on house arrest for the murder of our grandfather—the reason there was an inheritance—while our father showed up uninvited and chased the twins' mom, Mary (his first love), about like a lovestruck teenager. *Humiliating.*

My grandfather's death had ushered in the immediate requirements of his will and pulled Quinn, me and our recently discovered sisters into the nightmare I knew as Wentworth Manor. It only proved Wyatt Wentworth, a scion of industry, was savage from beyond the grave. An overdose may have sent him to heaven early, but he continued to taunt my parents from his new mansion in the sky, having bypassed them in his will.

"You're such a pessimist, Brinn. The rumor mill was utterly silent tonight."

"It only means they talked about us before they got here and ate our food," Gia, the mouthiest of our half-sisters, said. "If they were hoping for a catfight between sisters, they were sorely disappointed though."

We may have had three separate moms, but the jealousy everyone expected never happened. Once our stepsisters saw that our father was no better to us than the daughters he abandoned, the light of reality shone upon us.

Quinn stood again and pranced across the heritage hardwood floors as she lifted her skirt. "I could have danced all night," she said as she rose to her toes as if in pointe shoes. Her form was terrible, but that was always Quinn's issue with dance. She couldn't have cared less about ballet. If an activity didn't support her getting to the stables and riding her horse, her focus waned.

She'd been a better dancer than me by nature, but I trained ruthlessly until I rose to prima ballerina, only to have my body quit on me at the ripe age of twenty-three. The irony being that Quinn could still dance, while I could only sit on the sidelines and critique her form.

While Quinn was the picture of sun-kissed health, I was riddled with arthritis, my muscles had started wasting away from constant dieting to stay under one hundred pounds, and the *coup de grace*, I shattered my ankle into a million pieces and now relied on a metal one.

Gia clapped along to the silent music in Quinn's head. "That's so beautiful. Honestly, Quinn you move like a gazelle. You're so elegant all the time. I always wanted to learn ballet."

I kept my professional opinion to myself.

"You should totally learn it, Gia. What's stopping you? Brinn could teach you."

I grimaced.

"You could," Quinn said.

"I think she'd be better off with a real teacher," I said. "But Gia, you should take ballet, why not? It's never too late."

Mary, the twins' mother, agreed. "I love that idea! You've always moved so gracefully. I always saw you as a ballerina."

Mary fascinated me to the point that it felt creepy in the way that I watched her. She mystified me because I'd never met anyone like her. She'd had Gia and Sophia straight out of high school and hadn't ever married—even though she cooked, attracted men like bees to honey and didn't look a day over thirty. I couldn't fathom what kept her single and satisfied. I wanted whatever it was for myself. One thing was certain, she'd dodged a bullet in my father.

I wished I knew her well enough to ask her secret. Marriage was not going to work for me and instinctively, I knew this fact as well as I knew first position in ballet. Wentworth marriages were cursed, and I intended to break the chains that bound us by never getting married.

"I'm hungry . . . is there food?" Alisa, the youngest sister at twenty, moaned out loud from the sofa, where she slept curled up in a ball. The evening had worn her down; the light she emanated like pixie dust finally extinguished.

Only Gia's twin, Sophia, was missing from our afterparty gathering. Sophia, apart from looks, was nothing like her twin. Mostly, she was a quiet, now-unemployed social worker until someone needed defending. Then nothing could shut her up.

Mrs. Chen, the house manager, brought decaf coffee in a silver decanter along with cream and sugar and placed the leftover truffles on the heavy glass coffee table. It was just what we all needed, a little sugar high and respite from the crowd.

Although I'd been born into the spotlight, I abhorred parties filled with small talk and mean-spirited gossip. The only time I felt comfortable with an audience was when I danced. Ballet was its own world, and I was transported by the movement. Now I was left to deal only in reality.

"Thank you, Mrs. Chen," Mary said. "This looks delightful."

Mary appreciated everything fully. I silently added that characteristic to my list of things I wanted to emulate about her.

Mrs. Chen disappeared in her ghostlike way but returned shortly. "Ladies, you have a visitor."

"It's 2:30 in the morning, Mrs. Chen. Tell them to come back tomorrow," Quinn said.

"It *is* tomorrow." Mona Whitman entered the room as if she owned it and my stomach pirouetted.

"Grandmother?" Quinn was as shocked as me. "What are you doing in San Francisco?"

My heart thumped wildly at the sight of my maternal grandmother. The old woman never changed. Skeletal with crepey skin that wrinkled and gathered like a well-worn ballet slipper, she walked toward us like a drunken marionette, as if her scrawny legs could barely hold her.

"Is that any way to welcome your grandmother?" Mona pointed her long bony finger. "Neither one of you invited me to the gala."

"You were in Paris," Quinn said as she kissed both of the old woman's cheeks. Grandmother motioned for me to come and do the same and I did.

"Italy, actually," Mona said. "Northern Italy by the border with Switzerland. In the mountains. It's lovely this time of year. Absolutely fabulous and brisk. Just the way I like it." Grandmother said this for the benefit of the room—as was her way. While I despised an audience, my grandmother assumed any crowd gathered was there for the sole purpose of listening to her speak.

"Grandmother," Quinn interrupted, unsurprisingly without consequences, "let me introduce you to—"

"These are your partial sisters, I assume." She walked over to the spring-colored sofas and brushed past them in her stilted, atrophied gait like a zombie coming at them.

"This is Gia," I said. "And her mother, Mary." Both women stood to greet our maternal matriarch. I hoped Mona's skill at practiced politeness would win out over her disdain for Mary, who she saw as my mother's one-time rival for our father's affections.

After all, there'd been no real rivalry. Mary was simply his baby mama in Mona's eyes, a cheap thrill while he sowed his wild oats in high school. I wondered what Mona would say if she'd known Bradley (our father) said that Mary was the one true love of his life—a painful truth no one wants to hear about a woman who is not their mother.

Mona stood before Gia and Mary as my mind wandered. "I'm sorry, I lost my train of thought. Gia has a twin named Sophia, but she's off with her new beau." I didn't mention that

8

Joel, the new boyfriend, had been Quinn's fake fiancé for the media's false trail. In no time, Mona would be off to jet set into the wild blue yonder and once again, forget her granddaughters existed. Details hardly mattered.

"Charmed," Mona said to Mary as she put the tips of her fingers out to be grasped or kissed.

"They're Italian," Quinn said to force a connection between them.

"Southern Italian, I'm assuming?" Mona asked Mary.

I don't know if that's a dig, but it certainly feels like one.

"Campania," Mary said without inflection or attitude. She seemed too pure to be real.

"Hmph," Mona sniffed.

I'd only been to Rome, so I hadn't any idea what they were discussing. "What are you doing here, Grandmother?" I asked. "You're too late for the party."

"Well, I tried to make it for the gala obviously, but my plane was stalled in New Jersey. I spent the entire day looking at New York City from the Jersey airport."

"These things happen. Now we'll have more time to focus on you," I told her. Quinn scowled at me, but it wasn't like we had family to spare.

Mona twisted a giant blue sapphire ring in the light as she spoke. "I was most interested in what charities you've chosen for your foundations. Inheriting that kind of money comes with enormous responsibility."

"I thought you might be here for Mother," I said. "She could sure use the visit and some encouragement."

Mona's eyes flashed. "Tell me about this lovely soiree, darling. Who wore the prettiest gown? Are there pictures yet? Oh, this house may be weathered, but it will look so grand in the photos. The workmanship on the staircase alone is a lost art." She kissed her gathered fingers like a chef discussing the perfect meal.

9

"I think Mary had the prettiest gown," Quinn said, as if only to antagonize our grandmother. "She looks as if she's stepped back into Queen Victoria's court, don't you agree?" Quinn pointed out Mary's pale pink gown that hugged her petite body like a custom sheath and was the picture of femininity.

"I meant among the youth," Grandmother sniped. "Who was here?"

"Everyone," Quinn said.

"Was Evie Thorne here?"

Evie Thorne was not youth. She had to be sixty at the very least. "She was. Her daughter Vivien did the chocolate fountain."

"She must have loved that," Mona said sarcastically. "I don't know what it is about the young of today that they feel the need to work like the common man. Inheriting money is a lost art. Someone must keep society running and look after the poor. There is no shame in that."

Mary and Gia both shifted in their chairs. "If you'll excuse me." Mary stood, and my grandmother took in her lithe, curvaceous form in all its glory. Though Grandmother had blue eyes, I would have sworn they violently twisted into green. One would never know that Mary had two children who were thirty. She appeared younger than that herself and knowing how she cooked, it was unreal how tiny she was. *Ballet would have been so easy if I were gifted with that frame.*

My grandmother sniffed, the sin of envy everywhere on her person. It emanated off of her like a cloud of gaseous vapor.

"People were very polite about Mother," I said. "No one brought her or the case up. It was an evening to celebrate the future and that's precisely what we did."

"My daughter has been falsely accused," Mona said directly to Mary. "But you know how the world enjoys *schadenfreude* with the wealthy."

Mary smiled gently. "The girls were incredible hostesses.

You'd never know the stress they're under. They've done the Wentworth name proud."

Mona's chin raised. "Chelsea was at this event, regardless. My daughter has that effect on people. I guarantee that her presence was missed," Mona said in a rare positive moment regarding our mother.

One thing was certain. Our mother's presence certainly wasn't missed by our father.

CHAPTER 2

I wasn't off to a great start to the new and improved Brinn Wentworth. I already had one huge regret. At our party, I'd proudly announced domestic violence as my philanthropy pursuit—not knowing a thing about the subject. I'd been completely ignorant but acted like some kind of heroine ready to save all womankind at the party. Now reality struck, and it wasn't pretty.

Sophia, my new sister and former social worker, graciously hooked me up with a former business connection who worked in the spousal abuse arena. Monday morning, I stuffed a manila envelope (that contained nothing) into a navy Prada briefcase, which I borrowed from my mother's closet, and walked into the building of Garrick Kane & Associates alongside Sophia. The company, a security provider for the elite, did pro bono work on the side with abuse victims.

As we walked in, I realized there had to be good money in security because it was on the top floor of a high rise in the financial district. A penthouse suite usually reserved for the highest-paid investment bankers.

After exiting the gold-laden elevator into an empty foyer of mirrors, we were mysteriously buzzed in behind bullet-proof glass casing.

"Sophia, sheesh, what is this place? I feel like I'm in a spy movie. If he has a shark tank in there, I'm out."

Sophia laughed. "And you say Alisa is the one with the imagination. I think this appeals to men who imagine themselves in need of stealth security." She got closer and whispered. "All men secretly want to be Bond, so Garrick gives them what they want."

"Garrick sounds like a—"

"Shh!" Sophia put her finger in front of her lips. "You need his help, remember? Try a little humility."

Once in the office, I straightened my briefcase over my shoulder. Unlike the ominous foyer, the office was like any open concept place of business. Metal desks and low-walled partitions gave a 1950s vibe to the room, but it was all designed to fit in with the classic Bond vibe.

Sophia walked in like she was running for office. "Hey, everyone! I'm back. Did you think you got rid of me?" I followed behind her closely. She knew everyone's name and shouted it out at the top of her voice.

"Are you running for Senate?" I asked her. "Slow down."

"Sophia, you back at the Center?" a young woman asked her as we inched closer to the door we needed.

"Nope, still not working," she shrugged. "This is my sister, Brinn Wentworth. She's doing a project so we're here to pick Garrick's brain."

"Awesome." The woman smiled at me. "Welcome. I recognize you from the newspaper, of course. You used to dance, right?"

I smiled and nodded without saying a word and followed Sophia to the closed door in the back where the black and white nameplate read "Garrick Kane." She knocked quietly and my heart began to pound. I realized my ignorance for a subject that I had no connection to was about to rise to the surface—a very public surface. "Maybe I should come out and change my charity. This is a mistake."

"No, you can learn. This is such an important cause. I assume you selected it for some reason."

"This man is going to eviscerate me with my ignorance. What if he goes to the press?"

"With what? Brinn, no one expects you to be an expert. That's why we're here."

"Come in," a deep voice called back, and my heartbeat quickened. "Let's go home. I'll do something with the ballet. This was a mistake."

Sophia paid no mind to me and entered the private office, which was in stark contrast to the rest of the office. It had sleek cream walls and a clean, streamlined dark wood table as a desk that was covered with files, paperwork and empty coffee cups. Ancient metal filing cabinets lined the wall behind him, the top drawers open and overflowing with more paperwork. Another stark contrast—he had work to do, unlike my single empty manila folder in my mom's briefcase.

Mr. Kane had taken great pains to ignore any design efforts out front. I assumed he did things the way he'd always done them. His back was to us, and he held up his forefinger to let us know he'd be with us shortly. I took in the mess and had to force myself not to clean it up.

"That's no excuse." He didn't shout, but his voice held authority. "I want him off the case and we'll pull him in for a full review. Until then, get him off the street." He paused. "No, there's no excuse to leave a client unprotected, none. Call me back when it's done." He set the phone down gently and turned toward us.

I gulped audibly as he faced us. It was the man from the gala who'd lost his date, which couldn't have been a true story. No woman would lose a date that looked like him. That morning, I'd pictured Garrick Kane as a doddering, grandfatherly sage type. Instead, he was young and resembled a film noir gumshoe detective with suspicious, sexy eyes.

He could have pulled off a fedora without looking like a hipster code monkey in Silicon Valley. If he had, I might have searched for the Maltese Falcon on his messy desk. In essence, he was a man's man, and it wouldn't be long before he understood my ignorance on the topic of domestic violence. Garrick didn't seem the type to suffer fools gently and suddenly, all the confidence I'd gained after escaping to Southern California abandoned me.

He rose from his chair and hugged Sophia. "Sophia, I've missed you. I haven't seen you since you became an heiress."

Which means he hadn't seen her at the gala.

"Not since I got fired," she laughed.

"What's it like living in that famous mansion?"

"Living in the mansion feels the same as living in my papa's house, only I get lost more often and the food isn't as good."

He grinned. "How Joel got you, I'll never understand. Is there something in the water over in that manor of yours? Maybe I should come drink some."

"It's not in the bathroom," I said.

"What?" Sophia gave me an awkward look. "You should definitely come check out the house. I've got four single sisters, you know. Well, three," Sophia laughed. "One is too young for you."

"As a confirmed bachelor, I wouldn't dare enter such a danger zone, not for the water and certainly not for the temptation. A man has to know his limits."

"So that wasn't you at the gala then?" I asked him.

"The gala?" He played dumb and I was intrigued.

"How rude I've been. Let me introduce you two. Garrick Kane, this is my new-to-me, incredibly stunning sister, Brinn Wentworth. She's a former professional ballerina—a prima ballerina at that," She grabbed onto Garrick's wrist. "I just learned that means she dances the lead, so I wanted to show off my knowledge. Also, her awesomeness, I suppose."

"Impressive," he said to both of us—as if giving me a direct compliment might harm his ego. Watching him, I had to remind myself of my therapist's words that physical attraction was only a chemically induced reaction. *It means nothing.*

"She not only looks like this," Sophia went on flattering me in the most awkward way, "but she's brilliant too. She was in school getting her master's in finance so she can handle the family money for the rest of us, and I know she's going to be such a solid asset to your foundation."

"Is that so?" He looked me up and down, not with the same kindness he'd offered to Sophia, but with more distrust. His nature seemed stoic, slightly judgmental and cold.

In short, he felt like the younger, strikingly handsome version of my maternal grandmother and for that reason, I saw him as the dangerous entity he was. The hot factor could only add to his ability to do significant emotional damage to those around him. It didn't help that he didn't come clean about being in the manor that night. My walls were up and I thought about all the ways I could get out of this charity and find a new one that suited me.

"I think Sophia has painted a slightly rosy picture of me," I said. "I'm getting my master's degree because I can no longer dance, and I miss the structure." I closed my eyes. *Could I sound any more mundane?* Every time I spoke to a man I found attractive, it was as if I went out of my way to turn them off. Garrick's expression confirmed this.

"Brinn, it's a pleasure to meet you." He reached out his hand —as big as a baseball mitt—and shook mine with a sobering half smile. He knew how handsome he was and that annoyed me.

Sophia went on in her prattling way when she supported someone. "Listen, even though we've inherited the Wentworth fortune, I'm telling you, Garrick, the real treasure has come from finding my sisters. They are so amazing, and it's like we've known each other our whole lives."

He didn't reply and the silence extended to an unnatural length. I couldn't blame him. Sophia sounded slightly like a cult member. I had no doubt she believed what she was saying, but her zeal was over the top.

Sophia filled in the quiet. "Garrick, I'm not going to beat around the bush. This is why we're here. We're all doing some kind of charity work with our portion of that outrageous amount of money, and Brinn wants to take on the very serious issue of domestic violence." Sophia looked over at me. "Isn't she just the best?"

He said nothing.

"Naturally, you were the first person I thought of. Your organization has done so much for the city of San Francisco, and it felt like a logical connection. So here I am, connecting you two. I feel like with the two of you working together, domestic violence is going to take a hard hit—oh," She cringed. "I didn't mean that as a bad pun." She looked at me. "That was bad. I didn't mean that the way it came out—"

Garrick crossed his arms across his broad chest and addressed Sophia as if I wasn't standing there. After an eternity, he finally looked at me. "Why would a prima ballerina want to take on domestic violence as a cause?"

I stalled for a moment. "Because it's a serious issue in our city. I want to help women who may be stuck in terrible situations due to finances. The cost of living here has gone through the roof, and I can't think of anything worse than being stuck somewhere with someone who harmed me."

He stared down at me with his steely gray-green eyes, and I felt the weight of their intensity upon me. "You do realize that money is often a symptom of a much bigger problem. Many women offered the money to get out of their situation may not take it."

I didn't realize that, but I nodded.

"Domestic violence goes much deeper than throwing money at the issue. Often the real prison is in their heads after years of emotional abuse and even if you open the cage, they won't walk out."

I stammered and couldn't find the words. He seemed to have the same ability as my mother to shut me down with one stringent glance. "Well—I—"

"Miss Wentworth, have you ever met with a woman who was a victim of domestic violence before?"

"Well, no, but—"

He grinned in his belittling manner. "I bet you have; you simply didn't recognize it. Our foundation would love to have you partner with us financially—"

"No, you don't understand, Mr. Kane. The legacy of charity within the Wentworth family is hands-on. Anyone could write a check, but I want to get down and dirty with my philanthropy. I—"

"Write a check, Miss Wentworth. Truly, that's the best use of your skills in this arena. Write a check to our organization and I'll be sure it gets to the proper channels and saves as many women as possible. This is dangerous work. It would be irresponsible of me to involve you."

"I realize I'm not going to barge into an abuser's house, like Sophia here."

"I was fired for doing that," Sophia said. "Also, I got kicked by that meathead, remember?"

I gave her a scathing look.

"It's generous and thoughtful of you to have come here today," he said by way of offering me a breadcrumb of his humanity. "All of us at the foundation are grateful to Sophia for introducing us."

His condescension strengthened my resolve. "Mr. Kane, I don't think you understand me. I don't want to donate money to a cause. I want to further the support of victims and make a significant dent in lowering domestic violence in this city. I don't do things halfway and I won't know how to help without getting involved." I didn't know where all this was coming from, but his rejection fired me up.

"I'm sure that's true. You don't seem like you give up easily."

"It's not anyone's calling here on earth to be someone's victim." I stared at him expectantly.

"Forgive me, Miss Wentworth, I don't mean to be rude, but how is it you can be of help if it's not simply financial? Why don't you enlighten me?"

"I'll have to learn, I suppose." I shrugged.

He breathed in deeply and exhaled with force. "I don't have the resources for that."

"*I* have the resources to get any training I need. Tell me who to see."

He drummed his fingers on his desk.

"I plan to build a safe house. I can't do that without researching what goes into making a safe house. Sophia helped me find a property in the Haight that would be perfect."

"That sounds like an excellent project for you, but you don't need my help for that. I can let you know who to talk to for the design that works best for a safe house."

"Mr. Kane, my family has been donating large sums of money since before either of us was born. We're unmatched in the percentage that goes directly to the charity. That doesn't happen by writing a check."

"We obviously can't publicize these locations or call too much attention to the organization. Your presence creates interest and with that, press. Everyone and their brother will know where this so-called safe house is located."

"Mr. Kane, the press has made my life a living misery. I'd never—"

"Did you know that you were followed here today by them?"

I looked at Sophia for help, but she clammed up all of a sudden.

"No," I admitted sheepishly.

Garrick pressed a few buttons on his computer and turned the screen toward us. Sure enough, there was a photographer across the street when we'd entered the building.

"It's very important for the protection of women and children in these situations that safe houses and our tactics are kept secret at all times. That's impossible with you by virtue of who you are."

"So you're going to send me away when my money could help thousands? I thought you wanted to help victims."

"Miss Wentworth, if I were so inclined, I could probably find out from the *San Francisco Chronicle* what type of handbag you're carrying to see me today."

I looked down at my bag. "Chanel, for the record." I turned. "Prada briefcase, but it's my mother's."

Sophia laughed. "Those bags cost more than my mother's car."

I gnawed at my lip as Sophia said this—I knew she only wanted to lighten the mood, but it made me feel more shallow and ignorant than I already did.

Garrick sat down on the corner of his desk, crossing his long legs at the ankles. "You must realize that your public lifestyle does not afford the kind of anonymity our clients need. Your kind of notoriety is dangerous unless you'd want to use it for fundraising purposes. We have a dummy foundation that fronts our financial donations and keeps our partnership silent."

"I'll be the epitome of discretion."

"You announced your plans at a gala this weekend. It was all over the newspaper."

"I can assure you—"

He interrupted. "The only reason Sophia knows what we do

here is because she worked at the community center and sent us referrals."

His dismissal of me as a shallow socialite only irritated me more. Even if it was true, I was determined to prove him wrong. "Mr. Kane, I'm not doing this for publicity. My mother is currently on trial for possibly murdering my grandfather. The last thing I want to do is garner attention for myself."

"So you do have a personal connection to domestic violence."

"What? No, it's all a misunder—"

"I think what Brinn is trying to say," Sophia interjected to calm the rising tensions, "is that she wants to be involved on more than a financial level."

He narrowed his eyes and looked straight at me. "Why?" He sat down at his desk. "Why domestic violence?"

"Because things are not always as they seem. No one knows what really goes on inside a family system, not unless they live in it."

"Sometimes, not even then," Mr. Kane replied cryptically. "Often the abuse is so devious the family doesn't know they're abused. Not until they get out and are treated consistently with kindness and compassion."

I felt trapped, as if Garrick Kane knew every secret I'd ever kept and I'd been stripped of any covering I wore. Shame gripped me as if he'd seen inside my soul. Like he knew how my mother—and grandmother—felt about me. That I was the child destined for the "disappointments room" in the mansion. I knew instinctively that he understood Mother considered me her cross to bear as I was so hideous compared to her beloved Quinn.

"We should leave," I said to Sophia, but I stayed transfixed by Garrick's penetrating gaze. I crossed my own legs at the ankles like my mother told me to do so he wouldn't notice my "cankles."

"I'm not a foolish man, Miss Wentworth. I know how these things work and what's expected of me in my indebtedness for your generosity. Any nonprofit would be grateful to have you on board."

"Any nonprofit but yours. Is that what you mean to say to me?"

Sophia's eyes were wide, but she kept any opinion she had to herself.

"This is delicate work," Mr. Kane said. "No offense, but unless you'd be interested in teaching the children ballet offsite, I fail to see how your skillset will help."

I wilted in my chair, but I had to state my piece before I left. "Don't believe everything you read. I can assure you I hate the spotlight."

"You were a prima ballerina," he said with a laugh.

"That's not about attention. That's about art. When I dance, I disappear. I take flight and escape to an enchanted world—like a child disappears into Narnia by walking into the wardrobe." I'd gone to that magical place in my head as I spoke of it and grieved the reality that I'd never be there again.

He sat behind his great desk now, his expression confused by my virtual trip to la-la land. I needed to recover some semblance of normalcy, but I knew I'd choke on any word I spoke.

I stood. "Let's go, Sophia." I took one last look at the man who refused my money. "Mr. Kane, I realize that you don't know me from Adam, but you're making a mistake by underestimating me."

He cleared his throat. "Maybe, but I fail to see how teaching our clients the proper place for a shrimp fork is helpful to our organization."

I ignored his not-so-subtle dig. I put my hand on the doorknob as I shook at his rejection. "Let me ask you one thing, Mr.

Kane. Doesn't your superior attitude remind women of the life they're trying to escape?"

He rubbed his forehead as if I'd given him a headache, but I'd clearly hit a nerve. "One societal ill," I said. "If you could solve only one in domestic violence, what would it be?"

"I'd overhaul the court system so abusers couldn't manipulate the system to harm their families further." His answer burst forth like an explosion.

"I—I didn't know that happened."

"Court is the perfect stage for an abuser." Garrick looked me in the eye and for once, he wasn't talking at me, but to me. I softened like butter in the sunshine.

"Justice," I said quietly.

"Justice is very limited in the abuse game." He dropped his head. "Almost nonexistent." He looked back up and I saw the pain behind his eyes. "You're innocent, Brinn. Do yourself a favor and stay that way. Go find a charity that won't wreck your soul."

"I'm not innocent. My grandfather was murdered." Now it was me who looked down. "I don't know that he'll ever get justice. I don't know that they have the right suspect, but my grandfather would never give up on me. Therefore, I can't give up on him."

Garrick leaned toward me over his desk. "You don't think your mother did it."

I looked to Sophia shamefully and then back at him. "I don't know."

Both he and Sophia seemed disappointed by my answer.

"You're so young," Garrick said. "If you get involved, you might never get married or have a family of your own. I don't want that on my shoulders. Working with abuse victims changes you."

"So that's why you're a confirmed bachelor," Sophia interjected.

"I'm not ever getting married so it's not an issue." I straightened my shoulders to show my resolve.

He scoffed. "You'll get married and it's an issue for me."

"Marriages in my family are cursed. I'm breaking the curse by not getting married."

"With what, a magic spell?"

"Why is it so hard to believe I don't want to be married? Not all women have some kind of Cinderella complex, and I can buy my own glass slipper."

"Understood, but go find a public charity. One that can use your star quality."

I was fired up now. "You don't think it's a bit misogynistic to consider me too weak to do this work without seeing how I do first? I mean, there are women in combat." *I grew up in a combat zone, so I fail to see how this would be different.*

"Because I don't want a young, beautiful woman to hate all men because of what she sees in my foundation. I don't want to be responsible for that. There are good men out there."

"I'm a grown woman. I'm not your responsibility." I couldn't believe I was begging this man to take my money. *What the heck is wrong with him? Besides his obvious arrogance.*

"You don't even want the old Victorian in the Haight. With some sprucing up, it would be the perfect safe house."

He sighed. "No offense, Brinn, but if you want to renovate a house, call HGTV. The women who come to us are in danger and your being involved will only bring attention to their plight in the wrong way. If you'll excuse me—"

He made a motion for us to leave, but some unseen force held my feet to the industrial carpet. "This is important to me." And surprisingly, it was.

Sophia broke in. "Brinn, can you wait outside for me? I'd like to discuss something with Mr. Kane privately."

"Gladly," I said as I snatched up my handbag and fake briefcase. I sat outside the office, clutching the bags to my chest. Their conversation was easily overheard.

"Let her talk to one of your graduates from the program," Sophia said. "One of your speakers maybe. You're seriously going to let her walk out of here and thumb your nose at her money and time because she's famous."

"Sophia—you know that's not the only reason. Besides, she's not famous. She's infamous. Your new family is in the paper every day."

"She's lost dance and now her graduate program in finance because of these stupid will stipulations. If she were poor, wouldn't you have mercy on her for being stuck? She's trapped, Garrick. Isn't that your specialty?"

"She's only trapped for a time and then she can literally do whatever she wants to in life. I don't want to be some poor little rich girl's pet project."

"Garrick, you're better than this. I'm asking you to help my sister, as you would any client. You know that proverbial cage in a victim's head you're always talking about?"

"Money doesn't solve everything, Sophia. You know that as well as I do. Abuse straddles economic lines."

"Brinn's money didn't bring her here. I don't even know if she knows why she's here."

A long pause ensued, and I waited to hear why they both thought I was here. *Maybe they can tell me.*

"Are you going to tell me why she's here?" Mr. Kane asked.

"No, it's not my place."

"Sophia, you know she'll hate men—"

"You might be surprised. Her abusers are women, so we'll see about that."

I felt her accusation in my gut. *My abusers?*

"My gut says this is a bad idea. Why can't she go volunteer at the ballet or something? What is it she said? She takes flight there? She has no place in this underbelly of the city. She should be sipping cocktails on a yacht somewhere."

"Call Mrs. Donley and get her to meet with Brinn. The two of them will make magic out of that money and you don't even have to know she's involved."

"The work will corrupt her," he said.

"You're usually so insightful, Garrick. You're wrong about her. After your history, I'd think you'd understand. That you'd want to help her after your own childhood."

"You're just what the world needs—a pushy social worker with more money than Moses."

"Isn't it so cool?" The door opened but quickly shut again. "Garrick, you two have a lot more in common than you think."

"All right, I relent. I'll let her meet with a client, but if she flinches at the first sign of reality, she's done."

Sophia laughed. "Garrick Kane, you're the only man I know who puts so many rules on accepting free money, but fine, I'm sure she'll agree to that."

The door opened again, and Sophia came out to the chair where I sat.

Mr. Kane came out of his office with his long fingers wrapped around the door. "Brinn!" He held several books in his hands and a few pamphlets. "Read these. Abuse doesn't only mean someone gets hit. There's financial abuse, psychological abuse, maltreatment, neglect, trauma and more. Come back to me when you understand trauma-bonding and Complex PTSD."

I took the articles from him. "You won't regret this."

"I already do," he said with his left brow raised. Garrick Kane smiled authentically for the first time, and the action melted away my anger. I didn't think there was anything on earth I'd rather see again.

CHAPTER 3

"What was that about?" Sophia asked me once we'd reached the street.

A photographer clicked our picture and my face twisted at the invasion of privacy. *Exactly as Garrick predicted.*

"You!" I shouted to the photographer. He started to run, but he was no match for me and my bionic ankle. Ballet was history, but my lungs and legs still worked. "Stop right there!" I screamed, and he did. I faced him. "Who do you plan on selling that to?"

He shrugged. He was a grimy little man who hadn't seen this side of a razor for at least a week. "I don't know. Whoever buys it."

"I'll give you a thousand dollars cash if you erase it in front of me and don't sell it to anyone else."

"Brinn, what on earth?" Sophia, now out of breath, caught up with me.

The man held up his camera's display and deleted the photos without asking for the money upfront.

"You're trusting," I told him.

"I wasn't going to get much for it," he said offhandedly. "It's your sister they pay for."

"I'll give you fifteen hundred for being honest. You have Venmo?"

"Brinn, all his friends can track Venmo."

"Oh, you're right." I started to dig into my purse when the photographer informed me he also accepted Zelle. I sent him the money, and he tipped a pretend hat and gave me his card.

"I didn't mean any harm, Miss Wentworth."

"No, I know you didn't. I appreciate this."

"Brinn, what's up? First you give Garrick that weird speech about marriages being cursed, and now you're buying your own pictures?"

"I don't care if they take my picture. I care that they have my picture out front of Garrick's office. It would make all his fears true, and I can't have that."

We walked back to our waiting car and Sophia shook her head, as if disappointed in me. I was so used to that expression that it set me off.

"What did I do? Now you're on his side?"

"His side? No, there are no sides. I'm wondering what that drivel was you were spouting in his office. You're never going to get married? Marriages are cursed in your family?" Sophia kept shaking her head. "Garrick believed you. I could tell."

"Why wouldn't he? I was telling the truth. If you need proof, I'm glad to show you my family tree. What makes you think I'd ever want to get married?"

"Brinn, what happens when you fall in love?"

"I won't fall in love. I've seen where love gets my family in this world, and you can count me out." The driver headed to the Embarcadero. "If you're old enough to know you want to spend the rest of your life with your Prince Charming, Joel, I'm old enough to know I don't want that life."

"You're so cynical."

"So I've been told, but I'm not cynical. I'm observant." I pulled my hair back into a high ponytail and clipped it with the Italian barrette my grandmother brought me. She'd brought Quinn a Gucci handbag, so I knew who her favorite was. "Driver, take us straight home. The family meeting is tonight."

* * *

THE WILL REQUIRED we meet weekly to discuss the business realities of the mansion and our share of the fortune. I felt our grandfather's presence in the room whenever we met. *You handle the money, Brinn. You have my gift for numbers, but help your sister. Cripes all fishhooks, she'll spend anything and everything on the crazy horse.*

He wasn't wrong. I took my marching orders from him seriously. Finance and watching over my sisters seemed the most appropriate course of action.

After I dressed, I pressed the whole house speaker. "Wentworth sisters, the car is waiting." My voice boomed through the cavernous house, but no one gathered. I pressed the button again. "Our reservation is in ten minutes."

Renovation of Wentworth Manor began the following day, so we'd given Mrs. Chen an extra day off to prepare. A restaurant gave us the added bonus of privacy (that woman heard everything) and freedom from the dark walls.

Alisa, our youngest sister, peeked her head over the staircase. "I'm not finished curling my hair."

"It looks fine," I yelled back up at her. "Quinn pulled a lot of favors to get this reservation. We need to move."

The twins came out of the same room as Alisa, which I never understood. All three of them lived together, as if in one big dorm room.

"The back of Alisa's head isn't finished," Gia said.

"She can't see the back of her head." I clapped my hands together. "Let's go." I paused a minute. "And turn off the curling iron!"

"Yes, Mom," Gia sniped. There was a flurry of talking, and then all three disappeared into the third-floor room again.

"Arrgh!" I shouted.

"This isn't ballet school, Brinn. Chill out," Quinn said.

"Why does no one understand the concept of time in this house?"

"Maybe because it's like stepping back into 1920 and we're all lost in a time warp of epic proportions."

"You think this is funny," I told her. "It's your reservation. People wait months to eat here. We won't be allowed back."

"You worry too much. You'll need Botox by thirty if you keep this up. The more you nag those sisters of ours, the longer they'll take." Quinn hugged my stiff frame and pecked a kiss on my forehead. "You look beautiful, by the way."

"Thank you. So do you."

My whole life had been disciplined and I couldn't get used to life on the outside where people moved at their own leisurely pace. I'd really tried in Southern California too.

"Brinn, the renovation starts tomorrow. You're going to have a heart attack if you don't let things go. We're not in a military regiment on our way to the battlefield, we're going out to dinner."

"A little order would not hurt this family. I'm sure when Grandfather left us the money, he did not want us wasting more time on getting ready for the weekly meeting than the actual business of said meeting."

"You sound like you're eighty years old. Honestly, even Mona lives a more exciting life than you."

I scowled. "Rude. And come on, Mona can get it."

"Eww."

I giggled. Then I pressed the intercom button again. "Let's go, let's go, let's go! If you're not downstairs in ten seconds, the town car will explode. I repeat, the town car will blow."

Quinn shook her head. "Feel better?"

"Yes, actually."

Gia, Sophia and Alisa came running down the stairs. "Is there a fire?" Gia asked.

"There might be," I said. "Renovation might go faster. Burn the old place down and start again." I felt guilty for saying it, but there was truth in what I said.

As we climbed into the car, I shuddered at the imposing view of Wentworth Manor. Mrs. Chen stood in the doorway. That woman might as well be "Alexa"—because she heard everything.

Since Grandfather died, the rooms felt darker and more oppressive. I found myself sliding back into unhealthy habits while living there. I didn't eat enough. I weighed myself too often and I had nightmares that I was standing in line at ballet check-in—while the scales tipped into the obesity range. I kept waking up drenched in sweat. My posture had become more erect, and I couldn't relax. I counted down the days until I could escape again.

The house itself was part of the issue. The labyrinth of darkened hallways and stairs forced me to rush through life to get to the next destination, and yet I was going nowhere. Wentworth Manor just had a way of closing in on me.

My sisters talked over one another, so they sounded like a barn full of chickens. When the driver pulled up to the restaurant, barely a few blocks away, I pushed open the door as if I'd been deprived of oxygen.

"What's the matter with you?" Quinn asked me.

I tapped my ear. "It's a lot. I'm used to living alone."

Quinn laughed. "You're certifiable, you know. I told you to get a social life, but it's more serious than I thought. That car ride was five minutes, tops."

I fiddled with the collar on my dress and walked toward the small exclusive restaurant on Pacific Avenue. It was Michelin starred with a wait list of three months—unless your last name was Wentworth. The chef specialized in farm-to-table recipes, and Quinn thought it would be a good way to introduce our sisters to the finer attributes of gourmet dining. She managed to snare the only private room with but a few hours' notice.

"I saw this restaurant on Instagram," Alisa said as we walked into the old brick building. "The food bloggers rave about it."

"This restaurant is on Instagram?" I asked.

"Totally. Real foodies use Instagram to find restaurants. The food bloggers are cool, but you know, it's not my thing. I'm more into fashion. I only saw it because it came up on the hashtag since it's on the same street as our house. Hashtag Pacific Heights!" she sang with air quotes.

I heard myself sigh. I hated to admit it, but being around Alisa too long gave me a headache. I loved my new little sister, but she had way too much energy. I found her exhausting.

We were seated in a small room with a Gold Rush Era exposed brick wall and modern, rustic decor. It was crab season and the chef specialized in Dungeness crab risotto with dill.

"This crab is to die for. You haven't lived until you've had it prepared by a Michelin-starred chef," I said as I hoped my sisters would recognize the difference. "The presentation is unreal."

Gia made a face.

"What was that for?" I asked her.

"We're not complete hillbillies. We get it. We're at a fancy restaurant and it's not Fisherman's Wharf. Am I on the right track? Listen, I've agreed to this, but you're going to have to eat my mom's crab cioppino. I guarantee it's no contest."

I pressed my lips together.

"Thanks for letting me know it's different from Fisherman's Wharf though. As if I couldn't tell that I'm not eating outside from a paper bowl with the stench of fish all around me." Gia rolled her eyes.

"Gia!" Sophia snapped. "Be nice. For goodness' sake."

We sat down and were immediately brought glasses of pink prosecco that bubbled brightly in the champagne glasses. Our waiter, a handsome middle-aged man in a tuxedo, introduced himself as Wayne.

He placed leather-bound menus in front of us, though he suggested the tasting menu with the chef's creation. It was $275 a person, and honestly, I hoped it tasted better than Mary's *cioppino,* or I'd never hear the end of it.

Alisa took out her phone, ready to Instagram or TikTok, or whatever it was she did for constant attention, and took a photo not of the pretty champagne flutes, but of the prices.

Sophia pored over the menu. "Y'all know you can get fresh crab at the wharf for like six bucks?"

"We've established that," I said. "In a paper bowl with the stench of fish. Can we move on?"

"Touchy," Alisa said.

I tried to stay calm. "The restaurant specializes in seasonal epicurean dishes," I said, as the waiter disappeared. "The chef here has two Michelin stars. It's considered a sign of trust in his skills that you allow him to curate what you'll be eating. It's like allowing the artist to paint a canvas in front of you. Gia, being a curator, you should get that."

Gia looked unimpressed as she dropped the menu. "Nothing more seasonal than eating crab right at the wharf, fresh off the boat, but I'll give it a try. What's on the meeting's agenda tonight?"

Quinn took this as her cue but was interrupted.

"Oh my gosh, we've got to discuss contractors," Sophia said.

"Tomorrow the mansion will be teeming with them like cockroaches after the apocalypse."

I cringed. "Sophia, don't say that word in a five-star restaurant!"

"Contractors?" Sophia asked.

In an uncharacteristic lack of decorum, I dropped my forehead on the table. I longed for the quiet of my apartment in Santa Monica. I didn't like "acting like a Wentworth" any more than my sisters would, but it was necessary.

Quinn tapped on her glass to get the circus we now called a family back in order. "All right. Contractors. They'll bring chaos to the manor and according to the will, we have no choice but to live with it. If one of us moves from the home, the money all goes to charity—and not the charities we chose for the gala announcement."

"We know this," Alisa groaned.

"Knowing it and understanding the difficulties of being in a construction zone for months are two different things, Alisa." Quinn took a sip of her prosecco. "Tonight I thought we'd discuss how our charitable foundations are coming along and how to make the renovations more bearable."

"Seriously," Gia said. "Y'all have never had a hardship in your life? This will be nothing. A little noise, a few hammers . . . hot construction workers in jeans and work boots. I think we'll survive. What else you got?"

"Well, you'll be at work for most of the day," Quinn said. "The rest of us need to work on our foundations full time, so I thought it might be in our best interest to rent some office space nearby in the financial district."

Wayne returned and Quinn handed him her menu. "We'll all have the tasting menu. However, I'd like to order us each a starter of the caviar canapés."

"Very good, madam. Would you like the wine pairing option?"

"No, we will stick with the prosecco for the adults, and can you bring the young lady a sparkling water?"

"I want a Coke," Alisa said.

"Very good, madam. You'll enjoy our refreshing pomegranate soda." Wayne gathered all the leather-bound folders and escaped happily.

"What the heck is pomegranate soda? Are we even in America? Who doesn't serve Coca-Cola?"

"As I was saying," Quinn went on, "we may need to rent some office space if we're going to continue to—"

"Gia and I can just go to my grandparents' house if we need quiet to work," Sophia said. "We've got rooms on the second floor which have desks, and then there's the rooftop deck. You're all welcome there—"

I grinned. Sophia was without guile. She saw no difference between her grandparents' rundown Victorian in North Beach and Wentworth Manor in prestigious Pacific Heights, and I loved that about her. I'm sure the old house brought her a lot more happiness. "I thought your grandparents were selling and moving to the peninsula," I said.

"Over my dead body," Gia announced.

"Be that as it may, it's going to get very loud and chaotic in the house," Quinn continued. "I don't know that we'll all feel comfortable descending upon the twins' grandparents."

Quinn's commentary was pointless. There was never any true escape from Wentworth Manor. Just when you thought you'd found your way out, the long arm of its invisible power yanked you back.

The real chaos in Wentworth Manor came not from construction, but from the mess our parents created. If we were from a normal family, our father would have inherited the mansion and none of this would be our problem. But Quinn wouldn't discuss that. Instead, she focused on collateral issues that had nothing to do with the real problem—the crack in the

Wentworth family that was expanding and lengthening under our foundation. The fracture that could swallow all the sisters and our good intentions faster than the shaking San Andreas fault.

As if she'd read my mind, Gia picked up the briefcase beside her and slipped out a copy of the *San Francisco Chronicle*. "We can dance around the construction conversation all night, or we can talk about the real problem," Gia said. "We have a PR issue and if I've learned anything in business, it's best to tackle that early."

She put the newspaper on the table. Even upside down I could read the headline: While Wentworth Legacy Burns, Daughters Fiddle at Ill-timed Extravagant Ball." In smaller letters, it read, "Family parties like rock stars at crime scene."

"Murder," Gia said loudly. "Especially the murder of a patriarch worth billions is not going to be swept under the rug—no matter how fancy or new that rug might be."

I cleared my throat. "It may not have been murder."

"Brinn, honey, you need to wake up," Gia said.

"We're not discussing this in public," Quinn hissed.

"We can't discuss it at the mansion," Sophia said. "Everything we say gets reported right back to your mother."

Quinn's voice lowered. "We cannot allow Grandfather's legacy to be tarnished. The Wentworth name needs to be synonymous with philanthropy, not this scandal."

"It's a little late for that," Gia said. "Actions have consequences."

"Brinn?" I looked up to see Casey Sutton. He was someone we'd grown up with and who had a scandal of his own.

"Casey." I tried to find my bearings for casual talk.

Casey was a typical semi-pro golfer you'd see at the club, complete with dad bod and a head of wild hair that molded into the shape of his baseball cap. He always smelled like wet grass and looked as if he needed a shower.

"It is you," he said with false surprise. "Your grandmother told me that you might be here. I was in the neighborhood and—"

My grandmother . . . Casey was of the right "stock." Granted, he had no job or prospects. Word on the street was his family money was gone. Yet this is who my grandmother imagined for me. *That says it all, really.*

"Casey, hey, we're in the middle of a foundation meeting. You know all my sisters."

"Actually, I haven't met—"

I cut him off. "Seriously, it was so great to see you. We'll have to catch up sometime." I looked at my sisters again to remind him. *Meeting. Us. Go away.*

"I'm back in town for good," he said, tone-deaf to my oh-so-polite dismissal. "Maybe we could get dinner this week? I'd love to catch up."

"Yeah," I said, while my head shook back and forth to indicate no. "Maybe."

There was a day when I'd have given anything for Casey's attention. In high school, he was the man. He hosted all the best parties—not one of which I was ever invited to—and always had a posse of women following him.

"I heard you had a great party." Casey was now addressing the entire table. "Front page stuff, not bad," he rambled to my sisters while I watched his mannerisms. Casey was the buddy, the good ol' boy, the man society hyped as "the one to catch" and rescue from his wild bachelor life, but as a finance major, I saw things differently. I saw him as a liability.

There was a cycle of money in finance known as the three-generation rule—the first generation creates the wealth, the second generation stewards it, and the third consumes it like fire. Casey was the third. He consumed wealth so rampantly with flashy cars, golf memberships and private yacht vacations that rumor had it he didn't have a dollar to his own name. No doubt he intended to find himself a wealthy heiress who would be powerless against his charms so that he might continue spending recklessly.

He needs to keep looking.

Casey's financial situation spoke volumes as to his interest in me when one considered he wouldn't have answered my phone call back in high school. He was raised "right" according to my grandmother. *From good stock* as she'd say, a member of the Olympic club and the horsey set. I, for one, wasn't about to pull a *Downton Abbey* and marry a man to keep the old aristocracy going. *Casey needs a job, not a wife.*

"So?" he looked at me expectantly.

"What?" I asked.

"Friday night. Does that work for you?"

"I . . . uh—" *What did I miss?*

"Oh shoot," Quinn said, rescuing me from my trip to another realm. "We'll be in Napa this weekend visiting our father."

"Oh." He nodded. Casey stood over me with the freckled bridge of his nose and bologna-toned complexion, waiting for me to say something.

"We'll find a day soon," I finally said.

He glanced at the table of my sisters, assessing which one of us might be available prey and pressed his hand to the blue speckled bow tie he wore. "Ladies, if you're ever in need of an escort for the upcoming season, please don't hesitate to call on Casey Sutton. Quinn knows where to find me and I'm always at the club." He grinned but made no movement toward the doorway. "Look me up." Then he leaned in and whispered in my ear. "I'm sorry about your mother. I don't care what people are saying."

His words weren't said with malice. He really did seem to be offering his friendship, and he was correct in the fact that it was more than a lot of people would do. Being seen at the gala was one thing, hanging out with the Wentworth sisters on your own time was quite another. He took my hand and our eyes met.

"Thank you," I said with all sincerity. He nodded once and left the room.

The first course came, and it looked like a small, contained glass dome of Mexican flan. "This is Oestra Caviar Panna Cotta." Wayne, along with our two other waiters, set one of the glass domes in front of each sister, drew his hand behind his back and announced the course.

The disgust apparent on Alisa's top lip, she looked straight to Quinn. "You're kidding, right?"

"This is a delicacy and you'll be served this often if—" Quinn didn't finish her sentence.

"If I turn into you, and that's not going to happen. This literally looks like bait from when my grandpa took me fishing. I don't eat bait."

Sophia giggled and tried to recover by biting her lip.

"Seriously," Alisa said. "I'm not eating this. Can we get some chicken fingers or something? Maybe some mozzarella sticks? Real appetizers."

"Alisa, that is about $100 of the finest caviar, better than Tsar Nicoulai Russian caviar," Quinn said.

"Give it to him then. He's probably ruined his tastebuds with vodka anyway. I want some real food. Not something I can get at the tackle shop."

Quinn looked exasperated. She'd come naturally to the heiress lifestyle we'd been raised in. My half-sisters were more like me. They saw the absurdity in the pomp and circumstance.

"Alisa, the reason I brought you here is to give you the Michelin food experience." Quinn rattled on as she pushed the plate back toward Alisa. "This is the kind of meal that gourmands travel all over the world to enjoy from a world-renowned chef. We want you to get used to this so that you'll be welcomed in any home in San Francisco."

"I'm your dad's illegitimate daughter via his mistress who he met in a bowling alley. Those kinds of people aren't inviting me anywhere. I believe they call us 'trailer trash,' not that we were ever rich enough to have a trailer."

"I'm not doing it to punish you. Think of it as patronizing the arts. The chef is the artist, and we get to partake of his canvas." It was the second time Quinn used this metaphor, which was lost on Alisa both times.

"Do you want my masterpiece?" she asked as she shoved the plate back toward Quinn. "I don't want to be welcomed in a home that serves fish relish for dinner. Why is that wrong? What am I missing?"

"Brinn and I will share it. Gia? Sophia? Do you want some of Alisa's caviar?"

"It will be hard enough for me to choke this down myself," Sophia said.

"I love it. I'll have some," Gia said, relieving Sophia of the painful task of eating such a delicacy.

We hadn't made it past the first course and already we were splitting meals like we were broke high school kids at a city diner.

Wayne didn't comment or ask us about the caviar as the staff cleared away the empty dishes.

"The next course is fresh Dungeness crab baked in our wood-fired oven with hand-picked local asparagus organically grown in our garden an hour away."

Everyone ate the crab without commentary other than it was delicious. We'd found a cease-fire. The third dish came with much fanfare. It was set up as a sculpture with a central focus and several artisanal vegetables around it like its own edible galaxy.

"Squid with Buddha vegetables," Wayne announced as several other waiters placed the small plates in front of us.

At the word "squid" I panicked and stared at Alisa.

"This literally looks like what my mother throws away when she cooks," Alisa said. "Do you have any real food?" she asked the waiter.

Wayne couldn't help himself, he laughed. "Yes, miss. The tasting menu is not for you. How about some black truffle pasta?"

Alisa shrugged. "You can just put butter on it as far as I'm concerned."

"You'll like the truffles," Gia intervened. "It's a very subtle flavor. Do you like mushrooms?"

Alisa nodded and once again, we had temporary peace at the table. But we hadn't discussed one iota of business. *Our culinary lesson was a bust.*

I tried to support Quinn. "Alisa, there will be a lot of this at events and openings we're invited to. You can't wrinkle your nose at champagne and caviar," I said. "If anything, you'll have to learn how to politely decline."

"Seriously, what is the point of having money if you can't eat what you crave? Laugh all you want, but Taco Bell has killer food. I could be at home right now having a Quesarito, sipping a Baja Blast and watching *Twilight*. I'm so good with that life. Instead, I feel like I'm in church here worshiping at the great altar of gluttony."

"What on earth is a Quesarito?" Gia asked.

"Shh!" Quinn hissed. "Could we please not discuss the menu items at Taco Bell while enjoying a culinary feast made by a Michelin-star chef? I mean, is it too much to ask that for the one night we act like Wentworths?"

"Oh, you mean act like it's okay to overdose a patriarch who gets in our way?" Gia asked. "Because I'm not sure I want to act like a Wentworth, and Alisa is twenty. It is perfectly normal for her to want a taco over a gourmet tasting menu."

My cell phone chirped at the same time that Quinn's did and we both looked at each other in abject terror. We'd turned our phones off, so one of our parents must have used the "Find My Phone" app which caused our phones to beep even with the sound off. We both picked up our phones to stop the annoying beeping.

The text was, as we'd supposed, from our father. "Your mother has fallen. Found her crumpled in a fetal position in the kitchen. Going to hospital. Get there ASAP. San Francisco General."

"The only way to win the game is not to play," Quinn said.

I agree but pointed out the obvious. "The paper will print that we weren't seen at the hospital."

"So they will," Quinn agreed. "We have to make a stand at some point."

Our sisters stared at us questioningly, but we didn't offer an explanation. Was there any explanation that would help anyone understand our mother? Her desperate need for attention was so entrenched and evolved that she couldn't stand being forgotten about in her penthouse.

"Her breathing is labored," came another urgent text from our father.

"What is going on?" Gia placed her fork back on the table.

"Shut your phone down, Brinn," Quinn ordered.

I did as I was told, but I wanted to rush to the hospital. I was fearful this would be the one time Mother's need was genuine.

"Our mother has collapsed in the kitchen of their penthouse," Quinn said calmly. "No doubt she'll claim it's the ankle bracelet that tripped her up."

"You need to go?" Gia asked frantically.

"No." Quinn smoothed her blonde hair behind her shoulder. "Not today."

Our sisters didn't understand, and who could blame them. Our mother was diabolically selfish, but our father was the consummate enabler. He breathed life into her dramas. Instinctively, they knew the next trick that would garner them the attention they sought, like water to a dying man in the desert. Attention was their lifeblood, and their work together was a well-choreographed ballet of neediness.

Dad claimed he wanted to escape Mother, which is how he excused his affairs, so she'd have to let him go—but in reality, they'd become one being in their dysfunctional dance. They waltzed together in their malicious desire to be noticed.

We received one final text from my father as we shut down. "Everything's fine. Cancel."

That made me more nervous than the text saying she'd been hurt, and my leg started to shake as I wanted to leave.

Quinn was unfazed. "Since we're not renovating the ballroom to keep it historically preserved, we might transform that into a temporary office."

"Grandfather often lent out the ballroom to charities so they didn't have to pay a hotel to host their fundraisers. I think we should continue that tradition, but make the ballroom handicapped accessible with its own entrance so it can be used more often and by everyone. All in favor, raise your hand."

None of my sisters hesitated to raise their hands. Casey Sutton returned to our table, having overheard the vote. "Stellar idea, Quinn. Capital."

"Did you need something, Casey?" I asked him.

"I'm sorry, I forgot what I wanted to ask you. I got sidelined by how good you're looking. So refreshed. SoCal must have been good for you."

"Thank you," I said absently.

"You know my father is single. My mother passed away earlier this year."

I'd forgotten. How callous I'd been. "Oh Casey, I'm so terribly sorry for your loss. She was a delightful woman."

"Would you pass his business card on to the woman in the

pink dress at the gala? They had a grand time together and it's the first I've seen him smile since Mother left us."

All of us sisters stared at one another. Five eligible women with billions to their name and not one of us had a date after the ball. But Mary Campelli had suitors lining up like she'd called a new draft bill.

CHAPTER 4

"*B*rinn!" my grandmother bellowed. "Get in here now!" Her voice rose above the demolition and banging that the contractors created that morning. She called from the floral room, and I sprinted to get there quickly.

"Yes, Grandmother." I tried to catch my breath. I'd been reading the books Garrick gave me and his personal notes throughout stirred something within me that I couldn't name. His emotion-laden handwriting and detailed plans written alongside family court judge names and their failure to protect victims struck me deeply. The annotations in the margins did not compute with the cold, arrogant man I'd met the day before, and I wondered if his smile at the end was the true Garrick Kane.

"Brinn!" Mona screamed again as I stood short-winded in front of her. "I cannot stay in this noise. My masseuse left early. He said he could not work in this racket. You can only imagine my humiliation. I was left in my towel."

"It must have been awful for you," I said without a lick of sarcasm.

"I absolutely abhor construction. It's so beneath a family like ours to be in the midst of this kind of work. What on earth was your grandfather thinking to keep you here in this ruckus?"

"It's part of the—"

"Will's stipulations. Yes, I know. Your father's father always had a way of creating chaos in other peoples' lives."

Pot meet kettle.

"Grandpa loved this house and wanted to see us all restored —the manor and the family."

"He was a master puppeteer. It seems he is still at work. Your grandfather should have made arrangements for all of you to be far away from this dingy old house before construction started. In fact, he should have had you sell it immediately."

Well, he didn't. "Yes, Grandmother. Did you need something?" Just looking at her frail body incited me. I'd been raised to believe that bad posture and two extra pounds would destroy my person. Extra weight would render me unlovable and unworthy, so I stood up straight, spine up, shoulder blades flat, body centered, head erect. My body always in alignment, always striving for perfection. Whenever my grandmother spoke to me, my head instinctively went into ballet position and my shoulders squared of their own volition. But inside I was buzzing with rage, and I wanted her far away from me.

"I'm going to stay at the Fairmont," she said as if this was our punishment.

"I think that's a wonderful idea. You'll be much more comfortable there. Do you need me to order the car?"

She stood at the antique mirror and shifted her Gucci scarf. "Mrs. Chen has already taken care of it. If you should need me, I'll be at the hotel for the next month or so."

"You're staying in San Francisco?" I swallowed. "If you're staying in Nob Hill, you should see Mother. She's at the pent-house. Literally across the street from you at the Fairmont."

"Whitmans do not enter a house of ill repute, darling,

regardless of the circumstances. Your mother will understand. It's best for us all if I stay away."

"She's not in a brothel, Grandmother. She's in her penthouse with an ankle monitor. I'm sure she has it covered so you wouldn't be subjected to its ugliness."

"Shh!" she hissed. "Not another word. The sooner you girls separate yourself from that whole debacle, the better. When your mother is freed, she'll be back on the social circuit as if none of this happened." Mona dropped her head. "Though she'll never be welcomed back as she was. For now, this is something she must endure alone with your father. It will go away soon enough, sooner if we avoid the subject altogether."

The loyalty in my family was legendary. *One for me and all for me.* I loved my mother and father. I had no plans to turn on them, no matter what Joel and the police said. They were flawed certainly, but I couldn't believe them capable of overdosing my grandfather—neither one of them. Watching my grandmother's treachery gave me some insight into why my mother was so prickly. Mona had likely never issued a warm hug in her lifetime and my mother carried on the legacy.

No wonder I wanted to be like Mary.

"Mary," Grandmother said to speak about the twins' mother. "She must be very excited about her daughters' enormous windfall. Why don't you sit down and tell me about it before I go." She sat on the sofa and patted the seat beside her.

"Won't your car be here?"

"They'll wait. That's their job."

"I think Mary is genuinely the type of person who is happy for anyone to succeed."

"Well, be that as it may. She played the long game to get Bradley's money. I have to give her credit."

I attempted to redirect the conversation back to my own mother. "Grandmother, you're not going to see your daughter while you're here? She is innocent until proven guilty. She couldn't have done what they've accused her of—"

Mona gave a withering scowl. "A Whitman never puts herself in such a situation where her character can be questioned." Grandmother craned her long bony neck to lift her chin obstinately. "She should have never administered any morphine at all. No, I'll wait until Chelsea has been relieved of all charges before I see her. She'd want it that way to protect my reputation."

I doubt that.

"It would brighten Mom's day to see you. How long has it been?" *Let's be honest, Mona Whitman's presence has probably never brightened anyone's day.*

"How is that ankle of yours?" she screamed over the banging, which seemed to rise in decibels as she spoke. "Will you be back on the stage anytime soon?"

"Grandmother, no. Never again."

"Not with that attitude."

"I shattered my ankle. I have a new one that's made of titanium hardware. I can never go through an airport again without setting off all the sirens as if I'm packing heat." I kicked up my leg.

"Brinn, what a terrible expression. There are Olympians who run on prosthetic legs. You really should see what's possible for you."

"It's the Paralympics. There's no paraballet."

"Are you certain?"

"Well, no."

"You should look into it."

I'll get right on that. "Dance is history. It's time I used my finance degree. I'm going to be working with domestic violence victims and I'd like to use the knowledge to—"

Again, she gave the withering stare with her telltale smirk that I'd displeased her. "Brinn, sweetheart. That's very noble of you, but money is a man's job." Mona Whitman made a face like she'd just sucked a lemon. "I meant to speak to you about this charity of yours, it's so ugly. Domestic violence is such a messy business. You should get involved in supporting the arts—the ballet—something more in tune with your gifts."

"So I've heard."

Usually, my grandmother didn't care what I did. I was the "extra" while Quinn was considered the true heiress. Grandmother found me "too masculine." "Where in heaven's name did she get those ankles?" she'd ask my mother when I was little. "Her stubby legs are like tree trunks."

"Those are her legs, Mother," my mom would say. "She didn't get them from me obviously."

As if she read my mind, Grandmother reminded me of my fatal flaw. "If a girl with legs like yours can make it to prima ballerina, think of the little girls you might inspire." I took her words like bullets as a child, but now they felt sad. Pathetic really, how she worked so hard to fill me with insecurity.

I was good at ballet. I destroyed my body to be good. I withered to ninety pounds to be good—and still Grandmother thought I was fat. *I* thought I was fat. It took a lot of counseling to feel otherwise.

"Look how those legs grew into perfect Betty Grable legs." Mary, the twins' mother, appeared behind us, and I wondered how much she'd overheard. "You should have them insured."

I looked down at my legs. "Who is Betty Grable?" I asked her.

"She was the pin-up star of World War II—because of her legs. She had them insured for a million dollars back in the '40s. Imagine what that would be worth now."

I smiled. "Maybe I was born into the wrong era."

"Nonsense. In another era you might not have been able to be brilliant in finance," Mary said. "Is that why you picked domestic violence as a charity? Financial wits can really help a woman escape a bad situation."

"Not always, according to Garrick." I held up one of the pamphlets I'd been reading.

"It's a messy business," Mona said again. "And finance is for men."

"No one will ever handle your money with as much care as you will," Mary offered sweetly. "It's very easy for people like Bernie Madoff to run off with wealthy people's money because they are too trusting. Money brings out the worst in people."

Grandmother glared at Mary for her defiance. "What is it you're doing here exactly?" Mona asked.

"I was dropping off some items to Sophia and I wanted to invite Brinn to the restaurant for lunch. The girls and I—"

"Surely you don't mean in North Beach," Mona said, her nose upturned. "Across from the strip clubs?"

Mary, ever patient, smiled warmly at Mona. "You're welcome to join us, Mona. We'd love to give you a taste of Italy. You must be missing it."

"North Beach is not the north of Italy." Grandmother cackled.

"Well, no, but we have great sourdough. Something you won't find in Northern Italy."

I failed to see why Mona had to hate Mary so. It was humiliating. It wasn't like she was loyal to her own daughter.

"I'd love to come, Mary. I've been wanting to see your restaurant." I was slightly obsessed by Mary's life, and this open invitation excited me like nothing else had lately. It had the added benefit of annoying my grandmother.

Mona sighed and lifted her Louis Vuitton makeup case with both of her hands. "If anyone needs me, I'll be at the Fairmont."

I took Mary's presence as courage and maybe I wanted to impress her a bit, too. "Grandmother, you should know, when all is said and done, I plan to be on the board of Wentworth

Industries. I understood the direction my grandfather would have taken for the company and plan to work with his lawyer, Mr. Trunkett."

"Over. My. Dead. Body." Mona shot one of her withering glances. Even Mary gasped aloud at the angry force in my grandmother's reply, and I realized I'd aimed too high for the situation. You would have thought I told her I'd be working at the strip club in North Beach, not business.

"I think the world is a different place than when you and I grew up," Mary said, kindly acting as if she and my grandmother were from the same era. "Women today can do anything."

"Mary, is it a different era?" Grandmother asked. "Or do people just ignore propriety and do as they please now?"

Mary nodded. "The world is open now. Imagine if Madame Curie were born today."

"Forgive me, but women in our family do not work outside of philanthropy. It is considered beneath us. I realize this is a departure from your family's history, but we serve on committees. We raise money for the less fortunate and we throw soirees and galas, much like you saw here this week, for the betterment of society. It's not an easy path. With great wealth comes great responsibility, and charitable philanthropy is necessary and quite properly, a career in its own rite."

I want to curl up and evaporate.

"That's a worthy endeavor certainly," Mary said to Mona in her gentle, breathy voice. "But Brinn and Quinn seem far too bright for that kind of lifestyle. These young women can do anything they set their mind to *and* philanthropy. I'd be willing to bet they could have a career and contribute to their endowment and raise more money for charity. You know what they say? If you want something done, give it to a busy person. The girls don't need to play second fiddle to men in finance or any other endeavor."

Mary Campelli is definitely no wilting violet. Verbal shots have been fired and she never even raised her voice.

"You really shouldn't fill their heads," Grandmother said. "They'll do what they're expected to do. The girls will marry and continue to lift San Francisco in its civility. Their path was picked the second their grandfather left them his fortune."

"What if they don't get married?" Mary asked. "Or what if, God forbid, their life doesn't work out as planned the way it did for me."

I squeezed my eyes shut and prepared for the onslaught. I knew my grandmother believed herself above Mary's circumstances. Something so pedestrian as getting pregnant out of wedlock would never happen to her family. Of course, we had three new siblings who definitely proved life didn't always work out as one expected, but who was counting?

"I don't want to get married," I said boldly, using Mary's presence to stand up to my grandmother. "Ever."

"Well, you obviously don't need money, Brinn, but you'll need a man who understands what's expected of him in the upper echelons of society. Do you plan to show up to the symphony opening with a man who pops a can of Budweiser during intermission?"

I wanted her to be quiet. To hide our hideousness from the sweet heart of Mary Campelli, but for all her supposed manners, my grandmother had no artfulness when it came to her pretentious attitudes. Her ways had died out decades before and she refused to acknowledge it.

"For all your father's faults, Brinn," Mona said, "he puts forth a wonderful image and he only gets more handsome with age. He can bring an entire room to its knees with his charm." Mona looked toward Mary as if to see if her verbal arrow hit its mark, but Mary seemed incurious.

Personally, in regard to my father, I found him feckless, not charming. I loved him, naturally, but he never stood up to my mother. He allowed her to walk all over him. *And us.* It wasn't his big betrayals that broke my respect for him. It wasn't even his many affairs nor the inability to protect us from our mother's wrath. It was the tiny deceptions, the thousand thin slices to our veins that encompassed the whole of his character. The cumulative effect that stole our lifeblood drop by drop when he lied and called us insane for believing anything but his version of the truth. *It's this ugliness I want—no need—to escape once and for all.*

When Mary didn't take the bait, my grandmother goaded her. "Don't you find that Bradley is as charming as ever, Mary?"

Mary took her time to answer and before she did, she smiled at me. "Bradley is the father of my twins and therefore, he will always hold a special place in my heart. He gave me the greatest gift imaginable so if that's charming, then yes, I find him charming."

Charming like a snake remained unsaid.

"Will we see you at lunch today, Brinn? Gia and Sophia will be there at one." She handed me a business card. "Here's the address."

I bent over and hugged her small frame. Mary didn't stiffen like my mother, she softened and gripped me like I truly mattered. I didn't want to let go.

CHAPTER 5

$\mathcal{T}$he brisk Tuesday in January made me long for my beach apartment in Santa Monica. The cold, damp Pacific wind sliced through me like a dagger as I made my way to North Beach. I had the driver drop me around the corner. "Thanks for the ride," I told him. "I'll text you when I'm ready."

Mary's restaurant was on Columbus Avenue, the wide angled street across kitty-corner to the strip joints. It wasn't a street that was normally crossed by pedestrians and the two worlds hardly collided, but one couldn't help but notice the neon signs as they blinked glowing smut in the middle of the day.

The neighborhood was a stone's throw from the financial district and the mansion, but a million miles away in substance. I entered into the darkened restaurant and was promptly announced by a cluster of bells on the door. The place featured classic red and white checkered tablecloths with wine decanters that overflowed with spilled candle wax.

I'd worn a dark navy Tori Burch set for the occasion, as I didn't know what I'd encounter in the dark, dank little eatery besides what I imagined to be a legion of cockroaches. *Genetics obviously gave me a good dose of Mona's critical nature.*

Mary met me at the door. "Brinn, welcome! No photographers following you this afternoon." She looked around before shutting the door. "I'm glad you came. I was worried with your grandmother there you might get talked out of coming, and the twins were adamant about speaking with you outside the house."

"Grandmother went to the Fairmont. She's their problem now, and the photographers are usually more interested in Quinn than me. She photographs better and has more of a social life."

"I've saved a private table in the back for you. Come with me and I'll get you started. You're the first to arrive. My girls are always on their own timeline."

"I appreciated the invitation. Since I came home from Southern California, I don't leave the house nearly enough."

"Sophia gave me the card of your friend's father. Anyway, I texted him. Can you believe it? He called right back. We literally talked all night. I wanted to tell you this morning, but your grandmother seemed too interested in my love life for my comfort so I thought it could wait."

"Casey's dad?"

"Grant, yes. We met in the mansion and had a connection. He lost his wife last year." She dropped her head as if to mourn a woman she'd never known. "He's been alone for quite some time. It sounded like they tried everything."

"Oh—"

"Do you know last night, when we talked, he said he didn't know if he should call me. He wanted me to know that he wasn't wealthy like so many people at the party. As if I'd care, but isn't that the sweetest?"

"I—"

"You know, his wife died of cancer."

"I didn't know. I mean, I knew she passed, but—"

"They didn't get good care here, so they traveled all over the world to get her these expensive alternative treatments—"

"They did?" This was all news to me. I wondered how San Francisco had missed such juicy gossip.

"Anyway," Mary went on, "Grant said their family money was on the way out anyway after they got swindled by a money manager, but her illness took care of the rest. So he's about like me now. Getting by."

"He said all that?"

She nodded excitedly. "Well, he told me it's not polite to discuss money, but he wanted to tell me before I agreed to go out with him because he wasn't 'part of the pony set' like everyone else at the party." Mary positively glowed as she talked about Casey's dad while I reeled at my own judgment of Casey being without money.

I'll never be like Mary Campelli. Never. She simply loved people for who they were. I thought I wasn't like my grandmother, but darn it, the way I judged Casey and his father showed me exactly who I was.

"Are you all right?" Mary asked me.

"Me?" I put a hand to my chest. "Yes, of course."

"We're going out tonight." Mary grinned as she took my hands. "He said it's proper to wait until the weekend, but he doesn't want to. He said we aren't getting any younger and we shouldn't waste any time!"

"I beg to differ. You look even younger than when I met you," I told her honestly.

"It's the first blush of love." She patted her cheeks. "I can't believe I said that. I sound like a teenager. What on earth?"

"He's a special man," I told her honestly.

"Listen to me going on like a schoolgirl, come and sit down."

I followed Mary and for a small woman, she certainly moved quickly. I struggled to keep up with her as we passed the empty tables and the large mahogany bar. She sat me down at a round table and poured Pellegrino into a wine glass for me. "Can I get you some wine?"

"No, thank you." I covered the other glass. "I'm not a day drinker."

"Good for you." She lifted the bottle. "Oh, here are my girls."

Sophia and Gia walked into the private room; they were arguing as they came in and stopped abruptly. Each of them kissed and greeted their mother and sat down at the table with serious expressions and suddenly, it felt like we were at a funeral.

"Is something wrong?" I asked.

"I've got to get back to work so this won't take long." Gia wore a fitted cream pantsuit with a camel coat hung casually over her shoulders. "This may seem random, but Sophia and I wanted to talk to you about working with the abuse victims a—"

"And Garrick Kane," Sophia added.

"Oh, I thought you might be here about my mother's charges." I exhaled in relief. "I know. I shouldn't have picked such a difficult charity. I could have simply bought more time on PBS or opened a new homeless shelter in the Tenderloin, but after reading Garrick's assignments and his notes, I know this is where I belong. You'd never know what a heart that guy has, but it's everywhere in his notes."

Sophia's eyes widened. "Is it now?"

"It's nothing like that."

"We know you can do anything that you set your mind to. Do you know what the odds are against becoming a prima ballerina? You did that, didn't you?" Sophia's chipper tone was too much.

"What's this about?" I was leery.

"I've had a lot of guilt over that meeting. I felt you got side-swiped by Garrick and me. I think we should discuss—"

"Did Mona ask you to talk to me about this?" I asked. "I know she's not happy about my pick, but I'm already learning so much and I want to do this."

"We wouldn't listen to that old bat regardless," Gia blurted. "Sorry, I know she's your grandmother, but when she came for our mother, I was done with that broad. Honestly, I never met anyone with worse manners. How has she managed thus far?"

I laughed and relaxed slightly. "She's from a different era. Plus, she pays anyone who is around her, so they tolerate her for the paycheck."

"There's not enough money in the world for me to tolerate that," Gia said.

"If I know Mona, she won't be in San Francisco for long anyway. She comes into town, spreads her venom and disappears like a black widow, leaving the wounded to fend for themselves." I tried to laugh this off, but both my sisters looked at me sadly, as though they felt sorry for me.

Gia, being her typical self, ordered for us all. "Mama, give us all the special. We've got to get cracking." Then she looked at me. "We *are* here to talk to you about your mother and the accusations . . . well, the charges against her, but also the charity and how we think it relates. Because Sophia discussed this with Garrick, and we think it's important you go in with your eyes wide open."

"You talked to Garrick about me? I don't follow."

They looked at each other briefly and back to me. "There's no nice way to say this. Your mom is and has always been abusive. Your mom and dad together are unreal. Garrick and I think you need to address your own abusive past before you try to help anyone else."

"No." I was incensed. "I've already done that after I lost ballet. For the disordered eating I had. I'm not so broken that I can't help other people. You talked to Garrick about this?"

"I didn't have to," Sophia said. "You're a walking billboard to someone like him."

"Sophia, you're not working as a social worker right now, so you need someone to feel sorry for and offer therapy, I get it. I know my mother isn't like yours, but that doesn't make her abusive, nor a criminal."

"No, but—"

"Seriously, she's never even put a Band-Aid on me. How would she possibly know how to administer some kind of shot to overdose our grandfather? She has Mrs. Chen plug in her iPhone at night because it's too much for her. This murderess scenario simply doesn't add up, and what I think you're telling me is that if I don't believe your version of events via Joel, I'm too broken to help others?"

A look passed between Sophia and Gia. I felt cornered.

"Sophia, you have to believe my mother is guilty because you're too in love with Joel to think of an alternative."

"*I'm* not in love with Joel," Gia said. "But I've looked at the evidence and I think Joel's right about this. If you're going to work with Garrick, you can't stand up in court for an abuser."

"Then a court of law will decide if she's guilty, but you? My own sisters? Of course I'm going to be a character witness for my mother. She's my mother!"

Sophia looked down at the table instead of me. "We love you, Brinn, but in all honesty, we're not here for ourselves. Not even Garrick. We're here on behalf of Quinn."

I felt as if they'd all lined up and slapped me one by one. "I thought we were a *family*."

"We are a family," Sophia said. "That's why we're here."

"If I betray my mother, we're a family. Quinn isn't going to agree to this. She wouldn't have sent you as proxies. She would have talked to me herself."

My mind went to Garrick Kane viewing me as some kind of wounded bird trying to make up for a horrific childhood, and I was mortified all over again. *How could any of my sisters do this to me?*

"No one's come out and said it to you, so I'm going to," Sophia continued. "Quinn thinks your mother is guilty and she's testifying against her in court."

The breath left me briefly and my stomach twisted in knots. "She wouldn't go through with that. She'd talk to me first." Then I had no words. I wanted to slink under the table and disappear. Instead, I grabbed my Chanel by the chain and rose to leave.

"Brinn, come on," Gia said.

"This is between Quinn and me. It has nothing to do with either of you. It certainly has nothing to do with Garrick Kane getting my charitable contributions, so I'd appreciate it if you'd both keep your mouths shut when it comes to him. One thing you'll learn about society, ladies, is family business needs to stay family business."

"We have no horse in this race." Gia stood up and reached for my arm. "That's why we're telling you instead of Quinn. She's not our mother."

"I'm sorry my mother isn't sweetness and light like yours, but she's the easy target in this investigation. I may not be her favorite, but I know her well enough to know she had no reason to harm my grandfather, while Joel has plenty to gain by accusing her."

"Do you hear yourself?" Gia asked.

I was in attack mode. All I could hear was the two of them telling me something I refused to believe. "I have to remind you that you both have the Wentworth name too. The press isn't going to let you walk away unscathed if they prosecute my mother."

"What if she's guilty?" Sophia asked.

"What about Joel? Sophia, your boyfriend is the one who supposedly found evidence on my mother. That doesn't seem messed up to you? If anything, you have more horses in this race. I'm just trying to be loyal to my mother. Wouldn't you do the same?"

Sophia exhaled. "Quinn says she's testifying for you. For all the domestic violence you endured as a child."

They may as well have struck me. "Domestic violence . . . me?" *What on earth?* "Quinn must be trying to justify her betrayal of our mother. I need to stop her. There was no domestic violence." I turned on my heel, but Gia got in front of me.

"Sit down, Brinn," Sophia said softly, and I did . . . mostly because I was too numb to figure out where to go.

"My mother didn't do this. Quinn is going to ruin our family for what? If they have evidence, they have evidence. Why would Quinn do this? Ruin our family like this?"

"That's just the thing," Gia said. "Chelsea ruined your family. She took an upstanding man, an icon really, out of this world and sent him into the next—with no thought or regard to the consequences."

"She didn't do that!" I slammed my hand on the table and the glasses shook. After my pious beliefs on etiquette, here I was acting as if I was getting test results on Maury Povich. "Did you talk her into this, Sophia? To make Joel look better."

Sophia shook her head.

"Quinn wouldn't do this without talking to me first. If she really did ask you, know that your work is done here."

"The scandal is not going away. A life was lost. You were your grandfather's favorite, Brinn, don't you want justice for him?"

My eyes pricked with tears at the thought of my grandfather being lost, but I refused to be manipulated. "This will drag all of our names through the mud, and for what?"

"Because it's the right thing to do, Brinn," Sophia said.

"I'm not hungry." I stood up again to leave and Gia physically pressed me back down into the chair.

Sophia continued. "Before you work with Garrick, you need—"

"You know what? Never mind on Garrick. I'll figure something out. If he's not the right person, I'll give my money somewhere else. He can't be the only one working in DV in San Francisco."

"We love you, Brinn," Gia said. "We're sisters now. You don't need to do this alone. It's not your job any longer to keep your mother's secrets."

"This affects you as well as me." I squared my shoulders. "I'll grant you my mother is not the warmest bun in the oven, but when she finds out Quinn has truly turned on her? She's going to lash out and it won't be pretty. She'll destroy Quinn for not believing her."

"That's exactly what we mean, Brinn. That's abuse," Sophia said. "When someone tries to destroy you because you believe something different, that's emotional abuse. That's what we're trying to tell you. This is why you chose the charity you did. It's not an accident."

I scoffed and shook my head. "Sophia, I was there. You don't know what you're talking about. I'm not going to be a grown adult and blame my mother for my issues, and neither should Quinn."

"Quinn was the golden child. Not the target like you were."

"You weren't there, Sophia. It wasn't like that. I annoyed my mother." I let out a laugh. "I still annoy her. I'm not like her. Quinn is like her. They simply understand each other better." I dropped my head into my hands. "This will destroy my mother." I wasn't getting anywhere, but I was getting visibly upset with the twins acting as if they knew my life.

Mary entered and put her head on my shoulder, wrapping her arms around me. "Girls, the patrons can hear you over all the lunch rush. What's going on in here?"

Mary's presence immediately brought the stress levels down,

and I took a moment to drown my sorrows by gulping down the ice water on the table.

"We're telling Brinn that Quinn is going through with the testimony."

Mary frowned. "Maybe this is a conversation you might have in the mansion."

"No, because the mansion has ears," Gia said.

"Then go to Nonna and Papa's house, but this is not a public conversation."

"We were never abused," I said to Mary with my shoulders squared.

She patted my back softly and nodded her head while I spoke.

"I had an idyllic childhood and I love my parents," I reiterated.

"Naturally you love your parents," Mary said.

I felt bolstered by Mary's presence. "Joel must be filling Quinn's head with false memory syndrome. Neither of you were there. I lived it."

"So did Quinn. Her memories are very different from your own," Sophia said as she crossed her sinewy, muscular arms like I'd just told her little green men landed in my backyard and nothing could be more preposterous.

"Why was it so hard for you to come back to Wentworth Manor?" Gia asked while Mary put her hands on my shoulder and rubbed out the tension I felt.

"I was in the middle of my education, Gia. I did what normal people do. I moved out to start my own life. There's nothing nefarious about that." I shook out my hair and Mary took her hands away. "Which would you prefer? A beachfront condo on the Pacific Ocean or the mausoleum?"

"That's easy," Gia said.

"Ballet didn't work out, so I took a different path. That's

what you do in life. It knocks you down and you get back up and go in another direction."

"Quinn is going to relate some stories in court. We want you to be prepared," Sophia said, as if she cared about me.

"You still don't see the connection between your charity and your upbringing?" Gia asked. "For real?"

I was incensed. "There's absolutely no connection. I was not abused! And my mother is innocent of these charges. I don't want to see my mother rot in jail for something she didn't do."

"Girls," Mary said gently.

"Wouldn't you support your mother in the same situation?"

Everyone looked at Mary except for me, since she was behind me, and I knew what they were all thinking. *Our mother wouldn't ever be in this position.*

"They're going to bring up what happened when you shattered your ankle in ballet."

I shrugged. "Nothing happened. Catastrophic injury and I stopped performing. It was time anyway; my muscles were wasting away from the weigh-ins."

That wasn't entirely true. When I shattered my ankle, my mother was backstage and told me to get back out and finish the show. I howled in pain, and she told the director I'd be back and to nix the understudy. *But that was hardly abuse.* That was a typical backstage parent who understood the show must go on and that the audience was waiting. I felt terrible for letting the crowd down that night, but there was nothing to be done about it. My ankle was no more. It could no longer hold my weight.

"I'll admit, my mother doesn't have a lot of empathy."

"Why was she backstage at all? You were an adult. A prima ballerina," Gia prodded.

"Some people are better at mothering than others, but she did her best to be maternal when it wasn't in her nature. My ballet career made her proud and she wanted to be a part of it." I looked at my half-sisters, still conscious to keep my voice down.

"After meeting her mother, Mona, I assume Chelsea's lack of empathy is easier to understand."

"You did permanent damage to your body," Sophia reminded me.

"As all athletes who reach that level have done the same. It's no one's fault. It's just the way life is."

Gia and Sophia both remained silent. A waitress brought in three salads, placed them on the table and hightailed it out of the room. The tension was that thick.

"If my parents need me, I'm going to be there for them. *Both of them.* Thank you for lunch." I turned, and Mary moved aside this time.

"Even if it ruins your relationship with Quinn?" Sophia asked.

I tried to calm myself, but my heart raced, and I rose to my feet. "She's my sister. We'll work it out."

"Please don't leave, Brinn. We've got to talk about this."

"We have to agree to disagree," I said.

I looked at the beautiful salad on the table and my stomach turned. I couldn't bear to eat anything. Even being here with my stepsisters at their mother's restaurant felt like the worst kind of betrayal of my mother. Chelsea Whitman Wentworth was selfish. She was cold and always focused on perfection, but she wasn't a murderess. Nothing they said would convince me of this heinous lie.

"That's why Garrick treated me so strangely yesterday. You told him I was some kind of victim." I was shaking. "I never thought . . ."

"He makes his own assessments," Sophia said. "Even if you're mad at me, don't skip out on him this afternoon. I pulled a lot of strings to get Garrick to set up this meeting."

I couldn't even think about what they'd said about me to Garrick. Or why it should matter to me. I shot out of the restaurant trembling at their treason in every cell of my person.

Mary rushed out after me onto the loud, busy sidewalk. "Take this, Brinn." Mary held the unmarked white bags she'd grabbed from the solid wood bar. "Nobody leaves my restaurant hungry."

I couldn't turn her down. She'd done nothing to deserve my wrath. "Someone will be without food."

"He's a regular. I'll make him more. Just so you know, it's gluten-free, but you need to eat something. You're too thin as it is."

I wanted to thank her, but the expression told me it wasn't a compliment. I'd done so much work in Southern California. I refused to believe none of it showed, that people still saw me as weak and in need of a savior.

"Listen, I'm sorry the girls upset you, but their motive is pure, I promise you. They love you and they want you to be prepared if your mom is found . . . well, you know."

I took the bag and Mary put her hand to my cheek and stared at me intensely. "This too shall pass, Brinn. When people behave badly, it doesn't stop our love. Your father broke my heart, and yet he gave me my greatest gifts of my life. Both things are true." She dropped her hand. I felt the cold chill on my cheek. "People are complicated. If we loved only perfect people, we'd never love at all."

I nodded. I understood her meaning, but I wouldn't abandon my mother. Mother may have been a drama queen and desperate for attention, *but she was not dangerous.* I refused to believe she harmed my grandfather. If she did, it was nothing more than an innocent mistake.

I clutched the white paper bag and ran up the street before the waiting tears filled my eyes. Blinded by my mission, I crashed into a man rounding the corner. It was Garrick Kane.

He braced me by the elbows to protect himself from my velocity. "Brinn? Is everything all right?"

"You're all in this together, is that it?" I grimaced. "You were coming to lunch to close the deal, I suppose."

He looked at me questioningly. "Brinn, you look pale. Why don't you come sit down with me? Get something to eat."

"I'm not turning on my mother and I'm not a victim. No matter what Sophia told you. If you don't want to work with me, I accept that. You can just have the money." My background took over. "Once I check the charity financials, of course."

"What does that mean, you're not a victim? Brinn, come get something to eat."

I held up the bag. "I have something to eat."

"Will I see you this afternoon?"

"I won't let your client down." I jogged off to nowhere, as I had no idea where the town car was. I couldn't think straight and needed to move. I'd made a complete and utter fool of myself. I'd acted like my mother when she threw one of her tantrums. *I'll never escape my genetics. No matter how far I run.*

"Brinn, come back!" Garrick called after me. I turned the corner quickly and hid in an alley against a brick wall near the Greek restaurant. I caught my breath and whatever was left of my sanity. I hated when my emotions showed for other people to witness. I thought I'd numbed myself to crazy reactions. *I was healed. Why did I ever come back?*

My grandfather's will made it impossible for me to escape this drama when all I wanted to do was leave Wentworth Manor and never look back. I wanted to be normal again.

CHAPTER 6

I walked the short distance from North Beach through Russian Hill to Nob Hill. Some strange sense of loyalty landed me at my mom's penthouse. I needed to prove to myself that I could take her emotional punches and remain calm. That the work I'd done in LA worked.

When I walked into the sparkling glass entrance hall, the doorman recognized me immediately.

"Brinn, how I've missed your smiling face. It's been a long time. Your mother will be so pleased you're here."

I doubted that. "Good afternoon, Mr. Bennedetti, how are you?"

"Nothing much changes with me. Your father just went out a few minutes ago, but your mother should be here."

I nodded but didn't meet his eye out of shame. We both knew my mother was home. House arrest made that aspect obvious. It had been ages since I'd been to the condo.

"Would it be okay if you didn't announce me?" I asked. "I'd like to surprise Mother." *I.e., not face her rejection.*

"Is someone here?" He polished the gold buttons at his cuff with a handkerchief. "I'm sorry, but I can't announce anyone

68

right now. I'm on my break." He turned slowly away and dusted a plant. I took the hint and hightailed it to the elevator.

I pressed the code to the penthouse and waited for the shaky, swift ride up to the top floor. As I stepped out into the small exterior foyer, the door to the penthouse was closed. Since it took a code to get up, the door was usually wide open. I knocked and felt my mother's icy stare glaring through the peephole. No doubt she was thinking of some new way to punish me for not having visited. I shifted uncomfortably as I waited. I'd get her full wrath for having the gala without her, so I prepared myself for the onslaught.

You can do this.

She can't hurt you anymore.

You are worthy.

You are accomplished.

You are a prima ballerina, a college graduate . . .

"Mother," I knocked again, "it's me, Brinn. Open up. I brought you something to eat. Gluten-free, your favorite."

My mother opened the door partially and scowled at me. "Well, look what the cat dragged in."

For being on lockdown, she looked fabulous. Her blonde hair coiffed in a swept-up bun and her skin as luminous as ever, with a pale pink lipstick that made it seem like she wasn't even trying. Of course, I knew better. Nothing was more important to my mother than image and it was early yet for her. She generally didn't have makeup on until after two, but today I found her press-ready.

"Is someone here?" I asked her based on the state of her dress.

"I'm here. Where is your sister? Your grandmother?" She peeked into the tiny foyer again.

"Oh, you heard Mona was in town. She got in after the gala though. Plane troubles in Jersey."

Mother hadn't invited me inside. She let me stew in the

cubicle between the elevator and her penthouse like I was some kind of intruder. "Do I need a password to get in?"

More blinking. More silence. She was angry. I could hardly blame her, but I needed her to know I'd stand by her. That I'd found my bearings in Los Angeles, and I'd come to announce my loyalty.

"Mother, before you say anything, we had to have the gala. The will stated we needed to announce the charities publicly and time was running out. We thought it was better to focus on that positive rather than these insane charges against you."

"Who decided?"

"The sisters, along with Mr. Trunkett. There are very strict rules to the will's stipulations. Quinn and I wanted to remind San Francisco the Wentworths weren't going anywhere."

"I'm not going anywhere either, Brinn. I'm a Wentworth." She wore powder-blue slacks that served two purposes from what I could tell. They highlighted the icy blue of her eyes, and they hid the ankle bracelet she'd been forced to wear.

"Naturally, we're just placeholders, Mother. You'll be back. In the meantime, it's crucial to uphold our image as society's dignitaries, as you've always taught us to do." I looked around her at the sparsely decorated, all-white penthouse and waited patiently.

Mother offered a cold, dismissive glance so I'd know her disappointment. "Am I to understand that you were all doing me a favor by hosting a soiree in my home without me as hostess?"

Wentworth Manor wasn't her home any longer, but I wasn't going to correct her. "This penthouse isn't a bad place to be while you await trial," I said. "How long does your lawyer think this could last?"

"Oh, *him*. He's been useless to me. I'd rather be at the Napa house. At least then I could drown myself in wine, but he couldn't even accomplish that for me, so I'm stuck here in this tiny apartment."

The tiny apartment that's 5,000 square feet. Bigger than most people's homes.

My parents' penthouse bore no resemblance to Wentworth Manor. It was nestled atop the tallest condo building in Nob Hill with floor-to-ceiling windows that bathed the rooms in sunlight and/or fog. Sweeping views of the entire city to the end of the San Francisco Bay into the Pacific Ocean reminded one how small and intimate the city really was. A tiny glass balcony induced vertigo in the bravest of souls and I, for one, even with my ballet balance, wouldn't be caught dead out on the terrace in the buckling wind with only a sheath of glass to protect me from falling.

The kitchen was minuscule and as one might expect, unused. If my mother knew how to boil water, I'd never seen it happen.

"Mr. Bennedetti let you up? He never announced you. That man needs to be fired. All he does is gather gossip and overinflated tips while he ignores any security protocol. I'm in danger here. The real killer might want to silence me. Imagine going to my grave with everyone thinking I committed murder."

"Mr. Bennedetti must have been on a break, so I pushed the code and came up." I appreciated the doorman's action. Catching my mother off guard was the safest route for me. "No one else has the code to get up here and you've got the door, too. I think you're safe here." I needed her to know I was on her side and that I'd do anything so that she might escape these ridiculous charges and life could get back to normal—we'd be back to the society page versus the front page. Then all eyes would be off of me, and I could escape again.

"I can leave the apartment, just so you know. I just can't leave this block. We can eat at the restaurant next door. If the vulture press would leave us alone, your father and I might actually do that." She tossed her well-manicured hand. "It's fine up here. I'm only deluged by those newspaper sharks when I try to leave anyway. Did you see them circling when you came up?"

"No." I held up the bag. "I brought you some food," I offered brightly. "Gluten-free pasta." I silently prayed she didn't realize where it was from. Because one mention of Mary Campelli and my mother would lose whatever cool she had left in that frigid stance of hers. I held up the white bag again and shook it. "Mother, are you going to let me in?"

"You can understand why I'm a tad mistrustful. Are you wearing a wire?"

"Mother!" I opened my black jacket and pulled my shirt down. "Never. I'm on your side."

She opened the door wider and the light from the windows blinded me temporarily. "If you think I offed your grandfather, you can leave right now." She pointed an accusatory finger at the elevator.

"Of course I don't believe that." I walked in behind her.

"Put the food in the kitchen, I'll have it later."

"How are you feeling, Mom?" I tried to take her hand with the gentleness Mary had shown me, but my mother flinched and yanked her hand away as if my touch burned her.

"How do you think I'm feeling?" My mother had a way of snapping that was like a rattlesnake striking. She came out of nowhere with her venom.

I kept my voice light. "This will all be over soon. I'm hopeful your lawyers can get them to drop the case for lack of evidence."

"I wish I could be so confident, but there's too much injustice in the world. So many dirty judges. The judicial system and the press are stacked against me. This city has always been jealous of me. They're enjoying every bit of this debacle."

"I don't think that's true."

Mother stood in front of the windows. She was still so stunning that she took one's breath away. As a child, I was transfixed by her beauty. I looked upon her like an angelic being, and some part of me still saw that reflection of her—but that image had been dimmed a bit by the fear she invoked. As if she read my mind, she turned toward me, and I glimpsed the darker version.

"Where did I go wrong with Quinn?" Mother snapped. "I gave the girl everything, and where is she in my time of need? She hasn't come to visit me once. She hosted that gala in my absence as if I hadn't taught her everything about hosting and not so much as a thank you. Ungrateful little—"

"Mother, forget about Quinn—she's so busy right now and I'm here."

She looked me up and down. "Brinn, if I've told you once, I've told you a thousand times, you cannot wear all black without a splash of color. You're too young for that. You look grim, like a Victorian widow."

"Mother, is there anything you need to be more comfortable while you're here?"

She put out her hand. "I need to know my girls are with me. That you're taken care of."

"Mother, we're literally a few blocks away and we've inherited billions," I reminded her. "We are more than taken care of and it's okay to focus on yourself."

"I mean protected. Loved. *Married.*"

I sighed but understood her meaning. Our getting married to someone in society would prove to her that we weren't pariahs because of this ugly situation. That we'd be back. The thought was laughable if it wasn't so pathetic. *How protected was my mother in marriage?* I didn't see my father anywhere, which was our normal. Not to mention he'd been partying at the gala like he didn't have a care in the world—nor a wife. It was utterly humiliating.

"I don't want to get married," I told her, not for the first time. "As soon as this inheritance debacle is all over, I'm going back to SoCal to finish my master's." I'd said this a million times. It didn't mean my mother ever heard me. When one announced their plans to my mother, she promptly ignored them and schemed how she'd get them to change your mind.

"Nonsense. You'll never be accepted if you remain a third wheel. You need a man of your own and the time is now. Why would you go back to a town and live where no one knows you?"

"I like living that way, Mother. Out of the fishbowl. I don't need the limelight as you do. I want a quiet life, a—"

"That's not what you were born for. One can't escape their birthright."

How I hope that isn't true.

"I sent Casey Sutton to the restaurant the other night, did you talk with him?"

"What? I thought Grandmother sent him. How did you know we were going to that restaurant?"

"I have my ways," she said eerily.

Spies in the house still. I shivered and felt grateful Joel Edgerton, traitor that he may be, still lived at the house. The spies worried me for Quinn. If Mother found out Quinn meant to testify, I shuddered to think what might happen. I needed to make sure it was never discussed in the mansion. At least the twins did that much right that morning.

"Casey is such a quality young man. A marriage to his family would stop all the wagging tongues in the city. You girls would be right back on top where you belong and accepted in any home."

I felt the air leave me at the knowledge that my mother still cared about such vapid things when facing a murder charge. "Mother, you need to worry about your circumstances and let this go. I'm not getting married," I repeated. "No marriages during the year of living in the mansion, remember?"

"Well, any decent engagement would be two years anyway. Marrying Casey would be so good for the family. This ugly business would all fade into the background with that kind of society wedding. It would put us right back on top as a family of influence. Make the city forget about this horrible travesty of justice."

"Casey's nearly broke," I reminded her. I didn't mention why they were broke. For some reason, I knew my mother would find Grant's heroic care of his wife's illness a direct attack on her. I also knew it was fruitless to mention I found Casey nauseating. That would only encourage my mother to speak of my cankles and tell me I couldn't be too picky, especially now that I'd gained weight. I wasn't up for that kind of "advice" this week. I'd already been basically rejected by the charity I wanted to support. *Who turned away good money and put the donor through some kind of obstacle course?* Garrick Kane needed a good lesson on running a nonprofit. Namely, that money mattered.

"What does that matter if Casey is broke?" She caught a glimpse of herself in the mirror on the wall and halted as if enraptured by her own beauty. "You don't need his money."

"He doesn't have a job. Or a role, Mother. He literally lives off the kindness of others with his charms—which I fail to see. If Casey is meant for a Wentworth, it isn't me. His spendthrift ways would drive my finance mind nuts."

"He most certainly does have a role. He plays on the pro-am circuit in golf. He's a regular at the Olympic Club, so his father obviously still has some money left and if not money, then he's in the good graces of society, which may prove more valuable in our current circumstance. You have to think long-term."

"I am thinking long-term. I'm learning the financials so I can ensure the family's future wealth so that we can continue to make San Francisco better with our philanthropy. That's my only goal right now. And supporting you, of course."

"Don't be so naive, Brinn. You think everything is about money? Fortunes are bought and sold in a day. Society is more than a bank account."

I lifted a brow. "I think everything is about money?"

"You have all the money you could want, don't you? Your father's portion too, it seems, so I would think you'd be satisfied."

I scanned the countertop for some trinket to discuss. "Is this new?" I lifted a candlestick which clanged as it fell into pieces on the granite countertop.

My mother lunged for the silver. "Brinn! Honestly, these are seventeenth century Spanish Colonial silver. The pair of them cost me a fortune. How can a ballerina be so klutzy?"

"Why do they come apart?"

"They're baroque style, hand casted. They're made up of finely cast collars, each of them individually forged by a craftsman of the era."

"Shouldn't they stay together then?"

She rolled her eyes. "They're not copies. They're original. This is how they did it before machinery." She set the candlesticks back on the countertop.

"They don't really go with the modern style in here."

"Suddenly you're *Architectural Digest*? They're not for this house, but considering my current circumstances, they're here for now. I like to look at beautiful things. It reminds me that all is not lost." Mother's voice became more strained. The reminder of how easily I annoyed her made me anxious. When Quinn spoke, Mother hung onto her every word as if she dropped liquid gold with each sentence. With me, every word challenged her as she seemed to struggle to not smack me.

"Mother, I came to discuss what's going on—"

"Did you know that Casey gets asked for by name to play with Hollywood's elite as their second? He's played with some of the biggest names in politics as well."

"I don't really care about either of those things," I said. "I see famous people all the time in Santa Monica. I couldn't care less. We need to discuss the charges. I need to know your side of things."

Again, I got her stone-cold stare. *Just be quiet, Brinn.*

"Casey is solid husband material. You're not getting any younger."

"No, but I am getting richer, so I imagine I'm not spinster material just yet."

"You think this is funny?"

"Mother, I didn't come here to talk about Casey Sutton. I have no plans to stay in San Francisco after this confinement is over, so—"

"Don't talk to me about confinement, Brinn. Quite callous to do so." She moved the candlesticks piece by piece into the corner of the countertop. "San Francisco is your home. This is the life you were born into, whether you like it or not."

"Wentworth Manor doesn't have that kind of nostalgia for me and neither does San Francisco. I'll work with the charity while I'm here and then it's back to my life. If you can't decide what kind of life you want with billions, what good is it?"

"The shipping industry made the Wentworths a household name in this city and you have a responsibility to carry on that legacy."

I really don't, but I know it's useless to say so.

"I've already said I plan to be on the board of directors, but that's a few meetings a year. I can do that from SoCal." I changed the subject. "Have you and your lawyers discussed a plan of action to get these ridiculous charges dismissed?"

"Why isn't Quinn here?" Mother asked. "She's not taking my calls."

Because she thinks you're guilty. Naturally, I didn't say that. I shrugged, went to the kitchen cabinet and pulled out some bowls that had probably never been used. I served up the pasta without another word. Chelsea Whitman Wentworth always improved on carbs. And she nearly always shot the messenger, which I was determined not to be.

"Where is my *daughter*, Brinn? I need my daughter and I cannot believe she wouldn't be here for me at my time of need."

I'll never be Quinn. Mother focused her laser stare at me, obviously wondering how I might be useful to her now that I wasn't a star of the ballet or San Francisco society.

"I don't think you recognize how advantageous a marriage to Casey could be right now. It would give me the opportunity to fight these charges without all the city's eyes on me."

"Maybe Casey would be a good husband for Quinn? They both spend a lot of time at the club."

She walked toward the window and looked out over the city. "He's not right for your sister. She needs a manlier guy. Someone who can mount a horse from a standing position."

"Casey is not right for her or he's not good enough for her?"

"She has more sophisticated tastes than you. Her standards are different. She needs someone who doesn't care that he needs to compete with a horse, for heaven's sake. Casey is more relational than that."

"Who would you want Quinn to marry?"

"I don't know. Someone more Continental, well-traveled. You spent all your time in a ballet rehearsal, so you're more sheltered and your social skills aren't as refined."

That was the truth. "Sophia is marrying Joel at the end of this. That will have to suffice for a family wedding."

"Sophia," she hissed as she turned. "She's not a Wentworth. She's certainly not my family. It's vulgar to imply so. Marrying that heinous man who planted false evidence against me. It's criminal that they should be living in the family home while I'm here. To think my accusers are in my house, it's all too much."

Technically, none of us were Wentworths since my father's DNA test, but something told me now was not the time to mention this fact. "Maybe I should go. I'm buying a house in the Haight to renovate for families. It's a safe house, so it needs to be done on the quiet."

"This is what I mean about why Casey is good for you. Quinn would never choose such a vulgar charity. It's so distasteful. You cannot bring up," she gulped, "*domestic violence* at a dinner party. How do you expect to raise money for this? People want that kind of thing shoved under the rug."

"I don't need to raise money. I *have* money. I just need to help make a dent."

"Did you come here to rub salt in the wound? You have our money and don't forget it. If you're comfortable with how grandfather has left us out of his will for common guttersnipe pseudo-granddaughters, I know where your allegiance lies."

"Mother, you have plenty. Father has plenty. We *all* have plenty. I think you need to focus on your legal matters. I don't feel like you're taking them seriously."

"Nothing will happen, Brinn. I'm innocent and justice will be served."

"Mom, do you want to have dinner this week? I could have it catered. Or I could even come over and cook. We could—"

"Brinn, I want my life back. I don't want to have dinner parties and pretend I'm not dealing with some overzealous district attorney and his vendetta against people with money."

In a blip, I saw her fear. "I love you, Mom. I want you back in the proper spotlight where you belong." We didn't say we loved each other in my family, and I noted that she was flustered by the outburst of emotion.

"If that were true, you'd do as I asked and call Casey. He could propose by the end of the month. It's not as if you two haven't grown up together. What more is there to know about each other?"

I stopped serving the pasta and shoved the one bowl I'd filled toward my mother. "I'll do what I can." I kissed her cheek. It was obvious that I couldn't reach my mother without Quinn around and that scenario seemed impossible if my sister planned to testify against her.

My mother sat at the kitchen island with the pasta in front of her. I'd suddenly lost my appetite, like I always did when I was with her. "Eat something, you'll feel better. I'll come back soon."

Her arched eyebrow lifted, but she was defeated. "Will you?"

"I will," I promised.

CHAPTER 7

*J*ime with my mother drained me faster than the water in my grandfather's clawfoot tub. She always left me feeling empty and inadequate and I struggled to shake it off but took pride in the fact that I never lost control of my emotions while with her. She hadn't rattled me. I headed for the meeting Sophia arranged, grateful for the diversion.

Garrick Kane, under profound pressure from Sophia, set up an appointment for me to meet with Mrs. Katrina Donley, a litigation lawyer and apparently, a domestic abuse victim. The heat rose in my cheeks after our run-in on the street. He probably saw me as far too unstable to work with victims. And what was worse—he was probably right.

We met at a local church so Mrs. Donley wouldn't be seen at Garrick's security office and tip off her husband. When I entered the church, the scent of candles burned my nostrils and the sounds of the choir practicing echoed off the old stone walls. Garrick emerged from a heavy wooden door with his suit jacket off, his tie askew and his collar pleasantly disheveled. He looked, well, in a word . . . *hot*, and I fanned myself with the notepad I'd brought to take notes. *Why are the hot ones always so arrogant? So aloof?*

"Miss Wentworth." He nodded.

Another universal truth—why are the sexy men always so smug? Isn't there a nice guy in San Francisco who doesn't look like Quasimodo and doesn't have an attitude?

"Mr. Kane," I said with equal severity.

"Call me Garrick. If we're going to keep running into each other, we might as well make it official that we're acquainted. Friends?"

My eyes narrowed. "Why were you at the mansion the night of the gala? Why is that a secret? It's on the security cameras."

He looked past me and spoke through his teeth. "I can't tell you just yet, but it's nothing nefarious. I promise you."

"But you want me to keep it from my sisters."

"If possible." Then he aimed that sultry gaze at me, and I was hypnotized. This man could sell tickets to tour Wentworth Manor and I'd be first in line to purchase. I kept reminding myself of my therapist's words. *Just because you feel emotions around someone, it doesn't make them safe. It's simply a chemical reaction. As you start to feel more, these things will happen. Feel the feelings and move forward.*

"Are you ready for this?"

I nodded as I met the gray-green of his eyes. Questions about their origin stormed my brain. *Is he Irish? Welsh? German? What color was his hair as a baby?* "I read all the information you sent me home with."

"I'm impressed."

"I actually got more out of your personal notes than I did the books. You have a lot of insight."

"I like to think so." His eyes displayed a faraway look, as if he tried to recall what he'd written in the margins. "Brinn?" He snapped me back to the present.

"Yes?"

"Did Sophia fill you in on what you could say and what you couldn't say to our client?"

I lifted my writing pad. "She gave me a list and of course, your notes. I have it memorized."

He nodded curtly.

"Listen, if I was rude after running into you outside the Italian restaurant, I'm sorry. I had just received bad news. I meant what I said though. If you want me to donate, that's fine. I was way too pushy."

"It made me happy to run into you." Garrick stopped me from saying more. "It doesn't matter why you want to help. I should have been grateful on behalf of my clients."

"I know what this must seem like to you. Rich girl thinks she can save the world—maybe do your job better than you can."

He smiled. "I don't doubt that you could. I think it would be a mistake to underestimate you." He gripped the antique brass doorknob. "I've done a background check on you. No drug use. No run-ins with the law. No violent ex-boyfriends. For an heiress, you're pretty clean."

"I don't like to color outside of the lines."

"It was nothing personal. I don't like surprises and marijuana may be legal, but not in my organization."

I laughed uncomfortably. "One time, in college, there was this kid who was high all the time, he—"

Garrick's forehead crumpled as he stared at me. *What is it about this man that makes me produce random information?* I was generally quiet, but Garrick was the strong, silent type and his silence made me nervously fill in all those empty airwaves to quell the awkwardness between us.

Note to self: it didn't work.

He grabbed the doorknob again and gripped it tightly, as if rethinking if I should be allowed inside. Sophia managed to get him to acquiesce against his better instincts, and I didn't want to blow it.

"I've hosted diplomats and the highest of aristocracy. I'll be on my best behavior," I reassured him just as my mother might have. *Oooh, I'm so important. Please be impressed by me.*

He appeared uncertain, and the small lines on his forehead creased in thought again. The more he questioned my behavior, the more I acted like someone else. A complete idiot who rambled.

"I'm nervous." I gave a small shrug. "You make me nervous."

"Do I?" He gave a half-cocked grin as if that gave him pleasure.

"You're very intimidating, Mr. Kane. I'm sure you've heard that somewhere before."

He pursed his lips and shook his head. "Never."

This wasn't going well. "What did I do to make you dislike me?"

"I don't dislike you, Miss Wentworth, but trust isn't something I give easily. Not in my line of work. It's not personal. I just want to protect the clients."

"Not trusting people sounds like a harsh way to live." I said this, practically batting my eyelashes in mock innocence, as if it wasn't exactly how I lived my own life.

"I'm trusting you," he reminded me.

The weight of his confidence motivated me. For reasons I didn't understand, I longed to be worthy of this man's trust. It was not given easily, so all the more desirable.

"I understand. I'll be careful."

"Please do. She's still in active danger. Her husband is obsessive and controlling, but the most upsetting is he knows the law. He knows how far he can push the boundaries without technically breaking the law."

"That's terrifying."

"Know that I trust you, Brinn. If I didn't, you wouldn't be here regardless of Sophia being your sister."

I nodded while my heart swelled. Those were the words I wished my mother had said that morning.

"In other words, it's not you, Miss Wentworth. It's the notoriety that comes with you."

"I'll do everything to fly under the radar." I tried to connect with him. "You witness all these ugly things, so you assume everyone has a dark side."

"Everyone *does* have a dark side," he said.

Ominous. "I'll remember that."

"Look, it's not too late to back out of this charity. I'll come up with the excuse if you need one for the press."

I couldn't lie to myself. He was scaring the living daylights out of me.

"You sure you want to do this?" He clutched the doorknob so that his knuckles turned white. "Mrs. Donley is coming up on the most dangerous part of the cycle—she's getting ready to leave. She has two kids to think about as well."

"Garrick," I heard my voice tremble, "if it's not the right charity for me, I'll back out gracefully. I promise. The last thing I want is to put anyone in danger."

"I know." For all his gruff exterior, his kid gloves with his client drew me in. He felt her life was in his hands and carried the responsibility for it. Coming from a family of blamers, I couldn't help but find that inviting. This part of him restored my faith in humanity.

"Anything else I should know?"

"This case will be hard to hear. Extreme emotional and financial abuse, but she's well-spoken and wants to get the word out so she's willing to talk."

"She sounds amazing."

"I must reiterate that her anonymity is of the utmost importance for her safety. I'm only telling you her true name because I imagine you may recognize her from some of your parties. You two probably have mutual acquaintances."

His speech made me so nervous, my hands were shaky. He released the doorknob again and I was ready to grab it myself.

"Regardless of what happens here today, I still plan to renovate the safe house."

"Appreciate that."

I half expected the woman behind the door to have eight arms the way he built my fears.

He finally launched open the door. "Mrs. Donley," he said.

Inside sat a stunning blonde with perfect posture. She bore a striking resemblance to my mother except she was closer to my own age. I would have placed her right about thirty years of age. She had deep blue eyes which had an element of darkness to them that I couldn't place. On her wedding ring finger, she wore a diamond the size of a small ice cube in an emerald cut. My eyes couldn't help but focus on the jewel as she rose and the hand with the ring came toward me in a gesture of greeting.

"Brinn, it's such a pleasure to meet you. I know you by reputation, of course, and I've seen you perform. You were absolutely mesmerizing on stage. I was so sorry to hear of your accident."

"Th-thank you." I snuck a look back at Garrick to see if he noticed she knew me, but his poker face gave nothing away.

"I'm Katrina Donley, as I'm sure Garrick told you."

Garrick gazed at the two of us and I could see the conflict in his head. He had things to do but didn't want to leave me alone with this beauty who looked anything but frail. She looked like an Instagram model who made a living showing off how put together she was. I didn't know that this was the type of victim I had in mind when I said I wanted to help. She seemed quite competent.

"I have a million questions, but I don't want to upset you," I told her. "Just tell me if I get too close to a tender subject and I'll drop it."

"Absolutely."

Garrick stared at us as I sat down. There was a quiet agreement made between the three of us and though his jaw twitched, he exited the room.

"Thank you for agreeing to meet with me, Mrs. Donley." I took out my notepad. "I won't write down any names or identifying information."

"You don't have to be so nervous, Brinn. Call me Katrina and we'll talk, all right?" She brushed an invisible piece of lint from her pristine white slacks.

I looked again at the ring on her finger, which probably could have purchased a small island in the center of the Pacific. Silently I wondered if I could help a woman like her. She seemed a lot more put together than me. Legally, neither Sophia or Garrick could tell me anything about her, so I felt like I'd come into the meeting blind and bewildered. I'd already judged her, which Garrick's notes warned me about.

"You'll forgive my ignorance, but it seems you may have means to get free of your ex and I must admit, that makes me question so much of what I've read."

She laughed lightly. "It may seem like that, and I'll admit, this ring could be hocked for a pretty penny, but that won't free me from my situation. If it could, I'd be at the pawn shop within an hour."

I gnawed at my lip. "Can't you just divorce him? It's a no-fault state. I'm sorry, but I don't understand the issue if you're so unhappy."

"Just leave," she laughed. "The helpful advice from well-meaning but ignorant people everywhere."

Her answer sobered me up.

"Most likely, that's why Garrick wanted me to talk with you rather than a victim with fewer resources. Most likely, I'm one of his more complicated cases." She laughed lightly as if she didn't have a care in the world. "Leave it to me to strive to be the best in everything. Top of my class in law school and selecting bad husbands."

Honestly, I didn't think there was anything I could do for this client. I had *money* to help. I could get women and children out of a dark situation, give them a roof over their heads and a sense of safety, but it seemed like Katrina was making a choice to stay. She could book herself an Airbnb and be out tonight. *How can I help someone like her?*

"My idea was to provide—well, to renovate an old Victorian in the Haight so that victims would have a nice home with other families in the same position. They could empower one another and find work or learn new skills they might need to support their families."

"I know how a safe house works, Brinn. I'm a lawyer," Katrina said. "I know the law and I know my options, but it doesn't change my situation. Be very careful about who you decide to make a family with, it has lifelong repercussions."

"I'm not making a family with anyone, so I'm good. I'm all ears. Tell me why someone like you, with the means to make a good living and the looks to walk the runway, is stuck."

"I appreciate your honesty, Brinn. It's nothing I haven't heard before, so I'm happy to enlighten you. My husband is very powerful in town. In fact, he's planning on running for mayor. He's well known in your social circles, I'm sure."

"Not *Matt* Donley?"

"One and the same," she said softly. "Humanitarian, district attorney, mayoral candidate and wife abuser."

My jaw dangled. "But you don't need a safe house?"

"I will eventually, but I need a lot more than that. I need an escape route. That's where Garrick comes in."

"What is it someone like you needs?"

"I need the courts to take a fair look at my husband, and that isn't going to happen. Garrick knows it. I know it. My husband knows it. Women like me need legislation written that protects us from obsessive men who think they own their wife and kids. The courts treat everyone like both parties want a divorce and both parties will be fair and truthful in court. Funny thing is abusers lie. Easily, in fact. They're very good at it and I'll end up looking like the unstable gold digger who tried to take advantage of this *nice guy.*"

"I understand what it's like to be slandered, but even if he lies, the bank accounts, the property, it's all split down the middle. We're in a community property state."

She uncharacteristically cackled at me. *Cackled.* "Sometimes the money is in offshore bank accounts that you know nothing about. Your name is conveniently left off deeds and titles. Your passport is hidden for *safekeeping.* One thing is certain, the money is not where I have access to it to hire my own lawyer. Not that anyone would take my case." Katrina's full lips looked as if they'd been freshly plumped with filler, and I had a hard time focusing on her words. "What happens when a woman like me gets into court is she'll be called crazy, probably a drug addict, and the *pièce de résistance,* a terrible mother. He'll find any means he can to disparage me and steal my children right back into the home of their abuser. And the courts will help him do it. If I did get the divorce, he'll get the kids half the time and he'll spend every second telling those kids how awful and scary I am."

"Parental alienation," I said.

"The courts won't rule that custody should be half and half. He won't allow it. He'll use his power and means to get me out of their life eventually. Because he hasn't won unless he's destroyed me for wanting a divorce. So that's the big question. Do you selfishly go and let your kids suffer? Or do you stay and try to be the safety net?"

I sat back in my chair and gnawed at my lip again. Garrick was right. I was well out of my league. So much so that I had a hard time believing anything the woman said. It may have felt true to her, but was it? "What do you mean no lawyer will take your case? Do you need money for the retainer fee because—"

"I mean that no lawyer in San Francisco will go against him. He's a high-ranking member of the bar and he'd probably have anyone disbarred who worked for me. Everyone has something to hide. My husband would find it and his colleagues know that."

Here I'd been thinking I was going to help some poor woman to balance her checkbook and save the world.

She went on, "Your lovely house is a great idea, and it will help some women, but what Garrick is working on is much bigger. It's all-encompassing. It's fixing the court system."

"California is a 50/50 state," I reiterated.

"That's not how it works. People hide money. The poorer spouse doesn't have money to afford the discovery process to find where it's hidden. Many women like me will leave without a dollar to their name just to escape their abuser—even if he or she has more money than Moses. Those are the facts, unfortunately. The scales of justice aren't balanced, and please trust me when I say that I'm not staying for the money. I'd leave without a penny if I could, but I'm not leaving without my kids. My boys are seven and eleven, it's time. Every day is a battle, but it's time to go to war."

I remained quiet. I had to admit, I didn't understand why she didn't just leave, get a job and come back for the kids if necessary. It seemed like she attributed supernatural powers to the man. Katrina rose and walked toward the stained-glass window that depicted Mother Mary tenderly holding baby Jesus.

"You don't have children, Brinn."

I shook my head. "No, I'm not even married."

"Let me tell you something, no mother is going to leave her children with an abuser by choice. It's like leaving a steak to be guarded by a hungry tiger."

"The courts—"

"The courts will only help him abuse me further," she said again. "These are the truths Garrick wants you to understand. People want easy answers. There's no reason for what my husband does. No motive other than his lust for power. He'd hurt his own kids to hurt me. Try proving that in court."

"I'm only being devil's advocate here, but you don't think that sounds a bit paranoid?"

She laughed again. "Of course it does. He's banking on that."

I felt like the conversation had walked me in a big circle and I'd gone nowhere. "What does Garrick's foundation do that's different from just hiring a good lawyer?"

"For one, he hires lawyers from other parts of the state who won't be threatened by local powers. When someone is obsessive, the police can't act until they do. In other words, I get justice only when I'm dead."

I gasped.

"Much of Garrick's work is done on the sly—almost like a covert CIA operation. That's what he's trying to tell you."

The light of understanding came upon me. My money hadn't saved me either. I simply went along with the role I'd been given as a vapid socialite and ballerina. Not that I'd been hurt by my situation, but freedom wasn't measured in cash.

"You see why Garrick doesn't want any publicity." Katrina came and sat back down at the rough wooden table.

"I do."

"Give Garrick the money and let his organization handle things."

I nodded. "I will."

"He understands the idiosyncrasies and subtle ways that abusers gain control. I think you're amazing for caring though, I really do. If I were you, I'd probably shop all day and maybe hit the spa a few times a week."

My shoulders slumped. "Listen, for what it's worth, you've enlightened me. Not everything is cut and dry."

She smiled and her perfectly straight teeth were so white, they nearly blinded me. "I appreciate that."

"This is my mobile number." I gave her my calling card. "If you just need someone to talk or a place to run to. You and the children are always welcome at Wentworth Manor. We have security cameras everywhere. The only down thing is we're going to be starting construction on necessary repairs, so it's going to be loud, but regardless, you're welcome."

She twirled a long blonde tendril around her forefinger. "You have enough going on with your mother's case."

My face flamed hot and red from shame at the mention of my mother. Now I had to face Garrick Kane, who'd been right all long.

"I figure we have that in common," Katrina said as she pulled sunglasses from her handbag. "That's why I agreed to meet with you."

"Pardon?" I failed to understand her connection.

"High-profile abusers."

I shook my head. "Me?" I placed my fingertips on my chest.

"Once you've been beaten down by a narcissist, you learn to recognize the signs pretty quickly in others."

I scrambled to get my folder of empty, worthless information together and beat it out of the room. "Thanks again. Best of luck," I said as I escaped.

Garrick Kane stood outside the room like a wall, blocking my way. "Get everything you came for?" he asked me.

"Everything. Excuse me." I needed to flee before I got sick. I didn't make it down the church steps before I saw Garrick at my side.

"I owe you an apology, Brinn."

"You don't owe me anything." I waved my hand behind me. "Nice to see you again. I'll be in touch."

But Garrick kept my pace easily. Once at the bottom of the long stone staircase, he touched my elbow to get my attention, but I refused to meet his eye. The hopelessness of Katrina's situation made me ill and at the same time, she was worried for *me*.

"Katrina's great." I spoke down to the sidewalk. "Thanks for setting that up."

He touched my chin and forced my eyes up to his. "I'm sorry," he said. "I gave you that long speech about protecting Katrina, but I had an obligation to protect you, too." The sincerity in his eyes forced me to face the truth. *People feel sorry for me.*

"You all shouldn't believe what you read in the newspapers about my family. I don't need anyone's protection."

Garrick's tall stature intimidated me, but he moved to a lower step so our heights were more equal. "I'm trying to tell you that I was wrong. You're not some flighty socialite who wants publicity. The fact that I implied that reflects poorly on me as a human being."

"Thank you?" I didn't know what he wanted from me. But his complete turnaround unnerved me. I'd seen that switch flip in my mother before, right before she swooped in and took something that belonged to me.

He took my hand gently to keep me from leaving. I clasped his back, feeling the energy run up my arm; the magical, unspoken spark between us.

"I have an idea for how you can help the foundation."

"Katrina told me how it is. I understand now. I'll hand over the cash without fanfare. Just between us and the IRS."

"No." He tugged at his loosened tie. "You have this ability to change the atmosphere when you're in the room. The foundation can use that gift. I don't know why I didn't see it before."

"I need to go. I need to have my dress fitted for the ballet opening." I walked around him, but he took three steps at a time and stood before me again. *In all his masculine glory.*

"I'll be in touch soon," he said.

I won't hold my breath. I need to find a new charity. Stat.

CHAPTER 8

*O*pening night of the San Francisco Ballet season brought mixed feelings. The pomp and circumstance brought out the city's best efforts to revisit another more civilized era, when being dressed to the nines mattered. I cherished all the beautiful people in their billowing ball gowns and designer tuxedoes. The ambiance created a fairy-tale world that swept me back in time to when I danced. While I appreciated the opportunity to mingle with society at its finest rather than rehearse and prepare in the chaos backstage, I also resented and grieved the life that should have been mine.

I stared at my reflection in the illuminated vanity table. My expression, lifeless. I'd never laugh, cry or panic with my fellow dancers who understood the striving toward perfection. Instead, I'd sit in the audience as a blank witness to greatness.

Quinn came behind me and rested her chin on my shoulder. "How are you feeling?"

"How am I ever feeling? I'm fine," I said. It was well known that emotions weren't my strong suit, but *this* I felt.

"We've been through a lot this year. I thought it might be

harder. Although maybe easier for you without Mother there this year."

It was the perfect segue to ask her if she really intended to testify, but I couldn't bring myself to do it. Tonight had enough anguish. "You know, the first year I saw Sasha as prima leap into the air and land with grace, my soul died a little, but I'm getting to the point where I enjoy watching again."

The weight of my handicap made it seem as though my ankle were cemented into the floor beneath me, and I'd never take flight again. I was earthbound.

"Every year, it will get easier. The important thing is to keep facing it."

"I miss having wings."

"You still have wings." Quinn kissed my cheek. "You'll get to explain all the intricacies to our sisters. You can view the ballet through their eyes tonight."

"Alisa must be thrilled. She'll love all the fashion."

"Oh, didn't I tell you? Alisa decided she's not going."

"She got that incredible gown." I turned around. "What do you mean she's not going?"

"She already wore it on Instagram. She says her followers don't care what old people are wearing. We're old, apparently."

I laughed. "Washed up in our twenties. I thought the ballet opening would be the most Instagrammable moment she'd have."

"She says, and I quote, 'Who wants to hang out with a bunch of ancient people in grand muumuus and listen to elevator music?'"

"Tell her I'm sorry that ballet hasn't found the musical stylings of Cardi B yet. Maybe next year."

"You don't know that for sure," Quinn said. "There's some ballet company somewhere that is taking Cardi B to the next level."

"Heaven help us all."

She rubbed my shoulders. "I'm sorry dance was taken from you, but God isn't finished with you yet. He has some other plan for you."

"Well, whatever it is, it's not domestic violence as a charity." I stood and paced the room. "Quinn, what a fool I made of myself this week with that friend of Sophia's, Garrick Kane. He tried to warn me, but I didn't listen. I thought, when have I ever been overcome by my feelings? I went in so arrogant that I could fix everything."

"Maybe his charity isn't for you, but that doesn't mean you have to abandon the cause."

"The victim I met with? She was a rich stay-at-home mom. She'd had a good job before she had kids, but this man she married seems to have her trapped. She has everything a woman could want, except she doesn't really."

"I don't get it."

"The point is a safe house isn't going to help her. She looks over her shoulder constantly, turns her phone off so she can't be tracked. Her husband has access to anywhere she'd go. She has to stay in her lane, or she could lose everything."

"It sounds like you're mad at her."

"Maybe I am. I'm frustrated for her, but she made me feel hopeless and I hate that."

"That guy Garrot is an idiot."

"Garrick."

"You'd be an asset to any charity you picked and anyone worth their weight in philanthropy would know that. Forget him."

"It was so humiliating."

"As far as this woman goes," Quinn continued, "maybe she isn't who you help, but that doesn't mean you're worthless to this cause. That's Mom in your head. Life isn't all or nothing."

I brushed some powder across my face and put on the diamond studs my father had given me for my first prima performance. "It's not Mother. It's me. I want things to be perfect. I'm wired that way. I have to do what's best. Or at least, try harder."

"You'll be passionate again about the right thing, Brinn. Remember when you first came home from the ballet dorms? What were you, sixteen?"

"Fifteen."

"You were so impressed that the school had practice tutus." Quinn laughed. "'Practice tutus' you yelled as you danced through the house in your little puff of pink tulle." Quinn laughed.

I wonder if I'll ever feel that light again.

"You gave up so much for ballet, Brinn. High school. Proms. Friends. It's okay to grieve. This is terrible to have to watch others do what you're better at. You finally get to go to grad school and now, that's been taken from you too. But it's only temporary. You'll get to find your new path soon, I believe that. God is just saying wait."

"God is always saying wait. My entire life is one big yield sign. I can't even give away my money properly."

"This charity fiasco is a detour, but I know you, you'll make the most of it and find where you're supposed to be. If this isn't your charity, we'll do a press release and change it. Stop worrying."

"It's going to be hard to see Garrick again. Or that woman. I hope I never run into either of them. I acted like an imbecile whose money could fix everyone's problems."

"A little humiliation is good for the soul."

"Tonight will still be torture. I never liked Natasha and she's prima."

"Well, you look incredible. This gown is exquisite."

I looked down at my dress. I'd gone with an homage to my former dancing days in a couture Monique Lhuillier gown in navy blue. It was dotted with Swarovski crystals and hugged my frame tightly to knee level, then it flared into a sparkling skirt reminiscent of the night sky. "I'm grateful we don't have escorts. It's so freeing not to have to worry about small talk."

"Mother would have a fit if she knew we weren't having escorts again. Can you imagine what she would have said about us going to our gala alone? Much less the ballet opening."

I hadn't told Quinn I'd seen our mother. I knew she'd chastise me for my weakness.

"Sophia is bringing Joel, but he'd be there anyway," Quinn said. "He's so paranoid about us going out lately. I don't know what he thinks is going to happen."

"He'll feel better when this court date is over for Mother. Then we can all move on with our lives."

We averted our eyes and dropped the subject immediately. Neither one of us wanted to think about Chelsea Wentworth missing her first opening night.

Quinn looked nothing less than regal. She'd opted for a Zac Posen strapless periwinkle gown with a boned corseted top and a mermaid skirt. When she walked in it, it also shimmered like a magical night sky, which went with the ballet's Northern Lights theme.

"What did you help the twins buy?"

"Oh, those two." Quinn rolled her eyes. "They honestly think they're going to run out of money any day. I had to tell the stylist to hide the price tags so we could get it done already."

There was a quiet knock on my bedroom door.

Quinn opened it to the twins. Sophia and Gia both looked so stunning, they made me wish I'd been born a brunette—it would certainly be less time-consuming than the constant highlights to stay a blonde as an adult. Sophia stood in front of Joel, who I had to admit, looked like a fitness model in his tuxedo with a cutaway for the now black cast he still wore after being hit by a Smart car. He was using a black and gold Victorian cane that belonged to Grandfather. It went well with his finery. As a small party, we were worthy of any *Masterpiece* costume drama.

Sophia curtsied. "Sophia Campelli, heiress to the Wentworth fortune, is wearing Elie Saab Couture." She twisted the lavender gown with the navy tulle overlay with swirling sequin embellishments and small silk butterflies that made her appear like the perfect spring evening in the garden. "How's my heiress-speak coming along?"

"Right perty talk." Gia giggled. As expected, her gown was more daring, indicative of her work as the textiles curator at the museum. "Also, Elie Saab," she twirled. Her gown was a light sky blue and covered with different textures so it appeared 3D. An off-the-shoulder gown, the color highlighted her olive skin as though she'd just returned from Hawaii. When she turned, a brief but elegant train followed her.

"I can hardly believe I get to show up with the beautiful four Wentworth sisters," Joel said. "What a turn my life has taken. Maybe getting run over by a car was the best day of my life."

"Don't say that," Sophia snapped. "I'll never forget the imagery of you crumpled in the street. It was my worst nightmare come to life."

"It brought you to me, so I'd do it all over again." The two of them kissed as though they couldn't keep away from each other.

"Let's keep the romance on the stage, shall we?" I asked curtly.

Our sisters looked as if they'd been attending ballet openings forever and we were the novices. I wondered how the press would take our arrival, noticeably without the star quality of our parents. Luckily, no decent society dame would dare ask us.

* * *

THE WAR MEMORIAL Opera House in San Francisco was an oppressively designed historical theater built in the 1930s during the Great Depression in dedication for local heroes who died while serving in World War I.

Joel, with his hulking frame and stilted walk on the cane, hurried us through the red-carpet introductions and kept any journalist from asking us deeper questions beyond who designed our gowns. We skipped the pre-gala party for the same reason and were led quickly to our seats in the orchestra section. As Grand Benefactors, we'd be invited to mingle with the dancers and choreographers following the performance, but I couldn't handle that emotionally, so my sisters joined me in declining the invitation. As soon as photos were taken, I'd high-tail it home as if I were Cinderella herself and my carriage was about to turn into a pumpkin.

Once seated, it wasn't long before the theater darkened and the musicians' tuning halted. The maestro entered to rousing applause and the melodious sounds of strings began. I closed my eyes and let my body dance to the role I'd been taught so many years ago. It was almost as if I were there on stage meeting my wicked stepmother and watching my evil stepsisters dance comically to the spiccato bouncing bow on the violins.

The first act passed quickly and the prima ballerina, once my understudy, commanded the theater. The first act ended with a standing ovation, not out of politeness, but because she'd earned it. She illuminated the stage, and a jealous streak ran through my core like wicked lightning.

Intermission was why we were here. *To be seen.* The press was kept behind the decorated barricades and were only there to take pictures of the mingling guests.

"There's Vivien," Quinn said as she spotted her best friend. "Gia, Sophia, let's go say hello. She always sneaks truffles in her purse. We can get a sugar rush." My sisters pranced across the room.

I noted that Katrina Donley was across the grand hall, and

my muscles tightened. I'd made such a fool of myself meeting with her and I felt compelled to apologize. Katrina was resplendent in a backless red dress that clung to her yoga-fit frame like a Danskin bodysuit.

I walked straight toward her as she stood alone with a champagne flute in her hand. "Mrs. Donley, how gorgeous you look in that gown! Red is definitely your color."

The abject fear in her eyes reminded me of Garrick's warnings. *We aren't supposed to know each other.* I stammered for words.

Mr. Donley appeared by her side from out of nowhere. As handsome as any movie star, he appeared harmless as he smiled warmly at me. "Miss Wentworth," he said. "What a pleasure to finally meet you in person."

"Mr. Donley, I presume." I reached out a hand toward him and tried not to shudder as he touched me.

"Matt," he answered. "Please, call me Matt. I feel like I've grown up with you. Your family was always on that society page across from the comics, so it feels like I know you."

"What a pleasure it is to see you here, Katrina." I saw his eyes flash, just as my mother's did when she was suspicious. Nervously, I kept talking. "Matt, I don't know if Katrina has told you, but we've been trying to get her to join the board of trustees for *Encore*. It's the young professionals group supporting ballet. So far, she's ignored all of the committees' pleas, but maybe you can help her see the advantage of being involved. We need a new generation to embrace ballet."

His demeanor completely changed. "Katrina? You didn't tell me this." Then he looked directly at me. "Have you called the house? I don't remember any calls to the house regarding this."

"Not me personally. I think one of the mothers on the committee talked to her at the kids' school." I lied so easily that I knew that my mother's DNA contributed something. "I certainly hope she's been called and there hasn't been a miscommunication. Katrina's the perfect demographic to reach our younger audience. With her legal background and love for fitness, her name has come up again and again."

I had no idea if she loved fitness. I simply assumed that no one got a body like hers without a deep affliction to exercise.

He looked confused. "You may have been misinformed, Miss Wentworth. My wife isn't practicing law currently. Not for years now. She stays home with our boys."

Heavens. He's terrifying in his innocuous, passive-aggressive way. I felt the distrust in his voice and knew I was culpable in my thoughtless stupidity. Nothing in Matt Donley came off as dangerous or menacing. If I hadn't known the truth, I'd question Katrina's sanity for certain. Now I understood the true threat she was under. He was utterly predatory in that he seemed like the perfect husband. *Just as my mother seems like the perfect parent.*

"Mrs. Donley." Joel stepped forward alongside Sophia. "I don't know if you remember me, but we met at the Legal Warriors dinner years ago. I may have given your name to Brinn when she was looking for new patrons. I hope you don't mind, but young women who are cultured are getting harder to find. Aren't you running for mayor, Mr. Donley? Might be the perfect opportunity to get some campaign donors."

"It's quite an honor to be asked onto the committee," I reiterated. "We meet in the finest homes in the city."

I didn't understand how Joel knew I may have caused trouble and I didn't care. I was so grateful for his presence, I could have knocked Sophia aside and hugged him.

"Of course I don't mind." Katrina smiled and then quickly looked down.

Joel went on, "Once Brinn heard it, your name blew up like a wildfire in the board group chat. The industry can't wait for you to get back to practicing law."

"And you are?" Mr. Donley puffed his chest out toward Joel,

but it was pointless. Joel was large and built like a brick wall. Even on a cane, it was obvious Joel could take down Matt Donley with ease. Matt was minuscule by comparison.

"Joel Edgerton." Joel extended his hand. "Private investigator and former San Francisco police officer." Joel said this as the threat it was. "Allow me to introduce my girlfriend, Sophia Campelli Wentworth." Joel sang Sophia's name as though it were a favorite melody.

Mr. Donley's squared jaw flinched, but he caught hold of his reaction, visibly relaxed and thrust his hand toward Joel. "It's a pleasure. I'm surprised my wife made such an impression on you. Years ago, you say?"

"I do a lot of pro bono cases for officers accused falsely of criminal activity. She proved to be a good advocate for my fellow law enforcement, and one doesn't easily forget that. She's got an amazingly sharp mind."

The tension ratcheted up. I decided to take the focus off of Joel. "It's such a privilege to be asked to be on the board, Mrs. Donley, but I do understand if you're too busy with the children and all. We try not to take up too much of your time and most of the work is done off-season. I thought it might be good for your husband's campaign."

"She'd love to serve," Mr. Donley stated. "Wouldn't you, darling?"

"I'll have to think—" Katrina started to speak.

"What is there to think about?" Mr. Donley said. "Such an honor. It would be good to get out of the house now and again, wouldn't it?"

The lights started to dim on and off, and I made excuses and raced toward the ladies' room. I was wet with sweat from my close encounter and when I approached the restrooms, I saw Garrick Kane standing in his tuxedo with a tall, willowy brunette by his side. Her dress was cheap. I took amusement in that, but she was still a ravishing beauty. The two of them looked like wedding cake toppers in their perfection and in response, I felt my jaw tighten. She kissed Garrick's cheek and walked into the ladies' room as I approached him.

I wanted to confess what I'd done and tell him he'd been right all along. "Garrick, I—"

His eyes narrowed and under his breath, he whispered, "*Stop talking.*" I turned around to see Mr. and Mrs. Donley walking toward us and my hands trembled. Garrick didn't acknowledge that he'd seen them, but he pulled me in toward him, wrapped his arms around me tightly in an intimate embrace and kissed me full on the lips. He pulled away briefly and whispered in my ear, "Kiss me back like you mean it."

I melted like a wilted leaf in his arms and had no trouble obliging. I didn't need to be told twice. Garrick swept me up in his grasp and planted his firm, warm lips against mine again. My heart pounded in my ears like a snare drum. I was drawn into the most passionate kiss of my life. I tingled down to my toes at his touch as his mouth searched earnestly for mine.

Time stopped. All awareness of where I was disappeared into the sparkling lit starry sky of the War Memorial Opera House. I forgot everything but Garrick's touch, his desire for me. They say your life flashes before your eyes when you die, but my enchanting future played out before my closed eyes.

I envisioned myself in a whimsically romantic Hayley Paige wedding gown with a long lace trail. I held a red rose bouquet and strolled down the grand aisle of Grace Cathedral—the wedding march echoing off its stone walls. I smelled the incense burned earlier in the church. Garrick stood on the altar in his black tie and tails beckoning me with his boyish grin and unmistakable charm. The vision didn't end there. I saw our towheaded toddler with blonde locks with his father's steely green eyes and serious nature. We'd have a boy first and then a girl, and of course, an Australian Shepherd named Barbary after the rugged coastline of early San Francisco.

When Garrick pulled away, I felt breathless and weary as if I'd been on a time travel adventure and returned home struggling to find my bearings on solid ground. When I finally came around, all eyes were on Garrick and me, the audience's mouths held ajar, which took me back to the stage when I lay crumpled in a ball on my broken ankle.

The defiant child in me, who I'd forgotten existed, stood steadfast in challenge against anyone who dared tell me I'd done something wrong. I patted the back of my updo and stared right back. They were all simply jealous. I wanted to grab Garrick by the wrist and steal him away out of the opera house and down the grand staircase in my own retelling of Cinderella.

I was swiftly snapped back into reality by a harsh smack across my right cheek. I grabbed for it instinctively where it continued to sting. Garrick's date, in her cheap red dress and matching lipstick, stood fuming and positioned to strike me again with her now tightly wrapped fist. Garrick grabbed her arm before she could clobber me again. Not only was her dress low-rent, now I knew *she* was.

"What kind of woman hits another woman?" I implored. "At the ballet opening?" I rubbed the throbbing cheek. "Honestly, who did you get to hold your beer?"

I heard Gia laugh and I understood being around my Italian sisters had taught me a few things.

Garrick separated us and loudly whispered in his date's ear. The Donleys, who had been headed straight for us, were long gone as they wanted no part in our drama. Matt Donley obviously knew better than to get involved in a scandal before his run for office.

Gia strode over to Garrick and the woman who'd just struck me. "Did you just hit my sister?" Her voice took on her Nonna's Italian accent.

I held Gia back. "I don't need a warrior now, Gia. This is your moment to show San Francisco society who you are, don't let this girl ruin it." I leaned in toward her and shrugged. "I kissed her boyfriend, so technically . . . well, she's not wrong."

Gia shrugged.

"She's not—" Garrick started.

"I'm not what?" The woman crossed her arms and willed him to say she wasn't his girlfriend.

The bell sounded to announce the end of intermission, but we were the star attraction in the open rotunda, and the audience seemed averse to enter the auditorium. All eyes were focused on me, not because of a beautiful solo, but because I, Brinn Wentworth, kissed someone else's beau—in public, no less. Even my father did his cheating on the sly.

No matter what we did, the Wentworths were suddenly born to scandal. The good news was the Donleys were across the rotunda.

"Way to represent and redeem the Wentworth clan." Quinn was beside me now. She looked up at Garrick and whispered in my ear. "Well done though. I totally get it. He's probably worth the trouble."

"I didn't know he was taken," I shouted to Garrick's date while Quinn held my hand. His date didn't seem satisfied at the excuse, but I hardly cared at that point. Matt Donley was satisfied. And gone.

I heard the shutter click of cameras around me and instinctively understood the gossip rags would be filled tonight with news of my harlot status. I'd done the worst thing possible for our reentry into society. I'd collected bad press and given my mother another reason to get me married off to Casey Sutton. However, I'd also salvaged Katrina Donley's safety, and that was far more important.

Garrick looked down at his date, who still had fire in her eyes, but I watched his gaze trail Mr. and Mrs. Donley until they were safely inside the auditorium, then he clenched his jaw and looked toward me. "I need a minute," he said to his date.

He took me aside. "I told you this was a dangerous game," he said through gritted teeth.

I nodded. "You did."

I knew what he meant, and it wasn't the time to explain to him that I'd covered my tracks with Mr. Donley. Matt was interested in his wife being on the board of Encore and believed the story, but Garrick was correct.

The rotunda's faux night sky faded until the stars totally disappeared and everyone made their way into the opera house for the second half of *Cinderella*. The grand hall emptied. I didn't care what they'd say about me. Because that kiss affected me and stirred emotions I didn't know existed. I'd never wanted marriage—a family—and Garrick's kiss made me rethink my entire future in one momentary embrace.

He was like an instantly addictive drug and in the moment, all I could think about was how to secure more of it and get my fix. As he strode off to take his seat with his date angrily scowling back at me, I leaned against the wall with my sisters beside me.

"I *felt* something," I told Quinn. "I'm not numb anymore. Maybe I'm not as independent as I thought."

"None of us are." Sophia rubbed the top of my arm. "He's a good man, Brinn. I don't think there's a woman in this auditorium who blames you one bit."

"He only kissed me to cover my acquaintance with someone," I admitted. "He wasn't overcome with passion or anything."

"It didn't look that way to me." Sophia shrugged. "Lives have been built together on less. *Go get him.* All's fair in love and war."

"You're a romantic, Sophia, because you're in love. That's why people in love are so annoying to the rest of us."

"Garrick needs you in his life. He needs to believe in love again. You both do."

"You set this whole thing up from the start!" I accused her.

She raised her dark, perfectly shaped brows. "Maybe. Maybe not. I only know that Garrick Kane has been alone for far too long and so have you."

I watched his hulking frame until the door closed behind him. To Garrick, our kiss was nothing more than a business deal meant to protect a client. To me, it turned my entire world upside down. I'd already forgotten the sting of the slap, but the tingles from Garrick's touch remained.

CHAPTER 9

*T*he morning newspaper lay on the breakfast table. Under the glaring headline of the San Francisco Ballet's opening was a photograph of Garrick and me in a heated clutch. I'd like to say this publicity bothered me, but it didn't. I took immense pleasure in the picture. For once, I was on the front page for my own doing. It felt empowering. Beside that picture was another of my blurred face being slapped by his date—an action shot, if you will. Naturally, my eyes reverted back to the first picture, and I pretended the second didn't exist. In the photo, Garrick's eyes were clasped shut in our momentary burst of passion—well, mine at least—and the sight of it took me right back to the night before, fastened tightly in his grasp.

"Well, Mother should be happy she's out of the news this morning." I ran my finger along the printed page and tried to act nonchalant. The photos were in color due to the gowns worn for the ballet opening. I would be adding it to my scrapbook.

Garrick's kiss had softened and stirred something within me that I thought was long dead. I was enraptured and lightheaded

—alive again, not simply existing. If I never saw Garrick again, his kiss restored in me a hope for a fulfilling future without ballet. I was no longer dead inside.

Alisa came downstairs into the dining room and glanced at the newspaper. "How come every time someone in this family makes the front page, they're in a desperate clasp with some rando? Honestly, old people are weird."

"Alisa," I said in annoyance for her breaking my reverie, "nothing happened. There's a perfectly reasonable—"

"Nope." She put her palm up and shook her head. "I don't want to hear it, don't want to see that image again. I want breakfast, not to vomit. Old people kissing. Gross."

I thought it best to change the subject. "You should have come last night. I think you would have loved the ballet because you know the story of Cinderella."

"Is there a reason why you couldn't find some dark hallway in that creepy opera house if you felt the need to make out like a couple of teenagers in the rotunda? Not a good look, girl." She wrinkled her nose. "Craggy people kissing is just disgusting."

"Craggy? How old do you think I am? I'm only seven years older than you, missy. I'm not old. It probably just seems that way because my career was over so young."

"Still disgusting." Alisa popped a piece of bacon in her mouth. "Wasn't it like the classiest event of the year? Did you spike the punch, too?" She sat at the head of the dining table and tugged at her oversized sweater. "I knew I'd hate last night, so I did the posh thing and stayed home so I didn't embarrass the family by falling asleep in the audience, but you, Brinn! Of all people, you'd think a ballerina would know how to act at the ballet." Alisa cracked herself up.

Quinn laughed at Alisa's commentary as she entered the dining room dressed in purple Lululemons and a shiny black fitted athletic jacket designed to look like leather.

"Where are you going dressed like that?"

"The gym. Duh."

"The gym in the house?"

"No, there's like a hundred workers in the house. I'm going to the club," Quinn said.

"Who are you trying to impress?"

"None of your business," Quinn snapped.

Sophia stepped into the dining room and her eyes went straight to the newspaper. "Dang, that is a soap opera kiss if I ever saw one."

"For someone who was caught at the zoo acting like a pair of animals, you and Joel are in no place to judge me." I scooped some eggs onto a plate, salted them and sat down. "Besides, this isn't funny."

Quinn shrugged. "It's funny. Did you hear from Mother yet? She's going to be livid."

"I don't think I'll be hearing from her this morning." *Or any other morning.*

"I'd love to be a fly on the wall this morning in Madame Adrenko's breakfast room," Quinn laughed. "I bet she'd have your head mounted on the wall if you'd still been her prima."

"If I'd still been prima, I'd have no reason to have been in the lobby, would I?"

"Therefore, no reason to have your lips plastered on Garrick Kane's." Gia entered the room dressed in jeans that fit her like a glove and ankle boots with a spiky heel. For someone who never had money, she always looked like a million even before she'd inherited the money.

I looked at the newspaper again and happiness bubbled up in me—a high that made me crave Garrick's touch again. *It's this how marriage is supposed to be? How people become blinded and side-swiped into vows to love someone for a lifetime?*

It all made sense when I thought about how Garrick made me feel. If someone has the power to give you proverbial wings and fly with the angels, why wouldn't you commit? If brushing up against them rendered you unable to think straight or find the practical part of your brain, I understood how people rushed into marriage even knowing the inevitable crash that was to come. I was grateful that Garrick was just as opposed to the idea of marriage as I was.

While my sisters yammered on in the background, I searched for reasons to go to Garrick's office and explain myself. I'd done everything he'd warned me about and I wanted to tell him again, his foundation was off the hook. "Well, I'm full," I said as I reached for the newspaper and plucked it from the table.

"Wait a minute," Sophia said. "You begged off to bed early last night with some excuse, now we're ready to hear it. What happened last night?"

I dropped the newspaper. "Garrick was worried about a client. I had it all handled, but he overcompensated. That was what the kiss was about."

"I'll say he overcompensated," Gia said.

"And overcompensated some more," Quinn said. "Right there in the rotunda. Wait until Mother hears that we didn't have escorts, but you made out with someone else's escort. She's going to have a fit."

"Mother has enough to worry about," I said.

"She'll have you out with Casey Sutton before the week is out. Guarantee it," Quinn said.

"A girl could do a lot worse than Casey Sutton," Gia said.

"Oh yeah?" Quinn wiggled her eyebrows. "You want an introduction?"

"No. I'm only saying he's not hard on the eyes and he got his dad a date with my mom. How sweet is that?"

"Super sweet. I gotta run. See you at dinner." I rushed from my sisters. *I need to think.* I sailed by the contractors, up the stairs to my room and fell to the bed with the newspaper in front of me.

The bedroom door creaked open, and Sophia walked in—once again in her couture gown from the ballet. "Do you have a minute?"

"Did you just get back into your dress?"

She saw the newspaper and shrugged. "People will get over that. The worst part is seeing they always attach you to your mom." She made quote marks. "Socialite daughter of accused murderer Chelsea Whitman Wentworth."

"Don't you knock?" I asked her. "Why are you in your dress again?" I pressed.

"Gia dared me to put it on and float around the house. She said she'd give me her weekly allowance if I did it. The construction workers already talk about us. Why not give them something to talk about? Like we walk around in gowns all day."

"You and your sister have a strange way of entertaining yourselves."

"Don't we?" She laughed. "I never want to take this dress off, so the dare worked in my favor." She fluttered about my room like a butterfly in a garden before dropping herself on my bed. "Joel said I looked like a princess at the ballet, and I couldn't possibly top this gown for our wedding." Her voice was dreamy, which would have normally annoyed me, but after my kiss, I finally got it. There were some connections that couldn't be fought. "The workers won't be back here until tomorrow."

"That's part of the dare. I have to wear it all day today. You know, to get used to it."

"You two are a strange breed." I shook my head. "Did you come in here to make me feel better? Because you're not doing a great job of it."

"Well, I was worried about you. The newspaper article said the Wentworth sisters are known for their notorious stealing of men and to keep your husbands away from them."

"It did not say that." I grabbed the paper.

"It did. Well, not in so many words."

"I suppose that's why I never read the articles." I held up the paper. "I got stuck on the picture."

"I could see why you would. Garrick is hot. Seriously hot."

"I'm not a man-stealer. *We're* not man-stealers. Why would the paper even suggest that? When have I ever had a man? Much less one that I stole. It's been ages."

Sophia shrugged. "Technically, I am a man thief because of Joel. People don't know his engagement to Quinn was fake, so I did take my sister's fiancé as far as they're concerned."

"Oh, that's right."

"Then there's you last night. The article also references your mom stealing Dad from our mom, which isn't true, but people like that version better than the truth. Time smashes together and it makes a better story."

"Sophia, you know what last night taught me?"

"That Garrick Kane knows how to kiss?"

"Besides that. I realized when I was with Garrick, I not only felt something again, I felt safe."

"Yeah, he's in professional security," Sophia said. "It's sort of his job to make you feel safe."

"But I have never felt that way. For once in my life, I didn't care what people thought. I was just in the moment, enjoying it."

Sophia took my hands. "Really, Brinn? Not ever?"

"Something shifted when I saw my mom. She's never happy. It's not my job to make her happy. I probably can't make anyone happy."

"You can make yourself happy. That's allowed and it's not selfish," Sophia said defiantly. "It looked like you made Garrick pretty happy last night."

"Ugh." I dropped my face in my hands. "You have to help me find a new charity, Sophia. I cannot face him again."

"You faced your mother. You can face Garrick."

I shook my head. "I did exactly what he was worried about, Sophia. He's not going to allow me anywhere near that foundation of his after I nearly outed a client, and he doesn't have to. I told him I'd just donate."

Sophia shrugged. "Everything is fine now. You learned and you lived a little. Doesn't that seem worth risking humiliation for?"

"No."

"You felt safe," she reminded me.

I slumped against the headboard. "Right before I was slapped," I laughed. "The irony."

"You're so hard on yourself, Brinn. Why would you feel safe? In the few months I've known you, I've never seen your parents protect you. They never had a conversation about your new sisters that sprang out of nowhere, not to mention how to navigate the massive amount of wealth you inherited. Plus, your mother is possibly involved in the murder of your grandfather. Did you have a conversation about that?"

"We don't really discuss such—"

"How could you feel safe? Who protected you?"

"I've always protected myself," I told her. "Well, maybe Quinn has protected me. We protected each other." I'd been doing it since I was sent off to ballet school and I didn't know any other way.

"Being in Garrick's arms made you feel safe," Sophia said in a dreamy voice. "I think that's the most human thing I've heard you say since I met you."

"Do you think I'm a robot or something?" I tried to laugh it off. "It wasn't Garrick himself. I'm not a damsel in distress looking for a hero. It was the freedom that I didn't care what people thought."

"All those years." Sophia shook her head. "I longed for my father in our lives. Now I see that he wasn't really there for you or Quinn either."

"He bought me a car," I said in his defense.

"That's nice," Sophia offered. "Is that how he said he loved you?"

"We don't really say that in my family. We're not big on expression of affection. I think your mom has probably hugged me more than mine has." I tried to find the humor in my statement.

"My mom," Sophia said in her confident tone, "thinks she's everyone's mother."

"Well, she's good at it, so I can see that."

"You're going to be okay with whatever the newspaper prints about you with Garrick last night. People think they know right from wrong, but God looks at the motive and your motive was to protect Garrick's client. That's what matters."

"When you got snapped kissing Joel at the zoo, it didn't bother you that the press accused you of stealing Quinn's fiancé?" I asked her.

Sophia picked at the sparkles on her gown and shrugged. "I was in love. I knew the truth. What do I care what strangers think? Besides, Quinn's first love is that horse of hers and everyone knows it."

"Truth be told, the Wentworth reputation is not all that, is it?"

"People will think what they want to. That's why you have to do the right thing when no one is looking."

"I did the right thing by Mrs. Donley last night. I know I did." I shrugged. "Garrick's date probably didn't see it that way." I got up and put on a bracelet to match my cuffed white shirt. "Are you getting dressed for church? Or do you plan to stay in that gown forever and pull a Dickens on us?" She stared back at me blankly. "Miss Havisham?"

She sighed dreamily and laid back onto my bed. "It was such a magical night. I won't ever forget it. Joel looked like he'd walked straight out of a Jane Austen novel—he bewitched me. Did you see him in his tux?" Sophia rose up on her elbows. "By the way, how was Garrick's kiss? I'll admit, my old boss Bobbi and I may have discussed what it would be like to kiss Garrick Kane. He's pretty sexy, if you know what I'm saying, but from what I hear, he's not into monogamy either."

I didn't want to say what Garrick's kiss was like for fear I'd sound like a junior high school girl at her first dance. *Garrick's kiss was everything.* The first milestone that made me feel truly alive since I'd come home from school. Or danced.

"It was fine. Perfunctory," I lied.

"Perfunctory?" Sophia raised her brows, and she had that way about her where she saw right through me. "I've seen a lot of rom-coms in my day." Her eyes narrowed. "Have you ever watched a romantic movie that wouldn't be half bad, except the couple has no chemistry on-screen so the movie doesn't work because it's like watching a brother and sister together?"

"I guess," I answered. "It looked that way to you too?" I asked her. "Perfunctory?"

"No, not even for a second," she answered. "It looked like one of those rom-coms where you know the couple is sleeping together off set because their chemistry is so combustible it leaps off the screen."

I tried to hide my pure satisfaction at her comment, but my expression betrayed me. I lit up like that starry sky in the opera house. "Maybe that's why his date slapped me."

"Oh, I would've hauled off and slapped you too."

"Sophia, you wouldn't have. Your manners are ingrained."

"You two were inseparable and if you moved in on Joel like that, I wouldn't trust myself."

"No chance of that happening." I tried to keep the revulsion off my face. When you lived with someone like a brother—just no thank you.

Sophia rose from the bed and twirled again so that the Swarovski crystals on her dress sparkled under the light of my vanity. "Garrick didn't seem to be complaining and he's a serial dater. I doubt we'd ever see that girl again regardless of what happened between you two."

"The kiss served its purpose. I introduced myself to someone I shouldn't have from the shelter. Exactly as he had warned me previously."

"He's not wrong. This is life and death, Brinn. These women are often one wrong word away from a beating or worse."

I frowned at her. "I get it. I made a mistake, but nothing happened. I salvaged the moment before Garrick even kissed me!"

"I have friends who can teach you about working with victims if you want to learn the best way to—"

"No, it's fine. You're all right and I admit defeat. I'm not in San Francisco for long anyway." I stepped away from the mirror. "I'm going to walk away."

"Not after that kiss, I wouldn't. I think you and Garrick have a lot of unfinished business to take care of and I'd park myself outside his office until I knew what was going on between us."

"Don't be ridiculous," I told her. "Go get dressed for church."

"I'll lose the bet."

"Lose the bet." I pulled my hair into a ponytail and tied it up with the holder I had around my wrist. "You look ridiculous in the middle of the day. We need to go to church and give everyone the chance to talk about last night."

"Do you want me to come with you to Garrick's office tomorrow?"

"I'm not going to Garrick's office." I was steadfast. "He has a girlfriend."

"He had a date," Sophia said. "There's a distinct difference. Garrick is too serious for a girlfriend."

"Then why are you trying to push him off on me? She sure seemed to think she was his girlfriend. If he was interested, he would have made a move."

"He did make a move." She lifted up the newspaper.

"That was to save his client."

"Was it?" Sophia's single eyebrow rose. "He's not too serious to settle down when he meets the right woman. His date isn't someone he would settle down with."

"How do you know that? They always tell you that, but some leopards don't change their spots, and I'll be in Southern California in eight months. He was a lesson, that's all. I need to find out what makes me feel safe."

"Bobbi, my old boss, and I studied Garrick for a long time."

"Because that's not creepy or anything," I said.

She pursed her lips and went on, "He's all work, no play. Until I saw him last night and thought, *maybe not.* Maybe he's got a little game in him after all." Sophia grinned. "I should have guessed it by the sheer number of dates I've seen him with."

I didn't want to think about that. "The contractor is supposed to meet us at one at the new safe house I'm renovating. Do you think you can flitter back into this realm by 9:30 so we can get to church first?"

Sophia rose from my bed and twirled in her gown while she put the back of her hand on her forehead. "Oh, I suppose I could. You've had many moments of these princess events. I'm only getting started and I suddenly want to talk like Audrey Hepburn in *Roman Holiday.*"

"Well, you may be getting *too* used to it. Go get dressed."

CHAPTER 10

*T*he Victorian house in the Haight-Ashbury, purchased by the contractor, had stood abandoned for years. "I can't believe this house didn't get bulldozed by the neighbors," I said to Sophia.

"I'm sure they tried. It's absolute squalor. Be careful where you walk."

The homeless and drug-addicted had obviously called it home for many years. The yard was riddled with used needles and various drug paraphernalia and was strewn with stacks of garbage.

Sophia stood at the sidewalk and stared at the lilting house up on the hill. "The stench is unbearable from here. I'm not going any closer and I don't think you should either."

"Come on, don't be such a drama queen. This is my chance to say I did something for my charity and move on to start a new one before the press figures it out." I dragged her toward the house where the stench got worse, and our faces showed it.

"I can't!" Sophia squealed. "Someone might be in there still."

I climbed the steps to the front porch and the front door

stood ajar. "There's no one here and the contractor will be here soon."

"Nope." Sophia halted on the walkway and covered her nose with the back of her wrist. "This place is disgusting! Brinn, you're not going in? It's like a Petri dish. Just tell the contractor what you want and face Garrick already. This is stupid."

I was determined. "This is more than writing a check. One safe house and then I'll move into ballet as my charity. Please, Sophia."

She climbed the stairs to the porch. "No one said you weren't good enough. Garrick implied you needed training."

"This house has so much potential, Sophia. It's in the perfect neighborhood out of the way. Only money stands in the way. Garrick should trust me with that much and this way, I'll stay out of his hair and away from his clients."

"You don't have to prove anything. To Garrick or anyone." Sophia's eyes pleaded with me to not enter the garbage-laden house.

"We inherited the money for the sole purpose of bettering our community. What better way than to make this house livable and usable? To leave something better than we found it and put it to good use?"

She reached for my wrist. "I can get you trained to work with victims if that's what you really want, but this house. My Nonna would call for a priest to come perform an exorcism before she entered."

I ignored her and waved toward the shredded door jamb. "We're going to get it all stripped down to the studs and we'll power wash and clean everything with disinfectant. I'm more excited about this than the renovation at Wentworth Manor." This gave me something to do. To get my mind off my desire to leave San Francisco before the will's requirements were met.

"You do you." Sophia said as she slapped her hands together. "Meanwhile, I'm going to buy stock in Clorox."

"Just look at the footprint of the house. It has great bones."

"I see it fine from out here."

"This house will be perfection. We're going to bring it back to life."

Sophia shook her head. "I've seen a lot of crapholes in my day, but this one takes the cake. This is legally uninhabitable and probably should be condemned. I wouldn't save a two-by-four."

"Oh, it has been condemned," I told her. "The contractor had to get special approval from the city permit board to rebuild it."

Sophia's face squinted as if she'd never witnessed such seediness, which could not have been true with her social work in the Tenderloin district. "If someone from the community center tried to get this approved, there's no way. Their kids would be in custody within the hour and the house marked for the wrecking ball."

"Of course. It's not livable yet. Here." I came out onto the porch, opened a jar of Vicks VapoRub from my handbag and held it toward her. "Put this under your nose. It will help with the smell."

Sophia shook her head. "Come on, Brinn. Let's get out of here. I'm begging you. You don't have to prove anything to me. To anyone really."

"I purposely brought you, Sophia, because I knew you wouldn't be a snob. You're being a snob. I want your feedback on how to design a safe house."

"Not a snob, just equipped with a survival instinct."

"Come on, you've worked in that children's center that always stunk like sour milk and dirty kids. You can do this."

"I might have grown up poor, but we were clean," Sophia said.

"Except for the spaghetti hanging on the clothesline in the kitchen," I reminded her.

"If we weren't clean, we couldn't do that. By the way, it is bucatini which is way harder to make and needs to hang that way." She stopped. "How did you know about that?"

"Joel told us. He was fascinated by the fact that not only did your mother own a restaurant, but your grandmother makes her own pasta. I never saw anyone fall in love so fast."

"We're Italian. We cook. And my Nonna's food doesn't look like something you'd throw out—like at that so-called Michelin-star restaurant you took us to."

"Touché." I kept my hand in front of her face with the Vicks. "Are you taking some or not? I'm forcing you inside."

"Nope," Sophia said. "I want to live through this year at the manor. What if I step on a needle and all of this was for nothing? Joel can't marry a corpse."

"You won't step on anything," I promised her. "Because you have these orbs on your face called eyes. If you see a needle, move out of the way. It's not like a great white shark in the Farallon Islands. An empty syringe is not going to chase you to get its teeth in you." I started to hum the *Jaws* theme.

"Seriously, Brinn. If you want to pick a different charity, do it already. This house is like something out of *The Conjuring*."

I knew it seemed impossible, but I'd given my word and that meant something to me. I couldn't leave the domestic violence charity I'd chosen with nothing before I abandoned it for something prettier.

"These contractors are going to be dealing with all the debris soon enough, but you've been in these safe houses before. I need your professional opinion on how this one will stack up. Please, Sophia."

"My professional opinion is run before you sink your money into this dump." She brushed herself off. "Doesn't this contractor have an office where we could meet? This seems shady as heck."

I took a scoop of Vicks on my forefinger and smeared it under Sophia's nose. "Let's go."

Sophia started to cough and sputter as if I'd choked her. "This stuff burns!" She tried to rub it off onto her hand. "Now my hand stings. Brinn, I'm officially siding with Garrick now. Go support the ballet."

"Trust me, that's my plan." I pulled her inside the threshold of what had to be a former crack house. "But I announced to San Francisco I was going to help and I'm going to, even if no one knows I did it. I know I did it."

She grabbed a yellowed real estate flyer on the old table left inside. "Two million dollars? You paid two million dollars for a drug den?" She waved the paper in front of me. "Rich people have no sense about money."

"I haven't paid anything yet. I'm getting my master's in finance, remember? This house is an investment—$200k in this place and it's worth upwards of $5 million."

"This is why the rich get richer," Sophia sighed.

"You *are* rich now, remember?"

"Only if we make it through the year and all Dad's lawsuits are thrown out."

"Sophia, you're like Eeyore sometimes. This is the best neighborhood too. It's off the beaten path. On a dead-end street. There's literally no reason to be here unless you live on this street. Garrick says that can help with safety."

"Does he?"

"In his notes." I heard a knock from the brittle door frame. "Great, the builder's here."

I went to the door to look for the Marv Harris, the builder, and spied the two detectives who questioned me after my grandfather's death.

"Miss Wentworth, Steve Kendall and Rob Martin from homicide. Remember us?"

"I remember you," I said as my heart pounded. "What do you want here?" I looked around behind them for the contractor. "Did you follow me?"

"We'd like to ask you a few questions regarding the day your grandfather was killed. Do you mind coming with us to the station?"

I looked at Sophia. Panic in my throat kept me from speaking.

"She doesn't know anything, Officer Kendall," Sophia said emphatically. "She's already told you and the district attorney everything she knows. How long will this go on?"

"Until we're satisfied with the charges," he said stoically. "We just have a few more questions for you, Miss Wentworth. It won't take long."

"I'm busy," I said. "I'm meeting with my contractor this afternoon."

"We need you to come down to the station, ask you a few more questions so that we can get this case sewn up."

"My mother didn't do this. I certainly didn't do this. What more do you want from me?"

"There may be additional charges against your mother. We have a few more questions. Routine."

My blood ran cold. I stood under the crumbling wood that lined the slanted doorway. "I—I—my mother goes to church nearly every week. She's on the board of countless charities and has raised more funds than you can imagine. I think you have the wrong person and your rush to judgment won't let this go. So no, I don't want to come to your office, and I'm done answering questions."

Sophia's large dark eyes became so expressive in her apparent worry for my refusal.

"We're not generally in the business of railroading innocent people, Miss Wentworth. We're in the business of justice. Don't you think your grandfather deserves justice? Even if the man lived a long life, no one had the right to take his life."

"Naturally I want justice, but you have a theory and you're working backward to prove it's my mother. You're not looking at the facts." My whole body was trembling now. I was tired of being front-page news. "It's not my mother! You both need to get out there and do more police work. Stop humiliating my family!"

The men were unmoved by my outburst. "Did you notice any blue around your grandfather's lips the last time you saw him?"

"He was dying. He was an unholy color. I couldn't give you an exact tone, but I was back at school before he left us. He looked . . . he looked sick because he was a hundred! He'd lived a full life."

"Do you think a hundred is all anyone should live?" Officer Kendall asked.

"I didn't say that."

Sophia put her arm around me and helped me steady myself, but I felt chilled at her touch. It was her boyfriend, Joel, who'd first accused my mother. I knew she believed my mother was guilty. She probably talked Quinn into testifying so the will would stop being challenged. I eyed Sophia warily and moved out of her grip. Naturally, the contractor showed up at this exact moment. The officer lifted his palm toward the man.

"We're going to need you to come back at a different time," Officer Kendell said to Marv Harris.

Marv didn't blink an eye. He took his rolled-up blueprints, got back in his truck and drove off as if we'd never had a meeting in the first place. I'd have given anything to be in the truck with him.

Sophia whispered in my ear, "I think your builder might be on parole."

I faced down the detectives on the porch again. "Will you please leave?"

"I'm afraid that's not possible. We'd like to get you on record, but if we need to talk here, we're willing."

"Is this really necessary? I was in Southern California. I don't know anything about my grandfather's last day. I know he didn't look good when I saw him. That's all I can tell you."

"It's a Sunday afternoon, which is my day off," Officer Kendall said. "I'd much rather be with my family than chasing you and your sister around San Francisco, so yes, it's very necessary." He handed me another business card. "We'll see you at the station in say, half an hour?"

I grabbed the card so hard it wrinkled in my clutches. "Fine," I said through clenched teeth.

"I believe your mother to be a very dangerous individual."

"Well, you're wrong," I snapped back. *Selfish and vain, yes. Dangerous? Not so much.*

He smirked and jogged down the steps toward his unmarked domestic vehicle. "See you in a few, Miss Wentworth, and we appreciate your time."

I tried to maintain a straight face. I didn't want Sophia to know how nervous I was to discuss my mother with the police, but I was terrified. The house in the Haight-Ashbury looked as feeble and broken as I felt. This was never going to end. I'd always be a Wentworth and my life would never belong to me.

I GRIPPED the white steering wheel of the Tesla so tightly, I wondered if my handprint would forever mark the pristine leather. "I don't want your opinion, Sophia. I want the answer to this question. What do they say about my family in the real world?"

Sophia paused.

"Go ahead. I can handle it." I sped through traffic, following the GPS on my way to the station. "What could you tell me that's worse than they think that my mother killed my grandfather?" I stared right at her, with her mop of luxurious dark curls. "Spill it. All of it."

"You heard what they shouted at the ballet. Blood money. Our money is blood money because Grandfather was killed for it. They think we were all in on it. The whole lot of us."

"What else?"

"There's an entire contingency of people who hated Grandfather. They say he paid slave wages and took kickbacks on his ships so they could take shortcuts through dangerous passages. We are the benefactors to that."

That part was new to me. "No one killed Grandfather for money. We didn't know we were in the will. My parents didn't inherit anything except my dad's position on the board. That's so ridiculous. They had enough."

"Millions is not billions. You asked me what I heard, that's what we've heard. That your mother and father didn't know he'd bypassed them in the will, and they couldn't wait any longer for him to be gone."

I forced myself to listen to the nonsense Sophia was spouting. "Is that it?"

"The rumor mill also said Dad has a new girlfriend and your mother killed Grandfather in revenge. There's also a rumor your parents had financial trouble, like that guy you introduced us to. Casey?"

"That's not true!"

Sophia grasped my hand. "You said you wanted it all and I'm about to spill the tea. Are you sure you're ready?"

"Honestly, Sophia, the dramatics. I said I'm ready. I have to know what I'm facing in that police station. Tell me what Joel has told you. I know he's said something."

Sophia exhaled—the kind of haggard breath that makes you rethink all of your life's decisions.

"The police don't think your mother acted alone since the newspapers have reported that she didn't inherit any money."

"You thought this was information to keep to yourself?" As soon as I found a safe place to pull over, I did so.

"I was going to tell you," Sophia said. "But I thought the cops would have figured out the truth and dropped these interviews by now. They must need more to get the conviction before this goes to trial, but Quinn is worried your mother might point out a mastermind and claim she was coerced."

I smacked my head on the steering wheel. "I can't believe you didn't tell me this."

"You were on the front of the society page kissing Garrick Kane. I figured that was enough publicity for someone who hates to be in the limelight."

"Being in the limelight and another accessory to murder are two very different things, Sophia. They think my dad might have helped off his own father?"

"Either him or one of you."

"Honestly, Sophia. Why wouldn't you at least warn me?"

"When you went to see your mother, I didn't know what to think. Quinn says she's awful to you."

"I still love her. She's my mother." My eyes withered shut. "Oh my goodness. She wouldn't."

"Wouldn't what?"

"I don't want to jump to conclusions, but what if I'm her reasonable doubt defense?" My hands trembled and I forced them to my lap. "*I'm* her reasonable doubt."

Sophia didn't sugarcoat it. "Probably. That's what Quinn thinks, but she didn't want to scare you."

"I don't feel so well."

"It's going to be fine, Brinn. You did nothing wrong. We'll just go answer the policeman's questions and it will be over."

"You don't understand. My mother has this insidious way about her. She's almost hypnotizing in the way she can brainwash people into believing her truth. I don't think she killed Grandfather, but I don't think she's above looking close by for reasonable doubt either."

Sophia said nothing.

"I would never have hurt my grandfather. Never."

"Brinn, I know that. We know that. Your sisters know that. Everyone knows that."

"The police don't know that. Maybe they think because I'm majoring in finance that I love money, that I wanted my grandfather's money. Do you think?"

I hated the thought that came to me next. That my mother would never set up her favorite daughter to take the fall. And she and Father had that weird dynamic that left them enmeshed together with toxic glue. *That leaves me.*

"You wouldn't kill a fly, much less your grandfather. Stop letting your imagination run wild and let's get this over with. I'm right by your side. All of your sisters will be."

"I didn't even know he was leaving us the money. Did you?" I asked her frantically.

"I didn't even know Grandfather Wyatt knew I existed."

"No, of course you didn't know." I started to calm down a bit, but I was plagued by the thought *evil people always win.* They left the rest of us minions with their consequences. That had been my life experience and I didn't see it changing.

"They're charging your mother with first degree murder. Joel said they don't do that without evidence." Sophia looked me straight in the eye. "All your mother needs to prove is reasonable doubt. I hate to say it, Brinn, but it's probably you, Quinn or our father."

"But it seems she didn't pick either of them, did she?" I didn't need another reminder that I was the one who didn't matter in my family. I'd had a lifetime of watching it play out.

"You really don't get how much Quinn loves you, Brinn. She fights for you. That's why she's testifying to keep your mother honest."

"I can't believe she'd go against our mother. Sophia, our mother is slippery. She manages to wiggle her way out of any cage. She's on par with Houdini. I worry Quinn is going to pay for any lack of loyalty. I'm used to it, but she won't be able to handle it. I know her."

Sophia's expression softened. "Joel believes your mother acted alone and he believes the evidence will hold up in court."

The cars whizzed past us as quickly as the thoughts dashed through my brain. *Tell the police the truth.* It sounded so simple. But Katrina Donley couldn't tell the police the truth, so why would I fare any better?

"Joel really believes my mother did this." I let it sink in before I realized that meant most people thought she was guilty. "Do *you* think she did it?"

Sophia didn't actually answer the question directly. "If you had proof she did it, would you support your mother?"

"What? No, of course not. How could you think that of me?"

"Joel thinks the death wasn't about money. They can't prove motive, which will make this case difficult. Joel thinks your mother's motive was to gain the status of being the full matriarch of the Wentworth name."

I squeezed my eyes shut and shook my head back and forth. It felt like an out-of-body experience to think of my mother actually injecting something into my grandfather. I couldn't picture it. "I can't believe it, Sophia. Chelsea is selfish, I get that. But this—no. Her reputation is too important to her. She wouldn't have taken this risk." I stared down at my lap and brushed off the splinters of white paint I'd attracted at the house.

"We just want you to be prepared."

"Our family will never regain our reputation, will we?" I realized how little that meant to me now. How I'd been trained my whole life in its importance and how little I cared what people thought. *My grandfather is dead, and I wasn't there to say goodbye because I was so busy trying to escape the life I was supposed to live.* "I could marry Casey Sutton tomorrow and we're not coming back from this as a family."

"Casey is adorable. A girl could do a lot worse."

"He ate paste in kindergarten," I told her, and we laughed.

"You've been told your entire life it's your job to keep up appearances. This is not your responsibility. If you fight for her, it might be you who faces the consequences. You can't protect her forever."

"Sophia, she didn't do this. I can't go in there and throw my mother in front of the wolves."

"Then you best be prepared for her to offer you up as the alternative."

I loved my mother, and I wouldn't believe she was capable of murder, but I also knew deep in my heart that she'd use me as a proverbial shield. She'd done it my whole life. "I wonder if Casey would even marry me at this point. Do you think it would help the family out of this situation?"

Sophia sat back in her seat and gazed out the window. "You don't have to get married to Casey, Brinn. That's your mother's harebrained scheme and it won't work. Tell the police the truth."

"Sophia, please don't tell anyone this. I'm only confiding in you because you know I don't want to get married, and I don't think it would take people's eyes off of this anyway."

"You tell yourself you don't want to be married, but that kiss with Garrick says something else."

"Why does it say something else? Maybe I was just up for a really hot hook-up."

Sophia started to laugh. "No, for real."

"What's so funny? I could be the thirsty type if I put my mind to it. Maybe I want to bar hop every night of the week. Maybe I've been wild and free like Paris Hilton all along. You don't know."

"No offense, Brinn, but—"

"No. People always say no offense before they're about to say something offensive, so I'm going to stop you right there and we'll be good."

She ignored me. "Before I knew you and Quinn, I was in awe of how the two of you never had a hair out of place. Gia and I discussed how you could wear white all day and there wouldn't be an imprint of a mark on you—as if dirt wouldn't dare touch your immaculate image—it was actually repelled by your pure light."

I laughed, grateful for Sophia and the diversions she brought with her. For a brief blip in time, I forgot my mother was most likely throwing me under the bus.

"I thought you were on some other plane where mere mortals wouldn't dare go and you two danced about like the ballerinas you are and the rest of us can never hope to achieve. So no, I don't buy into your being the one-night stand sort. I also don't buy that your image is marked forever by your mother's sins. We'll get through this. Evil doesn't win. Evil doesn't flourish. The truth always wins out."

How I wish I believed that. I understood that even if my mother had committed such a heinous crime, she'd already done the mental gymnastics necessary to make it someone else's fault. "You don't know her. Chelsea Wentworth has this way about her. She casts off blame like yesterday's fashion and she'll do it again. None of us can go against her because she'll make us all pay."

"Not if we stand together. We're the Wentworth sisters now," Sophia said. "There's power in our numbers."

I wanted to believe in Sophia's world where goodness and light won out, but I couldn't underestimate my mother. The woman I knew behind closed doors was capable of so much darkness, and she'd cast her spell over the entire city.

We pulled into the police station. "You think they'll let me come in with you?" Sophia asked.

I shook my head. "I can take you home first so you don't have to wait."

"No, I want to be here." Sophia took my hand.

I nodded and walked into the precinct as if I was already headed to the gallows. I knew my mother's power and unlike Sophia's world . . . in my world, evil generally did win.

CHAPTER 11

San Francisco's finest placed me in a sparse interrogation room with mirrors around it. I assumed they were two-way mirrors and I was under intense scrutiny. Which didn't really bother me. I had spent my life under the microscope. The police weren't going to rile me with their mere questions, but as the minutes edged on, I became less confident.

I thought about my mother, so elegant in her ankle cuff. She'd already had a chance to spin her story web and create Brinn Wentworth in the image she'd imagined for the police. I wouldn't be here if that wasn't the case. Anxiety crept in like an invisible gas and my breathing intensified.

An officer burst in the doorway. "You all right?"

I drew in a few deep breaths and forced myself to calm down. I nodded and he exited as quickly as he came in. The seconds ticked by loudly on the black and white schoolroom clock above one of the mirrors. I plucked at the elbow of my sleeve just to pass the time.

Finally, at fifteen minutes past three, Officer Kendall came in alone and sat in the corner. "Miss Wentworth, I'd really like to thank you for volunteering to come in this afternoon."

Volunteering is a strong word.

"We have some questions about your mother's relationship with your father. And his father."

"I can't tell you much about that. I wasn't in the home that much. I was in ballet school, then I lived with the company. I was in college and then graduate school in Southern California."

He scribbled something in his notebook. "Would you say you're close to your father?"

I shrugged. "I guess. I mean, he's my dad."

"And your mother?"

"The same. She has her life. He had his and we went to social gatherings together like normal families." *There is nothing normal about my family, but I'm not about to admit it on tape.*

Officer Kendall looked up at me, his jet-black eyes searing through me. "When you heard your grandfather was murdered, who was the first person you thought might have done it?"

"The help," I answered honestly. "I thought maybe the nurse had gotten tired of doing that job and wanted to move on so maybe she handed him some extra morphine that evening. I mean, do we know for sure he was murdered? The coroner's report said unknown."

"It's been changed. To homicide." The officer watched me while he took note of my reaction. "Did you notice before your grandfather's death, any discoloration around his mouth?"

"You already asked me that. I told you, his coloring wasn't good the last time I saw him. He was dying and his pallor looked sickly like you'd expect of someone on his way into the next world."

"When is the last time you saw your grandfather?"

"About a week before his death. I drove up to visit."

"The last time you saw your father?"

"I suppose it was the night of the gala. He didn't come to the ballet opening, which surprised me."

"You don't know he's been in the hospital then?"

"My father has been in the hospital?"

"When is the last time you spoke to him?"

"The gala," I said again with more annoyance. "He texted Quinn and me the next night during the family dinner, but we muted him because we thought he was trying to get attention."

"Attention?"

"Quinn and I have been through a lot with our parents' drama, and we wanted to have our wits about us to make decisions regarding the renovation of Wentworth Manor. Part of the will is that we're supposed to see to the renovations." I pulled my phone out of my handbag and looked at it. There were a few missed calls from an unknown number.

"Something important?"

I shook my head and put the phone away before they took it from me. "No."

The officer took out a photograph and set it before me. "Do you notice anything about your father in this picture?"

My father was always pale, but in the picture, he looked like a corpse. "He doesn't look healthy. Is he all right?"

"Did you leave pasta at your mother's penthouse when you went to visit her?"

"Yes. I rushed out of lunch the other day with Gia and Sophia, my half-sisters. Their mother Mary sent me home with food and I took it to my mother's. I thought if my mother had something good to eat, she'd calm down a bit."

"Did you see her eat the pasta?"

"I knew she wouldn't eat it in front of me. She'd wait until I'd gone. My mother rarely eats in front of people."

He scribbled that down. "What do you mean calm down?"

I searched for the right words. I wasn't saying anything the way I wanted to say it. It sounded like my parents were monsters and I was giving this cop ammunition against them. "My mother has low blood sugar and when she hasn't eaten for a while, she gets hangry. It runs in our family."

"Hangry?"

"You know, hungry and angry."

"Does your mother get angry often?"

I sighed. "No more than a normal mother. She gets frustrated sometimes." *That's a complete lie. My mother lives in a state of perpetual unrest.*

"What kind of food did you bring her?"

"Gluten-free pasta. I knew she'd be upset about not being at the annual Wentworth Gala as the matriarch, so I wanted to make her feel better."

"And did she?"

"I don't know. Like I said, she didn't eat the pasta. She got snippy with me, and I left."

"Snippy?"

"Impatient. She wanted to know why I came alone to visit her without my sister and my grandmother."

"I thought your Grandmother Wentworth had passed."

"My mom's mother, Mona Whitman, is in town." I was making everything worse.

"Her own mother didn't go to see her?" He wrote that down too. "Why did you go without your grandmother and sister?"

"I don't know. They were busy, I guess. It was a last-minute decision to go see her."

"Her mom and your sister are too busy to visit your mom on house arrest?"

"They're very busy. We have a lot going on. My grandfather's will moved in three new sisters and the renovations started. The house is utter chaos even without these false accusations against my mother. My grandmother comes and goes as she pleases. She doesn't check in with me. You have to understand, my mother doesn't need a lot of . . . I don't know . . . emotional support? No one feels like they—"

"I thought you just said that your mother needs a lot of attention. She and your father create drama, you mentioned."

"Yeah, but emotionally . . . I don't know. She doesn't need us." I closed my eyes in regret. I knew those words would come back to haunt me.

The other officer came into the room. He sat down and leaned in toward me and stared me down in a way that made me want to confess to everything I'd ever done in my lifetime.

"I'm Detective Rob Martin," he reminded me. "Did you know your mother has failed her polygraph?"

I forced myself not to react. "Those tests don't mean anything. They don't allow them in court because of that, right?"

"Would you be willing to take a polygraph, Miss Wentworth?" Officer Kendall's voice had softened as if he were suddenly my friend again.

"Me?"

"We've asked your sister Quinn to volunteer for a test and Mary Campelli as well."

"Mary Campelli? Why on earth would you want to talk to her? She's basically a living saint."

"Isn't that where you said you got the spaghetti?"

"What on earth does Mary's pasta have to do with my grandfather dying? We didn't even know Mary nor our half-sisters when Grandpa Wyatt passed away. We didn't know they existed."

He didn't elaborate. "Did you add anything to the pasta after Mary gave it to you?"

"Of course not. I can't boil water. Why on earth would I add anything to Mary's pasta? She owns a restaurant."

"So as far as you know, nothing was added to the pasta dishes that you left at your mother's house when you visited her last in the penthouse."

"Correct." *What have my parents done now?* Any time there was drama, my parents and their incessant need for attention were behind it, but I didn't dare announce that or they'd both be accused of murder rather than just my mother.

"So do we have your permission to conduct a polygraph?"

"I—um—I'm worried those things aren't accurate. I'd rather not."

"This is not about your parents, Brinn." He looked me directly in my eyes as he used my Christian name, and it sent an icy chill down my back. "We're interested if you added something to the pasta that sickened your father."

"My father is really sick?"

"I told you earlier he's in the hospital. Usually daughters don't miss that kind of information when discussing the health of their parents. They have more of a reaction." His brow darkened as if he expected me to incriminate myself.

"I told you, my mom was going to the hospital for fainting. I thought that's what you meant."

"That's not a normal response to your father being in the hospital."

I shrugged. "I've performed Swan Lake on hairline fractures. What do you want me to do, resort to wailing?"

He leaned in toward me. "I want you to understand, your mother will be convicted. I'd like you to get her to confess so we can avoid a trial."

The door slammed opened with a bang and I jumped. "We're ready for her in the polygraph room." An older man with a paunchy belly and a bad sport coat chewed on a pen as he entered the room. The buttons on his shirt were stretched like they'd pop. He was one of those types who seemed like he was born sweating.

My nerves prickled everywhere as I came to the realization that I'd avoided all along. Perhaps my mother wasn't innocent. Some obscure part of me knew she'd probably done it, but I still couldn't will myself to believe it. I stared blankly at Officer Kendall, unwilling to react the way he wanted me to.

"Why don't you come with me?"

"I haven't said yes." I followed him into the hallway and noticed Mary Campelli standing next to a very rugged-looking Garrick Kane. He was dressed like a lumberjack in a green-checked flannel with jeans and a cowboy hat. The sight of them instantly calmed me.

"Officer Kendall."

"Garrick," he answered in equal manly measure.

"I'm going to take my client home now. I've been hired for executive protection, and I don't think it's in her best interest to have any more stress today. We'll have a lawyer for her by the end of the day. She will not be taking a polygraph at this time."

"You've been hired for protection, by who?"

"Mary Campelli for my client here, Brinn Wentworth." He smiled at the spritely mother of Sophia and Gia, who stood behind him. Her warmth filled the hallway and enveloped me in a protective hug that I didn't know I needed.

"What does she need protection from?" Kendall asked.

"I think we both know the answer to that question. You know Ms. Campelli, I believe, from your earlier interrogation." Garrick's voice was stern.

"We were simply doing our job, Garrick. We've got a second man poisoned and we're going to need permission from your clients to exhume the body of their grandfather."

"You know who did this," he said plainly.

"Wait," I said. "Who's been poisoned?" I was so confused. I just wanted to wake up and go back to my normal life. I'd go to as many stupid photo shoots as my sister wanted. *Heck, I'll even go to boutique openings.*

"I'll explain on the way home." Mary came toward me and crushed me into a hug so that I exhaled deeply and felt the love I'd never felt from my own mother. I melted into her embrace. *How wonderful it must be to have someone in your life who loves this deeply.*

"I'm doing you a favor, Kane. I just want to clear your client," Officer Kendall said. "The sooner she submits to the polygraph, the sooner she's off our list."

"That may be true, but she's been through enough trauma for a few lifetimes recently and I can't allow you to trouble her anymore. Not without a warrant."

"We need to know if our suspect acted alone."

"You know she did."

"Maybe, but I need a jury of her peers to know she did and who is she going to point the finger at? Your client."

"Chelsea has no peers. Not unless you have a jury full of sociopaths, which is what she deserves."

Garrick just called my mother a sociopath.

Words flew over my head like stray bombs, and I was lost. I just knew I felt safe beside Mary, and I wasn't motivated to go home to the stark coldness of Wentworth Manor nor face the harsh conversation swirling around me. *I want it all to disappear.*

"Shh," Mary hissed. "This isn't the time or place for this argument. Brinn, dear. . . ." She pulled back and looked deeply into my eyes. Something I never remembered my own mother doing—looking at me as though my opinion and my thoughts mattered. "You have a choice to make. You can either go home to the Manor with Garrick as your security guard or you can come home with me to Sophia's old room. Until the outcomes of your father's tests are finalized, we don't want you at home."

"What tests? Joel is at the manor. I'll be protected."

"He is, but we want you to have your own security detail or be in an environment where we can keep you safe. Your father is in the hospital awaiting toxicology tests."

I should have been terrified for my father, but I was more embarrassed that Garrick understood my family better than I wanted him to. *He called my mother a sociopath. My father may have been poisoned.* I'd been exposed in the worst way possible. Garrick understood where I really came from.

"Brinn?" Mary awaited my answer.

I didn't know what to do. I looked at Mary and all I wanted to do was go to the warmth of her Italian kitchen and home. To meet the grandparents who didn't want anything from the Wentworth money.

Then I gazed up at Garrick with his '40s gumshoe persona now wearing hunting gear, and I couldn't make a choice. I knew now that Garrick had been hired, he was too professional to ever kiss me again, and he now knew who I was, so Mary's offer won out.

"I'll go home with Mary."

"You're sure?" Garrick asked.

No, I'm not sure. I wanted to suggest I'd be safer if Garrick took me to city hall and married me on the spot—before I remembered that I wasn't the marrying type, and neither was he. My eyes pleaded silently with him as I gazed upwards. *Talk me into it. Tell me why you need to come with me and protect me.*

"Is my father going to be okay?" As if it was some kind of afterthought.

"He is resting comfortably in the hospital. He's not out of the woods yet, but all his doctors say his prognosis looks good," Officer Kendall said.

"I can't believe I didn't take his call yesterday. He must think I'm some kind of monster."

"We know you're not a monster," Mary said as she rubbed my back gently.

"We will get to the bottom of this," Kendall said. "If you change your mind about the lie detector test, the door is always open to you, Brinn. I'd like to see your name cleared. Think about what I said in regard to your mother."

"Consider Brinn's name cleared," Garrick's strong voice spoke again. "There's only one person who had the opportunity and it's not our Brinn."

Our Brinn.

"You don't think billions is a reason for motive?" Kendall asked.

"May I remind you that Brinn didn't live in town before her grandfather's death? She hasn't seen her father, nor had access to him."

"She had access to the pasta," Officer Kendall said. "I'm only doing my job."

"I'm doing mine. Brinn has not seen her father since the gala."

How on earth did he know that?

* * *

GARRICK, Mary, Sophia and I walked out into the winter sunshine. The fog hadn't come in yet, and the sky was a brisk blue with no heat from the sun. Officer Kendall stayed behind as we walked out of the station, as though he was trapped by the matrix of the doorway. Seemingly the same trap that kept pulling me back to San Francisco.

"I'll take the car home to the manor," Sophia said. I handed her the key. "I might go by way of New York City though for a little spin."

I nodded. I felt too numb to engage in light banter. "The Tesla won't make it that far. You better pick up the BMW on your route home."

Sophia smiled faintly. "It will be okay." She waved and left us.

"Garrick, why don't you come to dinner at the house tonight," Mary said. "We can discuss options and priorities to end this fiasco so the girls can get back to renovating the house. This isn't your burden to carry alone, Brinn."

"Mary, I've involved you far too much already. You had to take a lie detector test because you offered me pasta."

Mary gave a demure shrug. "And you shared it with someone else. There's no crime in that."

"My father is sick." It finally sank in as I studied Mary's kind face. *Where is my concern for him? Maybe I'm the sociopath?*

"He'll be okay. They've caught it early and we'll pray for him. I lit a candle for him this morning at mass."

I didn't know what that meant, but I appreciated it all the same. "I don't think my mother is capable of any of this, Mary." Which wasn't quite true, but I wanted her to reassure me.

"It's fine, Brinn. We want to keep you safe until the truth is exposed."

Garrick's deep voice interrupted my momentary peace. "I've sent extra security to the mansion. Your sisters will be monitored and everything they're eating will be tested. Just in case."

"This sounds like some crazy medieval plot," I said.

I thought when I lost ballet my life was over, but when I lost Grandfather, I realized my life had never actually begun. I'd never had a life of my own. Every time I started something new, the rug got whipped out from beneath me.

"This too shall pass," Mary said.

"Make some plans, Brinn," Garrick said. "For when this is over. A vacation maybe? Life on the beach somewhere. Something you can look forward to. You don't need to go to school again right away."

I felt the heat rush in. I hadn't been at school to begin with, and my lies were about to come bubbling to the surface. As much trouble as I was in, when I looked at Garrick's darkened brow, my only thought of the future included a private beach in the Maldives, somewhere off the grid with my own roughshod security guard, Garrick Kane. He had that effect on me, as if everything was okay when he was near. Even if it was only in my imagination, it was enough.

"I'd never go back to that mansion if my sisters wouldn't lose their inheritance."

"You'll have choices soon. I promise," Garrick said and the

way he said it, I believed him. His assuredness gave me the hope I'd been missing.

I stared at Garrick's broad chest in his lumberjack flannel, and I felt the sting of envy. *How can he promise anything?* Here was a man—a handsome, charismatic, muscular, roughhewn male who could have whatever he wanted in this world. How could he understand what it was like to be born into a family that scripted your future? He wasn't a leaf in the Wentworth River where the flow of unease bounced you from edge to edge.

Garrick's sober disposition seemed more intense than usual. I felt like he hadn't taken his eyes off of me since I'd become his "client," courtesy of Mary.

"I'd like you to keep as low of a profile as possible right now. If you want to follow through on that old crack house renovation—"

"How'd you know about that?"

"I told him," Mary volunteered. "Sophia said she didn't want to go in and Sophia grew up basically across the street from the strip clubs."

Mary wasn't helping.

"If you want to follow through with the house renovation for the domestic violence victims, I suggest you take a hands-off approach and allow your contractor to deal with everything. Let him send you the bill."

"Now renovating a house is too much for my fragile self?"

"It's just a caution for now."

"Come on home with me now. You need a respite and then you can go back to the mansion and fulfill your will require-ments. For now, you'll just be one of mine," Mary said.

"I think that's a stellar idea," Garrick said.

Mary nodded. "We can watch a movie or sit out on the rooftop terrace with the fire pit that Gia bought. We'll have a lovely time. She's made it like a *Sunset Magazine* porch out there."

A lovely time. I've heard that before.

"You'll come?" I gazed up at Garrick, who bore invisible holes through Officer Kendall behind the glass door.

Garrick's concentration broken, he looked down at me. "Pardon?"

"You'll come to dinner at Mary's? Just until I calm down a little?"

His smile was the balm to my soul until I faced the police again. "Of course I will, Brinn. We need to have a talk anyway."

My stomach flipped. I'll admit that talking wasn't what I had in mind. I wanted pure escapism at that point.

CHAPTER 12

I followed Mary into the Campelli household, an old Victorian house that appeared to lean to one side. The interior was very old-world. Two long, low-slung sofas in a garish pattern were covered by clear plastic sheaths behind a coffee table overflowing with newspapers. The kitchen on the right wall was no more than a round table and a small bank of cabinets with a stove that resembled a fireplace. A hallway that led out of the kitchen hosted some king of appliance—a water heater maybe—directly in the center of it. If "make-do" was a house, this would be it.

"Brinn? Would you like some wine?" Mary asked.

"Oh, no thank you. I shouldn't intrude. I'm really not in any danger, but I do love that you and Garrick were worried enough to watch over me."

"I'll be the judge of how much danger you're in," Garrick said. He was truly so handsome, and I wasn't above playing his damsel in distress. Something told me Garrick hadn't ever picked up a golf club in his lifetime.

"I hate to tell you both, but if my mother wants something to happen, it's going to happen." *No matter what you do.* I'd spent so much time living in fear, I was numb to it.

Amazing scents wafted over me. The yeasty scent of fresh bread and tangy tomato sauce coupled with garlic filled the entire downstairs area. It was no wonder Gia and Sophia had zero interest in moving to the mansion. It became clear why the Michelin chef's meal felt pretentious and ridiculous. As if we had something to teach the twins about food.

Mary stood behind her parents. The couple was old and bent but spirited in their movements. They shuffled across the small space to welcome Garrick and me.

The elderly woman dried her hands on a towel she wore on the waist of her olive-themed apron. *"Benvenuto.* Welcome." With her wrinkled spotted hand, she patted my cheek and then Garrick's. *"Coppia bella."*

"No, Nonna, they're not a couple." Mary smiled. "This is my mother, she goes by Nonna to anyone who enters her home. This is Papa."

We said our pleasantries and Nonna looked straight through us both as if she could read our very thoughts.

"Sophia and Gia?" Papa asked Mary.

"Just Brinn tonight. She is a famous ballerina!"

"Former," I corrected.

Nonna and Papa cooed their approval. "You too skinny," Nonna said. "Sit down." She pulled me to the table and pressed me down in the carved wooden chair. *"Mangia!* We eat."

Garrick sat beside me quickly. "You don't have to ask me twice. It smells like heaven in here."

Nonna put down a plate. Tiny slices of sourdough were decorated with chopped tomatoes, fresh basil and peppered with a light spray of parmesan. It was a work of art, even without the taste.

"If I'd grown up in this household, I would have never been a ballerina. A sumo wrestler, perhaps, but never a dancer."

"You were born to be a dancer," Mary said. "Do you cook, Garrick?"

He grinned at Mary. "You act like you don't think that's possible."

"I wouldn't underestimate you, Garrick Kane. Sophia tells me you've accomplished a lot for your young years." Mary pressed her hand on his shoulder. "And are you a great chef?"

"Not in the least," he laughed. "I can't cook too often. Nine-volt batteries are expensive, so I can't give the fire alarm such a workout."

"You make joke, huh?" Nonna patted his cheek again.

"You're welcome here anytime, Garrick," Mary said. "I can't tell you how I appreciated your fast response for Brinn today."

I felt a tinge of jealousy by their friendly interaction. I knew Mary had a good fifteen years on Garrick, but her charms captivated men of all ages. I felt invisible in their presence even while they talked about me. If I never saw Garrick again, I didn't need to watch him fall victim to someone else's magnetism. *Not after that kiss. No matter what the reason behind it was.*

"I'm happy to keep an eye on our Brinn," Garrick said.

"I don't need an eye on me," I said. "I thought that was just a show for the police. You didn't really hire him, Mary."

Garrick smiled directly at me. "I don't put on shows for the police, Brinn. Mary hired my company for executive protection until your mother's trial ends. She believes you're in danger and I agree with her."

"I'm not in danger." Even if I was, they were no match for my mother. No matter what Chelsea did, she'd come out smelling like a rose.

"Better safe than sorry," Mary said.

Garrick ate his pasta carbonara with relish. Nonna lit up as she watched him enjoy her food. There was something magical about Garrick Kane, and even Nonna felt it. Making him happy, watching him smile—he was the slow-burning fuse on a fire-work and when he lit up, everyone benefited by the explosion.

I finished eating my supper and suddenly felt like I was intruding. "I'd like to go home now," I said.

Garrick put his fork down. "Right now?"

"I need to speak to Quinn."

"You never asked why your father was in the hospital."

I choked on a bite and swallowed some water. "It's nothing sinister. My father always lands on his feet."

"Your father was indeed poisoned."

I abhorred my first thought. *Enough poison to where he was in danger? Or just enough to get himself on the front page?*

"Arsenic is not a common chemical compound to have in one's system." Garrick put his hand over mine on the table and the gravity of the situation hit me. Everyone at the table stared at me as if they expected tears that wouldn't come.

"Brinn, does this information make you *feel* anything?" Mary asked me.

"You think I'm like my mother."

"I think you're numb," Mary answered. "We're worried about you."

I still didn't want to see my father. Did that make me a sociopath? Maybe it did.

"You should know the police got a warrant for your grandfather's body," Garrick said. "They wanted to make sure it wasn't just morphine in his system."

"They're going to unearth my grandfather's grave?" I clutched my stomach.

"They've already done it," Garrick said. "No arsenic. Only morphine as reported the first time."

I exhaled deeply. "They didn't ask us!" My hand tightened into a fist. "They just went to his grave and desecrated it like he's a hamster buried in the backyard? My grandfather deserves to rest in peace. He did a lot of good on this earth and he's free of all this garbage. It's our turn to take up the mantle." I pushed my plate away. "Mary, before I go, would it be okay if I lie down for a bit?"

Nonna acted as if she understood nothing and piled my plate high with more noodles. There was a pungent salad in front of me with some type of oil and vinegar dressing and the empty bruschetta plate. My wine glass was filled to the rim. It was all very efficient, like some kind of production line for inhaling good food as quickly as possible.

Nonna mumbled something in Italian, crossed herself and said the magic word again. "*Mangia!* Eat."

"Of course you can lie down," Mary said. "Won't you eat a little more? You can't sleep on an empty stomach."

"I'm a ballerina. I can dance the entire *Swan Lake* on an empty stomach."

I ate a little more in silence as I noticed Garrick eye me warily. *What must he think of me?* I wasn't concerned about my dad being poisoned, but I was incensed at my grandfather's grave being disturbed. I wanted Garrick to understand but had no idea how to explain my feelings.

After the meal, Nonna insisted we leave her to clean the kitchen. She wouldn't hear of us washing up and I wasn't tired anymore. I just wanted to go home.

"Thank you for everything. I'll get out of your way, Mary." I pushed my seat back.

"We'll get out of your way." Garrick slipped my sweater over my shoulders, and I tingled at his touch.

"We'll?"

"You're not going home alone," he said firmly.

"Come upstairs before you go. I want you to see what Gia did to the terrace."

I didn't argue. Mary, Garrick, and I climbed the three stories of a creaky old staircase. The stairwell was narrow and dark. It gave Wentworth Manor a run for its money in creepiness with an old brick wall that probably dated back to the era after the 1906 earthquake.

Mary led us with a flashlight as the overhead lights weren't enough to overcome the seeping darkness. "These old stairs are so wonky and uneven. Watch your step. That's why we put in the chair lift." She pointed to the metal rail that spanned the wall.

This old house weaved around and loomed larger than it looked, but unlike Wentworth Manor, the home had an embracing soul.

Mary reached a wooden door at the top of the steps. "Wait until you see what Gia did for us on the patio. Before she decorated, it looked like garage sale leftovers." She flipped a light switch and thrust open the door. "But now—"

The terrace sparkled with twinkle fairy lights strung across the arched pergola and sprinkled generously down from the plants and shrubs. It provided the perfect amount of illumination and the whole courtyard was another world—as good as any spa escape on Instagram.

"Gia did all this?"

Mary nodded. A glass fire pit with electric blue flames licked at the sky and created color-filled sparks of light on the glass rocks below. Garrick wandered off toward the edge of the patio, which came well below his knee line and made me nervous.

"Garrick, get away from the ledge!"

He turned and grinned. "Not a fan of heights I take it?"

He moved toward the edge. I broke away from Mary and grabbed him and yanked him back.

"It's nice to know you care." He smirked in his cocky manner, and I remembered that he was being paid to be present.

"Mary said Gia got all this stuff on Craigslist," I spouted at him to avoid what his gaze did to me.

"We don't believe in waste in this family," Mary added. "It's like Mama always says, if they threw old things away in Italy, we'd have no history. A little history on something makes it more interesting." She pressed the bottom of her curls. "If I do say so myself."

"If there's history in you, it doesn't show." Garrick walked to the edge of the half-brick wall again and peeked over the ledge.

My green-eyed monster reared its ugly head at his compliment toward Mary. She seemed to sense my unease. "Stay up here as long as you want. Brinn, I'll put fresh towels on Sophia's old bed, and you can find your way around. I'd really rather you stayed here tonight. Her room is on the second floor. Worst case scenario, you'll find Gia's room instead and the sheets are clean in there as well." She stepped into the staircase. "Good night."

"Thank you, Mary."

"Garrick," she peeked her head out again, "being a security expert, I figure you can lock the front door on your way out."

"I think I can handle that."

The door closed behind her and then it was only Garrick and me. It dawned on me that I'd probably been set up, that Garrick was nothing more than an extension of the police force. He'd probably been sent to find out what I knew about my parents' latest scheme. I felt the full weight of his supposed betrayal and I was determined to give him nothing. It's what he deserved.

"I should get some sleep."

"You don't trust me," Garrick said. "But you should."

"Everyone who wants to cheat you says that." I laughed light-heartedly, as though I didn't have a care in the world.

"I don't think you're like your mom," he said. "If that's a concern of yours, you need to let that go. I only want to protect you from her. From anyone who would try to hurt you, actually."

How ironic that he had the most power to hurt me. He was the one who woke up my feelings. "Just a few months ago, I was a flighty heiress and former ballerina. When did having money become dangerous?"

"When someone killed your grandfather for it. By the way, I wouldn't call a master's student flighty."

I almost blurted that I wasn't a student, but I held my tongue. The truth would eventually come out.

"If you want to keep me out of danger, someone needs to convince my sister she'd better not testify against our mother."

"If you're really afraid of her vengeance, why aren't you afraid of her?"

I simply shrugged. I was too numb to feel afraid. My body was fresh out of cortisol. I'd been in fight-or-flight for so long, I had nothing left. As long as I ignored that awakening that happened when I was near Garrick, everything would be fine. Mother would get off, as she always did when it came to consequences, and we'd go along being the dysfunctional, disconnected family we were.

"Sometimes doing the right thing is the hard thing," Garrick said.

"And sometimes, doing the right thing puts you smack-dab in the center of someone's sight."

CHAPTER 13

*U*nder the starry San Francisco skyline with twinkle lights, I made my way to the secondhand sofas in front of the electric fire. As I sat, I noticed an inappropriate erectile dysfunction billboard directly across on the next building. I turned away and focused on Garrick's regal profile. It broke my heart to know that he and Mary discussed my lack of compassion toward my dad. I wondered how Mary could have any sentiment toward my father after all he'd put her through. I didn't like being their villain—probably being compared to my mother. I eyed him warily and calculated how long I had to remain to be polite before I could escape to my room or back to Wentworth Manor.

"I won't bite." Garrick patted the sofa. "Let's gaze on the beautiful view." He motioned toward the billboard and we both fell into awkward laughter. I was no match for him. He put me at ease like a tonic. But I sat feet from him with my back board-straight as if in ballet posture prepared for criticism.

"You've had a rough day," he said. "It's okay to relax."

I eased the tension from my shoulders and leaned into the loveseat. "I don't know anything more than I've already told the police. Your charms aren't going to give you a different story. I can only predict you'll never get a confession out of my mother. She's already done the mental gymnastics to convince herself she didn't do a thing—even if she did."

He got up and placed a blanket around my shoulders. The move softened me in a way that embarrassed me. I was putty in this man's hands, so I straightened my posture again. "I have no ulterior motives, Brinn. I'm here because I want to be."

"And you're being paid."

"I'd be here anyway. Being hired is merely the excuse I needed." He rose and came beside me, his handsome face mere inches from my own. "Why is it you'd believe I want to hurt you?"

Tears pricked at my eyes. "I'm not without feelings, Garrick. I'd never willingly hurt another soul. Not on purpose."

"I know that. Do you think I'd have let you near my client if I felt differently?"

"You and Mary talked about me."

"We did."

"I don't need your help, Garrick. I don't need anyone's help. If they think I poisoned my father, or my grandfather, or whatever else ridiculous thing they want to blame on me . . . global warming maybe? Let the cops ask their questions and I'll answer them. I have nothing to hide."

"Everyone needs help sometimes, Brinn. There's no shame in that."

"I'm in no danger. Well, no more than I've ever been as an heiress. Let's end this charade that I need protection. I appreciate your being there today at the police station, but you're free to go."

"Wouldn't I be a better judge of who is in danger than you?" Garrick asked. "May I remind you that you didn't hire me, so you can't fire me?"

"It's my life. You don't get to follow me around for no

reason. Who would hurt me? My mother's in lockdown and it seems like I'm her best defense as reasonable doubt. I'd say I'm safer than I've ever been. If something happens to me, my sisters get more money. They can't kill us all off without raising some suspicion." I tried to laugh this off, but Garrick looked horrified.

"Brinn, I don't want a false confession out of you. I want you to care that people are coming after you. I want you to protect your life and your freedom."

I brushed him off with a wave of my hand. "I hate money. I can't believe anyone's life is ever in danger because of money."

"That's because you have money. Don't change the subject."

"I can't imagine getting so passionate about something so temporary to this world. It seems stupid."

"Then be passionate about your future. What do you want when this is all over? You're in the homestretch."

I scoffed. "I want the heck out of here. I never want to see the Golden Gate Bridge or the Transamerica building again. I understand that you want me to care that my father may have been poisoned, that my mother is on trial for murder. I get it. I *should* feel something. But honestly, Garrick, if I felt all I've been faced with from people who are supposed to love me, I'd be curled up in a fetal ball and worthless to anyone. At least this way, I can oversee the renovations, get my sisters their money and get back to Southern California as soon as is humanly possible. That's it. That's all I've got as plans for the future."

"Believe it or not, I understand why you don't want to feel anything. I'm not asking you to, but tell me off the record, do you think your mother did this? Any of it?"

I still couldn't allow myself to believe her a murderess. "If she did, she would have justified it as I said, mental gymnastics. She would tell herself that my grandfather was suffering, and she helped into the next realm as an act of mercy. If she did it, she'll have the jury believing she did him a favor. Her words drip honey and going up against her is a worthless exercise. I'm frustrated that no one seems to understand that." I threw caution to the wind and looked directly in his gray-green eyes. "You've seen how the justice system fails your clients. Why do you expect me to trust it?"

"What about her poisoning your father?" he pressed.

My body involuntarily flinched. "I refuse to believe my mother is this diabolical. I still can't believe she'd physically hurt my father. Nor my grandfather. She needs attention, but not this kind of attention."

"What if the facts prove otherwise? Will you believe it then?"

"My mother's style is much more insidious. Like, she'd get my father thrown out of the country club or humiliated in some way by outing him with a mistress. She'd want to watch him suffer. She wouldn't kill him. That's too easy." I forced a laugh to hide my shame. "Where would my mother get arsenic anyway? She doesn't know where the laundry room is to find bleach."

Garrick's jaw twitched.

"My mother is shallow. She's stunning and always the star of any room she graces. She wouldn't put her reputation in jeopardy. The only thing my mother is a danger to is credit balances," I joked. "She shops so easily my father used to say it would be cheaper to divorce her in California than to stay married to her."

On consideration, I realized that was probably not the healthiest thing for your father to say about your mother. Garrick's expression proved it.

"I'm sorry your father said such terrible things about your mother. That must have been hard."

"Stop!" I shouted. "Enough with the fake sympathy. My parents are who they are. I never suffered." I rose from the outdoor sofa and listened for the traffic below to drown out Garrick's voice. I began to hum a song that always took me away from reality when I needed to go.

He walked up behind me and spoke softly in my ear. "I want to protect you, but I need you to fight for yourself."

I turned and slid down and leaned against the old brick half-wall. "I'm afraid to take the lie detector test," I said honestly.

"Why? You've got to be honest with me, Brinn. Your freedom could be at stake."

"Because I've been lying to everyone for years and once the police know that, nothing I say will be taken seriously. Like I said, my mother will get away with whatever she did and someone else will pay the consequences. If it's me, I'm resigned to it."

"Brinn, you can't mean that. You'd go to jail for something you didn't do?"

"I probably won't have a choice."

"What have you been lying about?"

I stared into his warm eyes, convinced he didn't deserve to be involved with the drama that was my family. I wanted to come clean. It made no difference now. "I'm not in finance school getting my master's degree. I have not attended one class. My whole persona is a lie." I waited for his reaction, but he didn't give one. "I do have a bachelor's degree and naturally, my grandfather's lessons, but I dropped out the first day." It was the first time I'd admitted it out loud to anyone.

"What have you been doing all this time in Southern California?" Garrick asked.

I didn't want to admit what a loser I'd been. Supposedly, I was escaping my parents' shallow ways, but the truth was, I'd accomplished even less than I had in the Sunday society pages. At least at a fashion week event, I got dressed for the day. Sometimes in Santa Monica, I never did.

"I did whatever I wanted to with no pressure from anyone. Some days I went to the Santa Monica Pier and watched the families, the couples on dates, the fishermen. . . . Some days I went to Disneyland with friends who had season passes."

"You probably needed the break," Garrick said gently. "You had a few years to make up for."

"I learned how to surf. I kayaked off the coast of San Diego. Oh, I got an expensive drone, and I flew it over the beach until I got caught by the rangers. Essentially, I lived the childhood I never got." I felt so much lighter exposing my secret.

"Your sisters don't even know this?"

I shook my head slowly. "Not even Quinn. Not even the friends I made down south."

"If your friends don't know you're an heiress, how do they think you afford this lifestyle?"

"They think I'm a tech guru and write code at night."

Garrick chuckled and it made me smile. "Don't you want to live the truth, Brinn?"

"No." I shrugged. "The truth sucks. The truth is my mom is trying to set me up for a future in the slammer. The truth is my ankle can no longer support ballet. The truth is, I'm alone and I'll never know if anyone wants to be around me for my money or me. You can have the truth."

"I want to be around you for you. Your sisters want to be around you."

I laughed. "Says the guy literally being paid to be around me."

"I know you're an honest person who has been forced to live a lie."

"I'm a liar. A liar lies."

"I don't believe that," Garrick said. "You lied to take care of yourself. All I'm asking now is you support Quinn while she tells her truth for the same reason."

"It's short-term thinking, Garrick. If my sister knows anything and says it publicly, our mother will not rest until Quinn pays for her betrayal." I grabbed the throw blanket off the back of the sofa, sat back down on the cold cement and tossed the throw over my legs.

"Cold?" he asked.

I shivered, but it wasn't the cold. It was the anxiety that plagued me in our uncomfortable conversation, but it freed me in a way. I was tired of being a chameleon in life; it felt good to unload the truth. *I probably should have found a pastor though and not the one man who makes me feel emotions again.*

He extended his hand and lifted me from the cold concrete. He placed the blanket on my shoulders and led me back to the sofa.

I looked him straight in those steely green eyes that rendered me thoughtless. "I'm afraid to check on my father," I admitted. "If I get involved, it starts all over again. My life will be stolen away again."

Garrick put his arms around me and pulled me close. "It won't," he whispered into my hair. "I'll never let that happen."

I want to trust him. I want to believe.

"Your mother will be convicted, Brinn. The evidence is overwhelming. You're being called to this fight. What if David turned away from Goliath and left it to someone else?" Garrick took my hands. I avoided his eye contact and instead looked down at the rugged hand that held both of mine in it. I inhaled his aftershave mixed with the dirty remains of the police station stench and the moist San Francisco sea air. The effect was tantalizing.

Garrick's voice was low and gentle. "If you won't fight for you, fight for me."

The knot in my throat tightened. "Why is this so important to you? It's my life. It has nothing to do with you."

His expression tensed and the exasperation with me pulsed off of him. The people-pleaser deep within me wanted to apologize and go along so he would like me again. So he would kiss me deeply like he'd done that magical night at the ballet. Even if that kiss was to save Katrina's skin, secretly I'd hoped it affected him as it had me, but he seemed focused on the job. On keeping me safe because that's what he was being paid to do.

"In my business, we have a threat level assessment test that we ask all of our clients to take. It measures whether or not the perpetrator or stalker is a safety threat to our client. What are the chances that he or she would commit a violent act if left to their own devices?"

"My mother could pass that kind of test with ease."

"No she wouldn't, because it's based on your answers. Your experiences with her. I need you to understand that your mother is a genuine threat. She's dangerous. Deep down you know this, but you don't want to admit it to yourself because it feels disloyal." He grasped the top of my arms so I'd look at him. "Your whole life has been about being loyal and being the good girl, am I right?"

I am the good girl. I didn't know how to explain being afraid of my mother's vengeance and taking steps to avoid it was being afraid of her. And also, doing what I needed to do.

"Have you ever bothered to Google me, Brinn?"

"Google you?" I asked. "Heavens no, why would I do that?" I didn't mention how many times I'd been tempted. Only to believe he had access to things like VPNs and cell phone records and then chicken out, thinking he'd know if I stalked him. *But oh, how I've been tempted.*

"Offering a large charitable contribution to an organization, it would be one of the first steps in deciding if you supported that nonprofit. Checking out its principals."

I shrugged. "Sophia said you were the real deal and your ratio for operating costs was low. That was enough for me."

"So it's Sophia you trust."

"She's been working in the underbelly of this town long enough. She would know if you were sketchy."

"*Why* haven't you Googled me?" he prodded.

"I don't use Google in the mansion or on my phone because I don't want the press knowing my business. A Google search is practically public record these days. Same reason I don't take nudes and leave them on my phone." Instantly mortified, I corrected myself. "Not that I have ever wanted to take nudes. But you get my point."

He fanned himself in jest. "I do get your point, but let's not use that analogy. You're my client now and I don't need to think about that kiss we shared."

I turned my head, only to see that blasted billboard, so I turned back again. "Do you want me to Google you?" I took my phone out of my handbag and perched my finger over the search engine.

Garrick plucked the phone out of my hand and gently pressed his thumb under my chin until I looked up at him and met his gaze once again. His eyes so serious and unyielding but full of warmth that inevitably made me feel safe. I felt the breath I'd been holding release.

"If you had looked me up, you'd find out how I got into this business."

He's so handsome. I didn't particularly process what he was saying to me, only that he looked so imposing and distinctive saying it. Even under the orange hue of the streetlights below and the dim bulbs strung across the patio, his eyes sparkled in a way that made him seem more alive. I was too fixated on his soft lips as they moved. I remembered his kiss and how alive I felt in that moment.

I closed my eyes in anticipation for him to kiss me again and transport me to that magical place where all the ugliness of life disappeared and there was only Garrick Kane and me. After a hot minute, I opened my eyes to see Garrick staring down at me.

"Did you know it takes a woman seven tries to get out of an abusive home?"

Way to break a mood.

"On the eighth," he went on, "she either gets out and stays out or she ends up a statistic."

His words sobered me right up.

"Garrick, I spent my childhood in ballet school and toe shoes. Am I missing why you're giving me these facts?" I let out a sigh. "I'm a dancer, not a philosopher."

"You're on your seventh time with your mother. It's time to get out and stay out."

I shook my head. "I'm stuck in the mansion for another eight months."

"Not the mansion," he said. "Get out of your head, where your parents are all-powerful. Their problem is not for you to solve. It's time you took care of you. It's all right to be selfish now."

"I shouldn't be concerned that my dad may be poisoned? Even though I know he probably ate something on a random bet at the club for attention. Did they check his pockets for Skittles? He loves those and they'll turn your lips blue."

"You think your dad ate some candy and that's why he became deathly ill?"

I was babbling now. "I don't know what I think, Garrick."

"I give up. Is that what you want me to do? Give up on you?" He stood and immediately I reached for his arm to stop him.

"You don't understand what it's like to be in Mother's good graces," I explained. "In her shining light, when you're the center of her universe for the moment and her attentions are aimed at you, you're the prima ballerina." I dropped my head in my hands. "I know it's pathetic. But it's . . . it's like a drug and she makes you crave more. If I turn on her, the alternative feels much worse than life in jail. I'll never feel that light again."

Garrick sat down beside me and pulled me into his burly arms. I crumbled into him and let my head rest on his shoulder. I didn't know how long we sat under the stars intertwined silently, but the traffic had died down beneath us. I only know I felt truly safe and for the first time, I didn't want to run anywhere. Maybe Garrick was right, and it was time for me to stand strong against my mother. To fight alongside Quinn because it was the right thing to do.

CHAPTER 14

"Good morning." A sedate Garrick Kane awoke beside me on the now-frigid patio. I snuggled into the warmth of his neck. His solid chest under my cheek made the ramshackle terrace feel like the most luxurious balcony on earth. Something shifted and Garrick let go and sat up straight. It was as if his security-conscious self woke up and returned full force. I instantly longed for the warmth of his caress—where I'd spent the night, nestled against him in the armor of his embrace.

"I'll be assigning a personal bodyguard for you today." He stood and I felt confused by his robotic actions.

"I—I thought *you* were my personal bodyguard?" I tried to step close to him and his entire body stiffened.

"That's no longer best in this case. I think it's best if we keep the professional aspects of this arrangement professional." He opened the door, stepped over the lip and I followed him down the three flights of the decaying staircase. If I'm honest, I chased him. *Chased* him, like a pathetic schoolgirl who longed for his attention. The way he switched was so familiar to me, and that was reason enough to see it for the red flag it was.

Mary met us at the bottom of the stairs as she must have heard the creaking boards. "You two must be freezing. You were out there all night?"

"We had an emotional talk and I guess it wore us both out," I said sheepishly.

"Well, I've made cappuccinos in to-go cups. They're still hot. Nonna made brioche with cream for you both. We figured you'd both be in a hurry to get your days started. That Silicon Valley mindset and all." She handed me a paper cup complete with lid. "Brinn, I can drop you off at the mansion on my way to work."

I was in no hurry to go anywhere, and I sputtered a few sounds rather than speak. When she spoke of the Silicon Valley lifestyle, I assumed she meant Garrick, who had a job. With employees. And a purpose. A job other than languishing around a mansion for eight more months.

"Mary, you should know," Garrick stated. "I'm transferring Brinn's case to one of my best men. Given her circumstances, I think it's best for everyone involved. If she wants to support the foundation, it's probably best we're not seen together."

It was Mary who sputtered now. "But Garrick . . . I specifically hired you because I knew—"

I stepped forward. "Thank you for letting me stay the night." I hugged Mary. "And for hiring Garrick for me. I'm sure his replacement will be more than adequate. You can't know what it meant for me to see you both at the police office yesterday. No one has ever been there for me like that, and I'll always be grateful."

She whispered in my ear. "Take Garrick's advice—whatever it is. He has your best interest in his heart. I'll get my keys and meet you outside."

I nodded while I hoped Garrick was about to offer to get me home.

Garrick and I walked through the kitchen and Nonna

pinched Garrick's cheek, *"Prestante.* Handsome, no?" she asked me.

I smiled while Nonna hunched over the table and lifted up white bakery bags filled with fresh bread that smelled as good as any professional bakery.

We said our goodbyes and exited out the garage to the back side of the house where Garrick's car was parked. He handed me the bakery bags. "Don't eat anything in the mansion."

I rolled my eyes. I couldn't help it. "If it's safe for my sisters, why not me?"

"You still think I'm making this all up for a job."

"I don't think you're making it up. I just think your experience leads you to a different result than me. My mother is selfish, but—"

"Seven times, Brinn. Wise up before it's too late." He lifted my chin with his thumb and kissed me softly on the cheek. "I can't bear to see you as a statistic. It would destroy me. Please do as I ask."

I nodded softly, weakened by his plea.

"You want me to fight for me," I reiterated.

"Brinn, even if your mother doesn't go to prison for what she did, personally, I think she deserves to go to prison for what she did to you. How anyone with your beauty and strength of heart could believe she deserves to pay for the sins of that awful woman is unreal. That alone is reason for her to be locked up for life. You're exceptional. Unparalleled. It's crushing that you don't seem to understand that."

If I didn't stand up for me, I'd never be in his arms again and that gave me resolve. "I'll fight for me this time."

"It's all I ask. I'll have a new guard to your house by 3 p.m. Until then, stick to the baked goods from Nonna."

"I don't want a new guard," I told him.

He gave one of his sideways grins. "That's precisely why you need a new guard. You throw me off my game."

"No one else will make me feel as safe."

"But you *will* be safe. I'll make sure of it."

"What if the new guard doesn't kiss as well as you do?"

He smiled despite himself and gave me another kiss lightly on the lips. "I'll have to fire him for letting my girl down."

I slapped his arm softly. "You!"

"I'll check on you tonight." He grabbed my hand. "Order in if you get hungry."

"Ahh, more freedom as an heiress."

Mary came out to the street and chirped her car's locks. Garrick opened the door for me. I stepped in while Mary went to the driver's side. He put his hand up in a steady wave as we drove away from him. I watched his brawny frame get smaller and thought, *We could solve all of our problems by disappearing to a small private island somewhere.* What good was being rich if it didn't allow you to escape your problems?

We could leave right now. We could disappear into the night on a yacht into the great Pacific and never look back. Maybe set up house on the shores of the Seychelles. With my money and Garrick's brains, no one would ever find us.

Then I laughed at the idea that Garrick and I, two creatures of extreme routine and habit, would ever do something so extraordinary based on a few stolen kisses and my own vivid imagination. He was probably only flirting with me so I'd do what he wanted. It felt like it was my mother or Garrick.

Mary drove me back to Wentworth Manor and she dropped me off in the circular drive. Just as I opened the car door, I received a text from Garrick. *"Your new bodyguard will arrive by 2:30 p.m. Kiss him at your own peril."*

I giggled and hugged the phone to my chest. *I still want my old bodyguard, but how I pray he isn't playing with my heart.*

I couldn't wait to see my sisters. I opened the massive front door with the code and rushed through the foyer. "Quinn? Sophia? Alisa?" I called. I passed a few workmen in their white coveralls and halted as I took in the changes. The mansion was completely gutted since the day before. The wood floors were taped off until they could be sanded. The marble portions of the wall were scraped clean, and all the lighting fixtures had been removed so that exposed wires clawed at me from every direction. My steps echoed as if in an empty airplane hangar, and the scent of sawdust hung in the air as it danced visibly in the sunlight streaks from the upper window.

We'd approved all of it. Now it hit me how this house would look like every other house in San Francisco, a white box with no personality whatsoever. I looked to the former marble walls crushed in small pebbles on the papered floor and my heart sank. *It's too much. We've done too much and harmed the integrity of the manor.*

I ran into the floral room, which remained unscathed from the construction. No one was around and the plans had been set. Why hadn't I realized? I had to get comfortable with the fact that the marble walls would be gone, but we could stop it before too much damage was done to the heart of the house. I fell into the sofa and lingered between sleep and wakefulness as I relived my night beside Garrick Kane under the brisk San Francisco sky. My mind had been focused on other things, not the things that mattered.

When I opened my eyes, all of my sisters had appeared. Gia was at my feet on the sofa, Sophia and Quinn were on the opposite couch. Alisa stood front and center in the room holding two giant plastic bags. "You're awake. Finally."

I wiped my eyes groggily. "I was awake," I said as I realized I must have drifted off to sleep. "What's going on? We have to talk about the renovations."

"Alisa is showing us her latest haul."

The smell of bacon hit me, and my stomach growled in response. Mrs. Chen's eggs were steaming on the sideboard and the memory of the fluffy whipped cream in the brioche was long gone. My promise not to eat in the mansion seemed over-reaching and unnecessary. Especially now that my stomach grumbled.

Sophia, Gia and Quinn were eating from their laps as Alisa waited for her audience to come to attention. "Are we finally ready?"

As I've said, Alisa had too much energy for me on a good day, but at eight in the morning, she felt like punishment.

"I'm not kidding you guys. I think this is my best haul yet." She stopped when she saw me close my eyes again. "Brinn! Wake up." Then she squinted her eyes. "Are you wearing the same thing you wore yesterday? Is that a walk of shame we're witnessing?" She snapped her fingers. "Get it, girl!"

"No," I snapped as I sat upright. "Where did you learn to talk like that? I spent the night at Sophia and Gia's grandparents' house."

No one questioned my whereabouts after that. Nor did they ask me how it came to be, which I found strange. My guess was a text that I was with Mary was enough to satisfy everyone.

"What are you doing here, Gia?" I asked her. "Don't you have work?"

"I called in sick today. I don't feel like fielding questions about your parents, so I'm staying here," she said over the pounding that started up again suddenly. "The whole poisoning thing—"

"My father is your father too," I said defensively.

"The builders are here, so let's be quiet," Quinn said to change the uncomfortable subject.

"We need to talk about that," I said. "They're taking out the heart of the home. We can't let them take away all the wood and the marble. It's art."

"That's so funny you said that, Brinn," Quinn said. "After Gia saw them take the marble off the wall yesterday, she had a fit. I told them to stop doing more on the walls and wood until we had a chance to regroup."

I breathed easier. I should have known Quinn would take care of everything. She'd always been the brains of this operation.

Mrs. Chen came in and shut the pocket doors to close off the rest of the house, but all it did was muffle the sound a bit.

Our little sister Alisa's online presence had become more directed as if she'd gotten some great marketing advice, but in truth, she was a natural. People loved her energy and her "Bohemian vibe" as she called it, and in turn, her numbers kept growing. I remembered when Quinn and I had been so nasty to her about how many followers we had, but she'd been right all along. We'd outgrown Instagram and posting pictures of our daily outfits—while Alisa had found her current purpose in life. She did it way better than we'd ever hoped to. How I wished that we could all worry about vapid stuff like that again.

Alisa's new channel was all about thrift shopping and making incredibly hip outfits from pennies and vintage clothing. She'd go to her local Goodwill and then go online to show off all the brand-name items and outfits she'd purchased and how to style them. She'd amassed a huge following as she tagged all the brand names alongside *Goodwill*. Or *Salvation Army*. Or *Your Big Sister's Closet*, the name of a local thrift shop.

As ludicrous as I thought it all was, I was so proud of her. The sisters always got the first look at the haul before she posted an artsy video with all the prices she'd paid, and brand names set to some *Twilight* tragic musical dirge.

She took each item out of the bag and snapped it so we could admire it. Most girls her age would be grateful for an unlimited shopping budget, but Alisa took to thrifting as an Olympic sport. It was more fun than buying something everyone had on the racks, she'd told us. Plus, it forced her to be more creative when designing an outfit. Alisa was a future fashion stylist and with the followers she'd amassed, she could start making her own living any day now. How ironic that she no longer needed to.

"Where's your mom?" I asked her before she got started.

"Actually, she's staying with Joel's family near Tahoe. She didn't feel comfortable here."

No one feels comfortable here, but some of us have no choice.

I looked at Sophia, who nodded that Alisa's mom was staying with her fiancé's family. My heart swelled at how naturally the families were coming together. Except, of course, for my parents. And our father. He kept a distinct distance unless it suited him. I loved that the professionals, the police officers and lawyers, had no better luck with my mother. It helped me understand all I'd been up against.

"I'm sorry your mom wasn't comfortable here, Alisa."

She sighed and put her arms, holding up a Henley, to her side. "The press has been harassing her at work about Dad and so she decided to take a break."

Oddly enough, there had been no press present at the police station, which is where all the excitement seemed to happen. I wondered if Garrick had anything to do with that. "I'm sorry. What's the press saying to her?"

"It's not your fault," Alisa said. "What do you think of this belt?"

"Beautiful," I said absently. "What's the press saying?"

"They were just asking her if she helped poison Dad or if they were getting back together now that your mom's out of the picture. That kind of thing. Slimy buzzards."

I pulled myself upright.

"So look—" Alisa held up a pair of leggings. "Lululemons. I found this old lady consignment and thrift shop and they have no idea what the young brands are. So you can cut a deal. Lululemons, size 2, basic black and I paid $5 for them. They're only from last season, too. Clearly, they don't know how to read the tags in this vintage store which makes them prime!"

"I think I'd rather pay full price than wear someone else's workout wear." I crinkled my face.

"Hello, it's called laundry," Alisa scoffed. "You just wash them. You have no idea what it's like to be homeless, Brinn. Having access to laundry is a luxury. Mom and I would wear our clothes multiple times before we could ever find a place to do the wash." Alisa dropped the leggings. "One time, she found this box of Febreze behind the Circle K and we thought we were living large because it would get us a few extra days so we could save our quarters."

The life Alisa lived in her short life. My sisters and I all stared at one another, the crimes of our father so readily apparent in what she'd endured.

"Alisa, I am so sorry you ever had to go through that. You deserved so much more. If we'd known—"

She shrugged. "It is what it is, we did fine." She pulled out the next item and went on about it and her deals of the century.

"No one recognizes you when you go in these shops?" I asked her. "They don't harass you?"

"I put on a baseball cap and keep my head down," Alisa said. "It's you and Quinn they're most interested in. Gia, Sophia and I are collateral siblings. No one cares about us, except maybe my followers, and they couldn't tell you who my father is."

"Collateral siblings?" Gia scoffed. "Speak for yourself."

"They're only following my mom because Gia and Sophia's mom won't give them the time of day. My mom's too nice. Mary just laughs at the press, so they follow my mom because she answers them."

If they were worth their salt, the journalists would find out about Alisa and her mom being homeless. *That's the story.* "I guess it's something we all have to get used to," I offered.

"I'm leaving when the money comes through," Alisa said without hesitation.

My heart died a little. I'd joked about how she drove me nuts, but I loved our new makeshift family. I loved how normal and comfortable I felt with my sisters around. I loved that my mother's situation hadn't tainted me in their eyes one bit.

"Where will you go?" I asked.

"My mom and I have been talking about living abroad. Maybe going to Costa Rica and living with the sloths or something."

"What about your charity? You're planning such great things for the homeless."

"Obviously, I'm not going to forget about my charity plans. Mom and I are really set on finding space where homeless kids can get internet access for their homework. When we lived in Mom's car, that and the showers were the hardest things. It's hard to keep up in school when you can't even download the assignment. Even if the schools supplied the laptops, they didn't come with WiFi."

Garrick's words about my mother came back to haunt me in that moment. My parents weren't simply oblivious to others, they actively harmed people by their careless actions. My dad let his own flesh and blood live in a car. I knew I had to go visit him for appearances, but I was already dreading it.

"I don't feel so well," I said. "I'm going to my room for a while if you don't mind."

Alisa tossed her clothing aside and came beside me. "It upsets you that I lived like that."

Tears welled in my eyes. "Naturally. I wish we'd known, Alisa. I'd have given you and your mom my room."

"It has nothing to do with you, Brinn. Look at me now." Everything Alisa said, her arms waved with excitement to the rhythm of her voice. "I live in a mansion. My mom's living it up in Tahoe rent-free right now because we have real friends who care about us, not just new family. Mom bought a brand-new Kia Rogue, and she got her first credit card for gas. It's all good." She rubbed my back tenderly. "We're on top of the world, and how could we appreciate all this good stuff if we hadn't gone through the bad?"

I covered my face with my hands. She was so happy with so little. So happy to have what should have rightfully been hers all along. "You're family, Alisa. I don't want you to move."

She hugged me and I realized how content I was. I didn't want to escape to Santa Monica. *I have a family now.*

"Don't be sad, Brinn. Mom and I are talking options. Nothing is set in stone. If you go back to Southern California, we will still have to come visit you."

"Brinn, what's going on with you?" Quinn asked. "You weren't this emotional when you shattered your ankle."

I sniffled. "We missed out on so much normalcy. When you wake up at Sophia and Gia's grandparents' house? There's fresh espresso and cream-filled puffs. But more than that, there are smiling faces. People who are delighted to see your face and concerned about your well-being."

"This is why I'm testifying," Quinn said. "Your well-being matters. Our well-being matters."

"I want to make everything all right," I told my sisters. "I still want to save my parents. I want them to be happy."

"It was never our job," Quinn said, putting her hand on my back alongside Alisa's. "You're twisting yourself in knots to make Mom believe in you. *That* is why I'm testifying. Your whole body was broken, and it still wasn't enough. She wanted you out on stage that night."

That terrible moment...I'd reached up to her. I'd begged for her attention, and she'd snapped at me about how weak I was. That broke me more than the ankle. "Garrick said it's time to fight for my own life. Escaping doesn't fix it. It's time to do battle."

"It's time," Quinn said. "Did you take your polygraph yet?"

I shook my head. "I'm afraid I won't pass."

"Why on earth wouldn't you pass?"

"I haven't been in school. I'm not getting a master's degree. I've been lying about getting my master's degree."

I had all of my sisters' attention at that point.

Gia laughed. "Oh, the horror of it all. Not getting your master's?"

"It's just that I went down there with that goal, but I ended up wasting so much time."

"Good," Quinn said. "Your entire life was scheduled. I'm grateful to think you finally did something for yourself. What did you do?"

"Disneyland, the beach, the boardwalk, oh, I kayaked . . ."

"That's what I wanted to hear billionaires did," Gia cackled. "Living your best life, girl."

I felt comforted by the fact that none of my sisters thought I'd committed an unpardonable sin. They actually supported me.

"The polygraph makes me nervous," I reiterated. "It's in my nature to feel guilty about everything that Mom does. I feel like she's our problem and we unleashed her on the world by not telling people how she was."

"How would that work, Brinn? The more you tried to tell people, the more she would have doubled down and donated to the person's cause if they started to believe you. No one knows what she's like, and it doesn't matter. *We* know what she's like. That has to be enough for us."

Alisa stood, wilted on the Persian rug with an old, pilled cashmere sweater in her hand.

"I'm sorry I ruined your show, Alisa."

She grinned. "This is way more important. It would be nice to walk the streets without someone yelling about Grandfather's murder. I try to tell them I never knew the man."

"They do that?" I asked.

"Oh yeah," Alisa said. "Blood money, they were screaming. Blood money, murderers, and my personal favorite, heirrorists. It's like heiress and terrorist put together."

"Clever," I said. "I'll take the polygraph."

"They legit do not care if you spent your life at Disneyland. They just want to know your true opinion on Mother and if you know anything."

That's what scared me. I knew the truth I reiterated, but what I really believed? That was terrifying.

"Quinn, I'll give my statement for the polygraph, but I want you to promise me you won't testify against Mother. It's not safe."

Quinn pierced the room with a guttural scream like something out of a horror movie. "You still don't get it, Brinn. She's getting worse with age and cockier, if that's possible. She's more empowered than ever and believes she'll get away with this. She thinks she can fool the cops as easily as she did us our whole lives. Could you handle it if she hurt someone else? For once in your life, you'd really have something to feel guilty about."

We were all so shocked to see Quinn wail like a vampire victim that we stood in a circle, our mouths all dangling open in disbelief.

"I'll take the polygraph today," I said. "I want to revisit you testifying."

"Get your coats, girls." Alisa said. "We're all going together. Brinn needs our support."

"Wait, what? No—"

But I had no choice. My sisters, all four of them, dragged me from the mansion like I was their rag doll.

CHAPTER 15

The five of us crammed into Quinn's Mercedes and sped to the police station as though our lives depended on it. (More than likely, Quinn was worried that I'd chicken out.) When we clambered to the front desk, I told the police officer at the precinct who I was.

"I'm Brinn Wentworth. Officer Kendall wanted me to take a lie detector test in regard to the Wyatt Wentworth death. Is he here?"

"Did you have an appointment?"

I looked back at my sisters.

"No. Could I make one?" I asked.

Sophia stepped forward. "Officer Kendall met with her yesterday. She didn't understand how the polygraph could clear her name. She'd like to take one now."

"Detective Kelly, please." A male voice spoke from behind us, as if Sophia was invisible.

I turned to give him a piece of my mind but quickly pivoted back when I saw Katrina Donley's husband, Matt. He wore a power suit, rather than the wifebeater tee that would have been more appropriate. He looked over me as if I were invisible and he certainly didn't recognize me as anyone more than someone standing between him and the conversation he was having.

His arrogance allowed me to take a good long look at him. He carried a Tumi leather briefcase and looked like your standard two-bit lawyer, the ambulance chaser type who advertised on midnight television. "Matthew Donley here to see Detective Kelly for a 9 a.m.," he shouted to the female officer behind the bullet-proof glass.

"Have a seat, Mr. Donley," she cooed at him like some coquettish schoolgirl and not a grown woman with a firearm at her hip. I could barely contain my disgust. *Aren't cops supposed to have some kind of sixth sense?*

Matt didn't recognize any of my sisters nor me. He was so self-important, so lost in his own world that he sat down and started staring at his phone, never acknowledging our presence. One would almost believe we had an invisibility cloak around us.

The young policewoman raised her forefinger at us as she called the detective and did Mr. Donley's bidding while we waited. At that point, I was too perturbed to wait for Officer Kendall.

"Let's go." I turned toward my sisters. "I'll make an appointment when we get home."

"Miss Wentworth?" Mr. Donley said, and I froze at being discovered. "What an odd coincidence how we keep running into one another after our first meeting at the ballet." He rose and handed me a business card. Matt Donley, *Criminal Defense Attorney.* "In case you need my services."

My teeth clenched. "I don't, but thank you." I wanted to ask him who would protect me from him, but I swallowed the words.

He raised a brow. "The newspaper says differently. Your mother's got a good attorney. I'd call him the best aside from me. But you shouldn't go this road alone even if they're only questioning you at this point."

"Which road is that, Mr. Donley?"

He dropped his head as if explaining directions to a child. "Being accused of a crime doesn't mean you've committed one, but even so, you want to have the best attorney money can buy in such situations. My consultation is free." He gazed at my handbag—a Chanel my mother had given me for my twenty-first birthday. "Since you have the best money, you should have the best attorney. And that's me." He tapped the card he'd just given me. "You give me a call when you're ready to talk and I'll make sure you're properly represented."

His voice alone makes me shudder. I need a shower after listening to his sales pitch.

"Thank you," I forced myself to say. I felt my temperature rise and practiced some yoga breaths rather than going for his throat. His conceit was off the charts. Even if I needed a defense attorney, he's the last person I'd call. I imagined that when I needed him most, he'd be outside doing a press conference. But more than that, it bothered me he knew exactly why I was in the precinct. It wasn't a secret that the whole family stood accused —until someone paid for the crime of my grandfather's death.

"Oh, and Miss Wentworth . . . Brinn, is it?"

It bugged me that he both knew and remembered my name. It sounded like poison dripping from his dangerous lips. "Yes," I answered.

"No offense, but I think it's best if you leave Katrina, my wife, alone for the time being. Any contact with her right now doesn't look good for my business. You understand. Especially if you want to retain me in the future."

"I won't," I assured him. "Want to retain you, that is."

"Katrina has a very soft heart. It's probably best not to mix business and pleasure. I'd appreciate if you didn't contact her about that ballet thing. She's very busy with the children and unlike some men, I consider that a full-time job for her. I'm sure you understand."

I knew he didn't want her having contact with the outside world and I took his concern for exactly what it was—control. "As far as Katrina goes, I completely understand. I was only trying to do her a favor. Encore is a very prestigious committee and it's the gateway to the office of protocol in San Francisco." I shrugged as if it hardly mattered to me.

I could see the conflict on his face.

"I'd heard you had political aspirations. That's what made me think of her, but no big deal. We'll find someone else."

I watched as his jaw tightened. My rejection hit him like a curled-up fist and landed exactly where I wanted it. I pictured him running on home to beg Katrina to contact me.

"It was nice of you to think of her, but as I said, she's very busy."

I didn't relent. "The meetings are held only at the most reputable of society houses and of course, The Olympic Club. Are you members?"

"We're not."

I nodded. "You'll tell her we'll revisit when the kids are older?"

I watched his confidence wane in his eyes and felt the satisfaction of harming this man's fragile ego. A man who would hurt his own wife—the wife God gave him to love and care for.

He recoiled at my suggestion but came back stronger than I gave him credit for. "If you want to do someone a favor, Miss Wentworth, you should relinquish your position on the ballet committee so that the scandal that follows you won't tarnish the good name of Encore and the San Francisco Ballet."

I saw Gia getting her Italian mafia face on and thought it was a good time to exit from the police station. I pushed her toward the door and turned to give a final thought to Mr. Donley.

"I appreciate that, but don't worry. The Wentworth name

will survive this scandal." I didn't add that when *his* truth came out, he might not. Instead, I turned to the female officer at the same time that I grabbed Gia and pushed her toward the front door. "We'll be back later. Thank you!"

We exited the precinct and all five of us stared at one another. "Now what?" Quinn asked. "You're prolonging the inevitable."

I shrugged. "I can't let that man in there know I'm taking a lie detector test. We need to make arrangements quietly."

"Fair enough," Quinn said. "As long as you do it. If we're done here, let's drop by the stables. We can eat at the club."

Quinn clung to her horse whenever times got tough. The prized jumping horse was nothing more than her expensive emotional support animal.

"I think that's a perfect idea," Sophia said. "We can discuss scaling back on the house. And maybe make vacation plans. I think we could all use the break and if we go together, Grandfather's will shouldn't be an issue."

I wasn't used to how my sisters attacked a problem. Quinn and I were taught to sweep conflict under the rug. We were more than happy to do that, but it kept rising like the smoke from a fire.

"I can go to lunch," Alisa said. "But I have to be at the shelter this afternoon."

"Why?" Gia asked.

"I've been taking the clothes I buy at the thrift shops and making outfits for the young people there, you know, styling them? I'm excited about today because I got a bunch of guy outfits. They're always too cool to come around when I'm dressing the girls, but I can see it in their eyes that they're interested. Who wouldn't be interested in style during high school?"

My youngest sister, who I'd found so vapid and extra, continued to shock and amaze me with her wisdom, which she came by naturally at the school of hard knocks. She'd already created a bit of her own empire in the last four months, and she'd taken to philanthropy as if she'd been born privileged. While I'd been jaunting around Disneyland and the beach like an overgrown toddler.

Alisa sat in the middle seat and when our sisters were engaged in conversation, she asked me quietly, "Who was that awful man in the police station? The lawyer?"

"What makes you think he's awful?" I asked her.

"There's not a sincere bone in his body. Anyone can see that."

"Anyone can't see that, Alisa. That's the problem with men like that."

"And women," she said. "No offense, but your mom is like that."

Alisa hit a target of her own and it was a direct bullseye. I probably needed to look at the world from her fresh perspective.

* * *

QUINN KEPT HER HORSE, Avery Lane, at the private stables which backed up to the country club. Most San Franciscans no longer bothered trying to keep a horse in the wealthy enclave of the tiny peninsula. Wide land swaths had long since been swallowed up by the lack of space, but if the mare left town, Quinn wouldn't be far behind.

I rarely visited the country club. I relied on the rest of the family to spend the required amount each month. The Wentworths had been members since the 1920s. Reputation and position still mattered there. Even with all the tech money in San Francisco, most millionaires wouldn't qualify for membership. The whole scene rubbed me the wrong way, but I suppose on some level, it worked. Mr. Donley could no doubt pay the $100,000 initial fee, but he'd be hard-pressed to find a sponsor. Matt's job would be considered beneath the membership—and judging by his character, he certainly wasn't someone they'd want on their roster. It was very easy to blackball someone from becoming a member. Just one vote and they were out.

Together, we walked into the elegant dining room and were seated straightaway. My sisters acted as if they owned the place because they didn't consider anyone better than themselves. *What a gift that line of thinking is. Where have they been all my life?*

"We're here," Gia said. "Let's give these old bats something to talk about, shall we?"

I couldn't have said it better myself, and I craved more of these times. "Does anyone know if the will's stipulations allow us to vacation together?" I asked.

"We could ask Mr. Trunkett. With the house renovations going on, I wonder if it could be arranged," Quinn said. "As long as we're together and managing the renovations, it seems plausible."

"There's the court date to think of," Gia said.

"You're such a fun sucker," Alisa said. "This isn't our trial. Let their mom deal with the crap she created."

"Alisa, a lady doesn't say crap," Quinn said.

"Whatever. I ain't no lady. Or haven't you noticed?"

Quinn scowled.

"I think we should vote on where we'll go for vacation," Gia said. "Because I'd pick a yacht in the middle of the Mediterranean. Somewhere that they consider San Francisco a Podunk little backwards town and won't care where we're from."

"The last thing I want on a vacation is to be stuck on a boat. You're a sitting duck." Quinn said, breaking her public scrutiny rule. As everyone stared at her, she changed her tone. "I mean, there are no horses. We'll fight over who has the best room. No, a yacht is a bad idea."

"Quinn!"

"It is. Next."

"Italy," I said.

"No, we'll be forced to see Grandmother if she goes home. I don't know about you, but I've had enough of her."

"Italy is a big country. Lots of shopping. No one cares who we are there. Fine leather goods, fashion, food. That's a vacation, right?" I used all of Quinn's favorite things in my argument.

"No," Sophia chimed in. "We can't go to the old country without my grandparents and mother, so I'm nixing that one. Because this is *our* vacation." She dug into her purse and grabbed a notepad. She ripped out five sheets of paper and handed them around the table. "Everyone writes an idea here and that's how we'll decide where to go. We'll vote. Just like we did on the wall colors in the mansion."

We all agreed without saying another word and took a moment to write down our ideas. The waiter came and told us the specials. He took our orders while the notes piled up in the middle of the table. We giggled about the police station. *If we didn't have bad luck, we wouldn't have any luck at all.*

"Only Brinn could walk into the police station ready to confess her knowledge and the officers scatter like cockroaches in the light."

"I'm glad you find the humor in my humiliation, Gia." I smirked at her.

"Brinn, lighten up. You need to laugh more, have a little fun. The weight of the world is on your shoulders and it's not your burden to bear," Sophia said, bolstering her twin's argument. "You know what they say, it's not your circus, not your monkeys."

"Does everyone have a passport if we vacation internationally?" Quinn asked.

A hush came over the room and our eyes were drawn to the doorway as Casey Sutton entered. He held the room captive and for the first time, I noticed how much charisma he possessed.

The room of diners turned to him as if a movie star graced the club with his presence.

Casey had been such a fixture in our lives since kindergarten that I never gave him much notice. He was like the annoying little brother that we didn't take seriously. Yet I watched as the entire room paused and grew silent, as if mesmerized by him in his fashionable golf gear. He removed his plaid golf cap as he entered the dining room and the young ladies at the corner table giggled.

"Are they gawking at Casey?" I asked my sisters.

"Casey's hot," Gia said.

"Casey?" Quinn and I asked in unison.

"Casey's hot," Alisa and Gia reiterated.

Quinn and I exchanged glances. "I guess we've known him too long."

"Or maybe not long enough," Gia said and made a growling noise. "I think—"

"His family is going broke," Quinn said.

"If you judge a man's husband potential by his bank account," Gia said, "you're going to end up with someone exactly like our father and you might deserve it."

"Gia!" Sophia hissed. "Quinn isn't like that. Apologize."

"Mama always said if you marry for any reason other than love, you'll regret it."

"Mama never married."

"We're just saying if we wanted to pay a Hemsworth brother to be our date or even join us on vacation, chances are we have money enough to do it. But who wants that person who can be bought?" I'd made things worse. And Casey didn't deserve my judgment.

"I don't think a Hemsworth could be bought," Alisa said. "But if he could, sign me up to crack that piggy bank."

"All we're saying is that Casey," I lowered my voice, "is

running out of cash. So how would you know if he wants you for you or your money?"

"I guess I'd have to use my discernment," Gia said. "See, this is your problem, Brinn."

"My problem? What about Quinn?"

"Quinn has embraced the hard truth about your mother. You keep ignoring it and look for the good in her. Even if it isn't there. Contrast that with being paranoid about every man you meet."

"I'm not afraid of men!"

"When was your last date?" Gia pressed.

"Last night," I said triumphantly. "I slept on Garrick Kane's shoulder."

"My mom is literally paying Garrick to be with you, but you're worried about Casey?" Gia clucked her tongue. "You're wasting your life in fear of making a mistake. Some of the best things in life are mistakes. You get up, brush yourself off and don't do it again. Lesson learned. Next."

Gia made everything sound so easy, but I wasn't the casual dating type, and I never would be. Maybe my personality was too serious . . .

"Casey looks like that hot actor from the '50s—the one who died in the car accident, what's his name, Sophia?" Gia said.

"James Dean?"

"No, the other one. The guy Elizabeth Taylor had a crush on, but he batted for the other team—"

"Montgomery Clift," Sophia answered.

"Yeah, him. Casey looks like a younger blonde version of him. I'm here for it, that's all I'm saying. And if you're going to make a mistake in life, Brinn, let it look like him."

As if our thoughts summoned him, Casey walked over to our table in his fresh young golf gear. He *was* handsome. Strikingly so, I supposed. *But it's Casey!* That thought felt like finding out your brother was attractive to the opposite sex. *Just gross.*

Gia stood as Casey approached and her linen napkin slid to the floor. Casey took in the vision like he was a parched man in need of a tall drink of water and she was the glass. If Casey ever had designs on me, it became evident he'd been served a new, hotter spicy dish from North Beach, which rendered me invisible. Casey, a natural salesman (read: professional flirt) was suddenly at a loss for words and tripped over his own tongue.

"I . . . ah . . . " Then he said nothing more. He looked to me for assistance—his mouth wide open but silent.

"Gia, meet Casey." I waved my hand out between them. "Casey is on the pro-am golf circuit and Gia is my half-sister. She works at the art museum in textiles."

Normally, Casey had a compliment at the ready. He would tell us something like, *In a world full of compact cars, you ladies are the Ferrari. Or . . . How are you all related? It isn't fair that God bestows so much gorgeousness on one family.* I waited for his expected line of baloney, but it didn't come. He simply stood there enamored with Gia's beauty and her perfect hourglass shape, apparent even when she was seated, while he sputtered small sounds.

"It's a pleasure, Casey." Gia smiled coyly and when Casey didn't reply, she excused herself to the restroom. His gaze followed her until she left the expansive dining room.

I snapped my fingers in front of his face. "Casey, are you still with us?"

As if the noise broke the spell, he looked down at me. "Yeah. Sorry, yes, Brinn. I had an urgent message for you."

"For me?"

"It's from my neighbor." Casey's eyes were on the doorway anxiously searching for Gia.

"Your neighbor?"

"Katrina. She said it was urgent that I find you. I texted you, but you must have changed your number. Not that I'm offended or anything." He cocked a brow. "I finally texted

Quinn and she told me you were on your way here, so I decided to rush over."

"I changed my number after my grandfather's will and well, you know . . ."

He pulled out a dainty baby-blue envelope, the kind that had to be hand-carried to its destination because it was too small for the post office to deliver. "She said not to get back to her directly. You women and your secrets. I didn't even know you knew each other."

"Just casually," I told him. "I wanted her for Encore."

"Oh, she'd be perfect for that. Her husband has been prodding me to sponsor him for the club ever since they moved in next door. I don't know if that is what this note is about or not."

"Really?" I feigned ignorance. "Are you going to do it?"

"Nah, I can't really vouch for him." Casey shrugged. "Something's just—off—but you didn't hear that from me."

"Your secret is safe with me."

Casey came lower so the rest of the table didn't hear. "Guy works with white collar cheats all day. I told him I was on my dad's membership anyway so I couldn't sponsor him even if I wanted to."

"Is that true?"

He rolled his eyes. "Of course not. Sometimes you're so gullible, Brinn."

"So I've been told."

"I guess Gia isn't coming back." His broad shoulders slouched.

"She had to call in to work, I think. We've been on a family errand."

"Nice to see you all," he said to the collective table. "I've got an afternoon tee time, so I'll catch you all later." He looked down at the note he'd handed me. "I'm just the messenger and she said not to mention me."

I nodded. "Got it."

After he walked away, I ripped into the small envelope with my forefinger and saw Katrina's flowery handwriting.

Brinn,

He's found my plans.

Contact Garrick right away, please!

I can't have his number on my cell.

Don't try to reach me on your own.

Katrina

I looked at my sisters, their vacation votes sitting in the center of the table sans mine and Gia's. "I need to go."

"Whatever it is, can't you just make a phone call?" Quinn asked. "We've got a vacation to plan."

I shook my head. "I have to go see Garrick. It doesn't matter to me where we go. As long as it isn't Disneyland."

"Garrick?" Sophia said. "You just left him this morning."

I felt fear deep in my gut. Katrina barely knew me. She'd enlisted Casey and had him track me down? *Something is very wrong.* "It's about my charity," I exaggerated.

Silently, I prayed for Katrina. I didn't know her well enough to know if maybe she invited drama into her life, like my parents seemed to. But her plea seemed heartfelt and legitimate. I went with my gut instinct. Finally, I felt like I might have something to offer, even if it was simple access to Garrick Kane.

CHAPTER 16

The country club's veranda boasted sweeping views of the bay and the Pacific Ocean. Perched over the tip of San Francisco, the sight would make anyone feel on top of the world. I pressed Garrick's personal number and my stomach fluttered as I waited to see if he'd answer from an unknown number. I waited. And I prayed I hadn't imagined our connection. I wasn't much of a praying person, but ever since my mother had been arrested, it had become a way of life. Maybe Mary Campelli's outlook had inspired me. Her quiet spirit and acceptance of the raw deal she'd lived was something I now aspired to.

A woman answered Garrick's cell. "Hello?"

"I-I'm sorry, I must have the wrong number."

"Are you looking for Garrick?"

"Yes," I said, disheartened. *What did I expect?* My handsome guy with the swagger of Indiana Jones and the mystique and uprightness of Perry Mason, what was I expecting?

"This is Vicky, his assistant, is this an emergency?"

"I think it might be. One of his clients contacted me because she can't call him directly."

"And you are?"

I didn't answer. "Her husband has discovered her escape plans, I think."

"That constitutes an emergency," she told me. "Who is this?" she asked again.

"It's Brinn Wentworth."

"Hang on."

There was silence that seemed to stretch on forever as I waited. Until the smooth baritone of his voice answered. "Garrick here."

"Garrick, it's Brinn Wentworth."

"Brinn," he said gruffly in his sexy, gravelly voice that reminded me so blissfully of waking up on his shoulder. "Did you think I've somehow forgotten the woman I spent the night with?"

"Garrick!"

"You know what I mean. Alongside. Is that better?"

At the moment it didn't sound better. It sounded platonic. One thing I definitely did not want was to be friend-zoned by Garrick Kane, but I quickly remembered this wasn't about me.

"I'm at the club." I nearly smacked myself for leading with this. It was like announcing my uselessness.

"Are you calling me to tell me the special of the day?"

"What?" Recognition hit me. He'd made a joke. "No, I'm not calling for that. Prime rib though, if you're interested."

"I'm not," he laughed.

"I shouldn't be beating around the bush. This is serious. I'm calling because my friend Casey—"

"Casey Sutton?"

"You know him?" *Is there anyone in San Francisco who doesn't know Casey Sutton?*

"I do," he said without giving anything away. As was his norm.

"Casey gave me a note today. From Katrina Donley. I think she may be in trouble."

His tone became severe. "What did it say? Read it to me exactly as she wrote it."

"Brinn,

He's found my plans.

Contact Garrick right away, please!

I can't have his number on my cell.

Don't try to reach me on your own.

Katrina"

"Thanks, Brinn. I'll be in touch."

"Do you have my number?"

"You just called me."

"Right. Garrick, one more thing."

"What is it?"

"I don't know if this is important, but I saw Mr. Donley when I was at the precinct this morning. He was meeting with an officer. I assume about a case, but he saw me there. I don't know if it means anything, but I felt compelled to tell you so you're not surprised by it."

"When is the new house you purchased in the Haight going to be ready to move into?"

"Not for months. It's not even worthy of being a crack house at the moment," I told him.

"Katrina is too high profile to send to one of my regular houses. Her husband has access to those places through his job." He paused. "At least, I'd worry that he does."

I could hear him typing as he spoke with me, obviously already on the case.

"I can get her an Airbnb under my name until you find something permanent, but she and the kids are always welcome at the mansion, too."

"I'll handle it, Brinn. We have protocols in place. Thanks."

"Wait a minute, Garrick, I want to help."

"Do you mind getting an Airbnb for tonight? It can't hurt. Plan B. That way if Matt does have access to anything here, you've got it covered."

"I'm on it. Any particular neighborhood you prefer?"

"Pacific Heights. We'll hide her in plain sight."

"You know she's welcome at the mansion if she needs to come. I can put her and the kids in the guesthouse out back and she'd have privacy and wouldn't have to move. We've got security at the house."

"Hmm," he said as he continued to click away on his computer.

"Joel is there. Plus, you're sending me another bodyguard this afternoon, right?"

He was quiet for a length of time, and it made me uncomfortable.

"Tomorrow actually," Garrick said. "I've got a guy finishing up a job. Joel assured me he's got you until then."

"So you're worried about the mansion?"

"Listen, Donley thinks he's smarter than everyone else and you have enough troubles in that mansion." He tapped away on his computer as he spoke. "I've got enough reservations about you being in the mansion," he said.

"You do?"

He paused again. Garrick Kane was very particular about every word he said. Most of the time, he said nothing at all, which brought out something in me that tried to force words out of him. "Too many points of entry," he finally said.

"I understand." I couldn't refute that.

"If you want to help, say a prayer. This guy Donley has one of the darker natures I've seen in my cases. That's when he's in public. I shudder to think what he's like behind closed doors."

His words sent shivers down my spine. Garrick wasn't

someone who created drama for drama's sake—the antithesis to my parents. The fact that I could hear the apprehension in his voice over Katrina's circumstance made me more nervous. He'd been clacking on the keyboard the entire time we spoke, so I knew he was already making arrangements for Katrina. Garrick's solitary focus on her safety unnerved me because he clearly wasn't the type to be easily startled. Suddenly I understood how I'd played with fire that night at the ballet. Mr. Donley wasn't one to trifle with and I wished I'd never started this journey.

"If you hear anything else, I want you to call the line you've called, all right?"

"Yes," I said.

I stayed quiet on the phone following his lead. If I had to venture a guess as to Matt Donley's character, I would have chalked him up to a cheesy salesman at worst. The kind of guy who might be seen selling accident liability insurance on television—or calling about your car's warranty. I did not see him as someone who actually posed a physical threat to his family or others. I supposed that was the point and why Garrick was so leery of my involvement. Monsters didn't necessarily look like monsters.

Matt Donley hadn't scared me with his threatening behavior, but now I realized that was probably some deficit in me. The fact that a licensed professional like Garrick Kane saw the urgency in Katrina's letter made me wish I'd never pushed my way into his foundation. This was a place I couldn't afford to fail.

Garrick finally spoke again. "I don't want you anywhere near this, Brinn. Do you understand?"

"That's why I called you first thing."

"I know this guy's type. He will transfer his rage to you without a second thought. He's strategic and he's three moves ahead of us all."

"How would you know that?"

"We have assessment tests but basically, it comes down to experience. He hides his abuse well. I bet at this very minute he'd have no less than fifty people at the station to speak on his good character. Mostly likely, he's already prepped those people by insinuating his wife is crazy, an addict of some kind or a child abuser."

I felt breathless at his assessment and slightly guilty for doubting him—or Katrina. "Why would—"

"Don't bother trying to figure it out. He doesn't need a reason. He's playing his own game in his head, and he intends to win without telling the other players that there's a game going on."

"Garrick, call me and let me know what's going on. I'll be praying for Katrina."

"That's the best thing you can do. I'll do my best to call you with updates, but ignorance is your best friend right now. I'll have enough eyes in the mansion too, so feel free to eat anything."

I hated hearing the business tone in his voice.

"I'll order an Airbnb in my name when we get off the phone. Katrina doesn't have to use it."

"I already have my people on that, but I appreciate your help." Garrick's cold tone forced me to question our connection. *Was there one?* Or had I created it all in my head? "Talk soon," he said before he hung up.

His cool demeanor made me feel like he'd given me the proverbial pat on the head and sent me away. Just like my parents did when they were done showing us off to guests.

Sophia emerged from the club and found me pacing on the veranda still holding the phone in my hand. "Is everything all right?"

"Garrick has two sides, doesn't he?" I asked, while I secretly wished she'd deny it. "One minute he's warm and nurturing, the next, he's like a robot."

"I don't think so," Sophia said with a distinct look of pity in her expression. "I think he's confused about his feelings for you while you're currently his client."

I stared out over the golf course that sloped down and stretched toward the Pacific Ocean. "I should have never taken on this charity. Everything about it is over my head. I should have taught ballet to underprivileged kids or something. After I know this client is safe, I'm out."

"Do underprivileged kids need ballet?"

I stared straight at her. "As far as I'm concerned everyone needs ballet. For the beauty, for the discipline, for the proper way to hold oneself. It's foundational."

"Far be it from me to keep ballet from the masses." Sophia smiled. "Are you coming back in for lunch? We need your vote."

"I don't like how Garrick makes me feel. It's uncomfortable." *And yet, the most comfortable.*

"Well, like you said, maybe it's not the charity for you."

"Garrick makes me feel that same breathless need to impress, like my mother. I hate how I act around him, like I have to dance for my dinner while everyone in the restaurant is staring at me like I'm out of my mind."

Sophia rubbed my shoulder. "You're trapped in this situation for another eight months. Maybe making lifetime decisions isn't your best option right now. It's okay to have some harmless flirtatious banter, Brinn. Lighten up."

Is that all it was?

"You're right. Obsessing over petty stuff beats facing a polygraph."

"We're all here for you. You've got this. The case doesn't rest on you. It's just a matter of telling the truth again to the machine."

"You all don't get it though, Sophia. My mom has this ability to make people believe everything she says. There is this part of me that feels like if she wants me cornered, I'm already as good as guilty." As I said those words, I suddenly understood Katrina's fear. It didn't have to make sense to others. We lived with the truth.

"I think you're right. Focus on Garrick for now. We're not going to let your mother twist you up this time."

"He rescues damsels in distress for a living. I don't think I'm at his level of flirtation."

"Garrick? Yeah, and dudes in distress too if we're being literal, but don't forget, we all saw that kiss. You can act as innocent as you like, the truth is out there."

"Pardon me if it's hard to believe a man being paid to be near me—"

"You really don't get it, Brinn, do you?" Sophia lifted part of her lip as if she was disgusted.

"Get what?" I asked her.

"In the real world, you're out of Garrick's league. Not because you're blonde, gorgeous, a ballerina and a billionaire. Even though any one of those things is enough to put off a working man like Garrick. . . ." Sophia took me by the hands. Her family was so touchy-feely, and I was barely getting used to it. "Put someone else's name in those qualities. You don't see yourself as the world sees you. You see yourself as your mother has told you that you are, and no offense, but your mother is warped beyond measure. Honestly, I could forgive her more easily for what she did to our grandfather than what she's done to you."

"Grandfather is dead," I said, astonished. "I'm definitely not out of Garrick's league. Did you see his date at the ballet?"

"I saw her." Sophia squeezed my hands again. "You're so serious about everything, Brinn. I can't see you being casual about anything, which is why I think you and Garrick are perfect for one another. You both act like life is like a late library book that you must return immediately or the world will blow up. It's not even *your* library book, but you both seem to wear the strain of others on your shoulders like Superman's cape. Why not fight crime together?"

"As if you don't do the same thing as a social worker."

"But we're not talking about me," Sophia said. "If you really are serious about wanting to date Garrick—about not being single for life like you unrealistically decided for yourself—then you're going to have to let your guard down and take a risk."

"I'm not going to humiliate myself and chase him, if that's what you mean."

"That's not what I mean at all. You're allowed to change your mind in life, Brinn. There's no hard-and-fast rule that something you decided under duress in your parents' house of trauma has to be for a lifetime. What do you *want* now?"

I never really knew what I wanted because I'd never been allowed to decide much in my life. Once the will stipulations were over, a life in finance seemed like the safest choice, but that's not what came out of my mouth. "I want to feel alive again." I slipped my sweater off in the rare afternoon warmth. "I don't want to feel dead inside anymore."

"Then you need to start with your parents," Sophia said. "I say that as a professional."

I failed to see how my parents had anything to do with Garrick's effect on me, but my body recoiled at the idea of dealing with them. *Life should definitely come with a manual.*

CHAPTER 17

*a*fter being released from the hospital, my father fled to the Napa family estate in the wine country. Bradley Wentworth never met a crisis head-on; he always had an escape route. Maybe that's where I'd learned it. When the going got rough, my father got going.

I'd set up the Airbnb for Katrina and her boys before we left town, and Sophia assured me that it seemed like as good a time as any to deal with my father.

Sophia and I drove the sports car, a BMW i8 that my father gifted me after I shattered my ankle. The sight of the sports car still made me angry. Dad made a big show of presenting the car outside the hospital when I was released. It had a giant pink bow on the hood, and he stood in front of it like a game show model with his arm extended in a flourish. *Seriously, the drama.*

I couldn't even drive this "gift," but he'd called the photographers, so I painted a showy smile on my face as was my habit and acted surprised. *As surprised as I could handle without tumbling over on crutches.* Thinking about it made me enraged all over again. I'd just lost everything that mattered to me, but I plastered on my cultivated smile and grimaced from the pain as I lowered myself into the completely impractical sports car with a stick shift. So had I had a working leg, I still couldn't have driven it.

The first time I slid into the passenger seat with my dad at the helm, I was the antithesis of the ballet grace I'd been known for. He didn't seem to notice. Not even when I knocked my head bending so low to get in the car after my injury. Of course, that's the picture that the newspaper ran with.

The i8 was a showy car that handled like it was on rails, but it was impractical with attention-seeking doors that opened upwards, so when I moved to SoCal, I left the car in the garage and bought a used Subaru Crosstrek for school.

The Crosstrek was still ten times nicer than what most students drove, but after the high-end Beamer, it felt like a beater car. That was the first sign that I'd grown accustomed to the money, and while I liked to believe I could easily live without it, some days I did question my resolve.

Lost in my thoughts, I pressed the accelerator and shifted as we crossed the Golden Gate Bridge into the Marin Headlands.

Sophia made a show of grabbing onto the arm rest as if she was on the world's scariest roller coaster. She pressed her foot against the floor as if she were braking and asked me, "Do you know how fast you're going?"

"No," I told her. "That's the beauty of this car. It feels like you're standing still no matter how fast you're going."

"Waze says you're doing eighty-five," she said, holding up her phone so I could see it.

"Seriously?" I pulled back on the pedal. "Doesn't it feel like we're going forty-five?"

"It's so low to the ground, I feel like we're about to take off in an airplane."

"I'll take that as a compliment."

"It's not a compliment," Sophia said. "When this will fiasco is all over, Joel and I are getting married—"

"And?"

"And I'd like to live to see my wedding day."

"This thing has amazing crash tests." My laughter escaped. Sophia was so easy to mess with, sometimes I couldn't help myself.

Sophia gave me such a side-eye that I felt as if it were physical. "This car doesn't suit you at all."

"Well, it's not me. It's my consolation prize from my dad when I shattered my ankle and lost ballet. Since he couldn't show up for me emotionally, he bought me something completely impractical that showed he had no idea who I was inside. I figured it would be a balm to his weary self to see me in it today, but the truth is, I miss my Subaru."

"Trade this thing in and buy five of them," Sophia snapped.

"Let's look at the bright side. If Grandfather's money doesn't come through, I can always sell this and put a roof over our heads."

"Really?" Sophia's voice softened. "You'd put a roof over *our* heads."

"Sophia, if we didn't get a dime, you wouldn't get rid of me. You've done so much for my soul. I can't even think of what my life was like before you. The five of us are sisters always."

She held my hand. "Truly, I hope everything works out. I'd be sick if I'd missed this year of my grandparents' life for a payout that may not happen. I'm doing this for them. And my mom. They deserve to never worry. The allowance alone allows for that." She sucked in a deep breath. "At least you don't have school debt. Unless you decide to have a new wing built for yourself."

"Touché." I hated being reminded how different we were. *I have money. She has love. If given the choice, I know what I'd choose.*

"Seriously, you think this may not happen? That changes a lot for Gia and me."

"It will happen," I reassured her. "But it will be a bitter battle to the end, I think. There's the company itself battling for their share and who knows what my parents have up their sleeves. It's better not to be complacent when it comes to greed. I know my grandfather and he made sure that will was airtight, but people can sue for anything, so there's that."

"I used to be so jealous of you and Quinn. Every weekend in the society page, seeing your gorgeous outfits and the sparkly life you all seemed to live, but now I understand."

"Understand?"

"I don't want you to take this the wrong way—"

"Conversations that start like that always end in the wrong way."

"Hear me out. I used to cry myself to sleep at night because you had a father and we never did, but it was the same man. We felt like we were less-than because our father didn't want to be around us but seemed to be so wonderful to you and Quinn. It left this hole in my soul that was life-altering."

I was glad my eyes were on the road and I didn't have to see the pain my father had caused her.

"But now I know that you never really had a father either. He doesn't seem present or to have any clue what his daughters are going through. I mean, a sports car when you're recovering from a life-changing injury seems offensively tone-deaf."

I looked at Sophia briefly as we buzzed up the highway to the Napa Valley.

"I know the car was his way of saying he was sorry. It was his attempt and I have to appreciate that. It's what he's capable of." I wished it was more, but I needed to be grateful for what was there. "What did you think when you met him?"

"I was taken aback," she said honestly. "He was so handsome, and it felt so unreal to see him in front of me after only seeing him all those times in the newspaper and imagining who he was. I thought this hole in my heart would be filled, but then there seemed to be this visceral wall between us. I felt it go up the second he looked at me and thought I was my mother. It was like he was missing some kind of connection chip and didn't know how to relate to others. He only knew how to pretend for others as if he was acting in a role."

I wanted to turn the car around. My whole life I'd wanted to believe my father was the man who was my rescuer and protector, but it was never true and going to see him now felt like buying into his reality. He'd never protected me or Quinn from a thing. In fact, there'd been times when he'd blamed us for circumstances and thrown us under the proverbial bus to protect his own good name. I looked over at Sophia, grateful she was here to keep me grounded. I'd need her today. My father had a way of turning my world upside down and I vowed today, I would not end up apologizing to *him*. A small but worthy goal.

* * *

MY PARENTS CALLED the Napa Valley house The Country House. As we drove up the long, winding driveway, I realized how utterly ridiculous that moniker was. It was country like the queen's Balmoral Castle was country. A large French chateau-style estate set on twenty-five acres upon a ridge overlooking Napa Valley, the house boasted expansive views of the iconic amber rolling hills with the hopscotched lines of the grapevines and the punctuation of several ancient oak trees.

Derek, my father's butler, greeted us in the portico, opened the doors and helped us out. Sophia stretched and looked over the valley. "I mean, wow."

"Right? We can go wine tasting while we're out here."

"I'd love that," Sophia said. "This house . . . this property. I can see Joel and me getting married here."

"Well, hopefully, my father will still be talking to us and that's a possibility."

"Solid point," Sophia said.

"One thing you need to know about our father is that someone always has to be at fault. You don't have to fix a problem, but someone definitely needs to be blamed. Once that happens, the problem gets swept under the rug, never to surface again. So don't go in there thinking we're going to resolve anything. We're just letting him know we're glad he's alive and someone is to blame."

"That seems emotionally healthy," Sophia said sarcastically.

"Derek buzzed you were here." My father strode out of the open double doors of the country house as Derek swept away the BMW. Dad wore a heather-gray sweater with a Burberry scarf wrapped casually around his neck. "Sophia." He acknowledged my sister and both of us were astonished, mostly that he knew which twin it was. It helped that Sophia dressed like a schoolteacher and Gia, a corporate princess. Father always took notice of clothes and I figured that's how he knew it was Sophia.

"It's nice to see you," she answered without using his name or the word dad.

He came alongside her and kissed her cheek and then mine. "Are you staying the night? You didn't let me know you were coming. I'll have Derek ready some rooms."

"I don't think so. I may have some urgent business back in the city with the charity. We have to attend to some legal items, too." In the midst of his hospitality, I wanted to remind him he was suing us for the inheritance.

"That's right, your domestic violence work," he rolled his eyes. "Does your father being poisoned enter into that realm of your concern? Or is that too dirty for you to get involved with?"

"I'm willing to hear your side of the story," I said without committing.

"You didn't even check on me in the hospital, Brinn. I was lying there alone and only one person bothered to come see me.

I know there's the lawsuit, but that's business. I'm still your father."

Guilt began to gnaw at me, but Sophia gave a short nod, and I knew I could do this. "I didn't think you were really in the hospital. I've been busy. They want me to take a polygraph test at the police station."

"You never did know how to prioritize people, Brinn."

I threw it right back. "Are they certain it wasn't food poisoning?"

He narrowed his eyes and if looks could kill, I'd be dead in the portico. "You believe your mother." He looked at Sophia with his hands in the air. "Do you believe this? Her mother is trying to frame her for the murder of my father, and she believes her over me. Unfathomable."

"I didn't say I believed her, Father. But I have to wonder why, if you think you're in danger, you'd come here to her house?"

"In the state of California, it's my house too. At least until we're divorced and the settlement has been made."

I didn't think that was true. My mother had been very specific about her family home when she'd inherited it and I thought it was kept in a separate account, but again, I'd be arguing semantics rather than what mattered.

"Regardless, it's Mother's home. Why would you come here?"

"I'm here for the simple reason that she can't be, Brinn. It's not like I'm welcome in my own ancestral home. Since when did you become so suspicious of your own father?"

"You *are* suing me, Dad."

"That's not personal," he reiterated. "My father made me a verbal commitment and yet his will set out to ruin me. It has nothing to do with you."

I sighed. "Fine, Dad. I don't want to talk about the lawsuit. We'll let the lawyers deal with that."

"Then why are you here?"

"I wanted to check on you because I love my daddy." I went in for a hug and he stepped back.

"I passed my polygraph; did you know that?" he pressed.

"No." Though I had little doubt my father could trick a polygraph. Lying was like breathing to him.

"Your mother failed the test miserably. Did the police tell you that?"

I felt like I'd seen a ghost when my grandmother emerged from the country mansion.

"Grandmother," I said, astonished. "What are you doing here?"

"Is that any kind of greeting?" She put her bony left hand out and I reached for it, shaking it awkwardly. "Bradley, what have you taught these girls of yours? How will they run Wentworth Manor without the most basic of manners?"

"I'm thrilled to see you," I lied. "I thought you were at the Fairmont."

"Bradley, I wasn't even properly welcomed after the gala." She turned to me. "Wentworth Manor is a flurry of activity, which during renovation, is still your duty to maintain order. Your mother would have moved out, but since it isn't possible, she would have ensured the chaos was kept to a minimum. Between you girls in and out of the place and the contractors banging at all hours of the day, I couldn't hear myself think. The presidential suite at the Fairmont was booked, so when I found out your father came up here, I decided to join him."

"Alisa was living on the streets with her mom, so Wentworth Manor is quite an improvement for her."

Father and Grandmother both pursed their lips and turned toward the house. I hoped I wasn't becoming just like them with my shrouded barbs.

Clearly, my mother was a selfish woman, concerned only with her image and beauty. She lived for a compliment and waited with bated breath until the next one appeared. It was like oxygen to her. But seeing my grandmother side with my father, I had mercy on her.

"Well, you may as well come in." Mona turned, as if we weren't welcome.

We followed her into the expansive living room with two back-to-back sets of furniture that created two distinct living rooms in the same space. My father had our full attention and took the opportunity to tell us his side of the story.

"I've been telling the doctors your mother isn't right for years," Father said. "They didn't listen."

"Dad, I—"

"You know what happens when you get poisoned, Brinn? You get vertigo. Your ears ache and the migraine is like nothing you've ever felt before. I'd rather be dead than experience that headache again. I slept for thirty-six hours, and do you know how many of my five daughters came to check on me?" He held his fingers in the shape of an "O."

"You're suing us!" I clapped back again.

"Enough with that. You sound like a broken record. What does that have anything to do with it? I'm your father. Business is business. Trunkett knows that. It's not personal."

I sighed aloud. "You keep saying that. It feels pretty personal. We're already stuck in the house for a year. Sophia can't get married until this is over. It's a huge inconvenience, and you want to come in and make all of our efforts for nothing! Grandfather made his will the way he wanted it. You have enough, why do this to your daughters?"

"How awful for you to be stuck in a mansion in Pacific Heights. The *struggle* is real, is that what you want me to believe? You know where I'd like to be recovering right now? In my home."

"Why are you here?" Mona asked me.

Sophia's eyes were wide, horrified. I imagine no one asked her why she came to see her family.

"By the way, you don't need protection from me. You can call off your goon," Father said.

"My goon?"

"That big guy. The private eye you hired."

"I didn't hire—"

"Garrick?" Sophia asked.

"That's his name. I told him to stay the heck off of my property and that if I saw him here again, I'd shoot first and ask questions later."

"Dad, you don't even own a gun," I said, as I processed the thought that Garrick was here. "He couldn't have been here. He's working on a big case."

"If you want to fear one of your parents, maybe try the one that's poisoning people."

"Dad?" My father wasn't usually angry or bitter. I didn't recognize this version of him, and it scared me. Not for myself, but for what my family's future looked like. By his words, he separated himself from my mother. With grandmother here, what did it all mean? I didn't blame him, but we had entered a new era and I wondered if he would finally get my mother to admit her wrongs.

"I wanted you to know I didn't appreciate you sending that gorilla over here, Brinn. He drove up here like he owned the place. You know I'd never hurt you. Nor any of my daughters."

Tell that to Alisa.

"It won't matter soon," he said. "We're going back home to stay in the penthouse with your mother."

"The woman who poisoned you?" All hope of justice died within me at that point. I had to stop listening to what people said and take note of their actions. It was the only way.

"Allegedly," my grandmother said. "It seems perhaps her actions may be attributed to this . . . this tumor in her head. It must be from her father's side of the family. We have no cancer on my side." My grandmother said this as if it was some kind of badge of honor that no one on her side had died of cancer.

"What tumor?"

"Your mother's tumor. She has a brain tumor so that's why she's been acting this way," my father said. "That Chelsea, she just always keeps a man on his toes."

"Dad, you're not going back there. Even if that's true, she might hurt you again."

"You see, Brinn," Grandmother said. "That's how much he loves her. These other women are nothing to him compared to my Chelsea."

"I thought you weren't going to see her until this was all cleared up."

"It is all cleared up, Brinn. Your mother is a very sick woman, and this is all a result of that."

Sophia's mouth was ajar. Shame covered me like a veil. What chip was my family missing that these conversations were part of my life? My mother could get away with anything and she'd still be loved by her minions. Meanwhile, I struggled with perfectionism and settled for scraps from parents who barely tolerated me. I gasped for breath and chugged the water that Derek set beside me.

"What did Garrick want?" Sophia asked, apparently trying to take the heat off of me.

Mona and Father acted as though nothing was said. "You're welcome to stay as long as you like, but Mona and I should get on the road before the traffic gets too bad over the bridge."

"You're really leaving? Dad, I came all the way over here to talk to you." I glared at my grandmother. *"Privately."*

"And we talked. What else is there to say?" Father asked me. "Your mother isn't well and that needs to be our priority. We need to get her doctors ready to testify."

"Dad, she tried to kill you."

"It's called forgiveness, Brinn. If you honored your parents as you're commanded in the Bible, maybe you'd have more of it within you. No one is perfect."

"What about Grandfather's death?" I asked.

He patted my shoulder. "Until this lawsuit is over, I've been advised not to discuss the will or your grandfather's death with you girls."

"Father, if you walk out of here now, I'm done!" I shouted. "Done! No more games. No more covering up for you and Mom. I'm done, do you hear me?"

"You're making threats now? If I don't do as you say, you'll cut me out of your life? Well, aren't you like your grandfather after all."

He strode out to the portico with Mona scowling back at me as she followed. If only the city of San Francisco could see them now.

"What just happened?" I asked Sophia.

"I have no idea. But first he was angry you sided with your mom. Then he said it wasn't your mom's fault because of a tumor, and now they're going back to live with her because . . . because they're all intensely crazy and if you understood this, you'd be as crazy as them."

"That about sums it up," I said.

"It's pure insanity."

It felt good to hear it from an outsider. "I don't know how long I can stay around this, Sophia. The money isn't worth my sanity."

"It's not worth any of our sanity, and if we have to walk away, we walk away. All of us. We have enough. We can sell Wentworth Manor. That gives us more than enough."

"It doesn't give Quinn enough to keep that horse."

"Then she'll sell it. Do you think your mother really has a tumor?"

"I doubt it. She probably paid someone for their cat scan." I hated how bitter that sounded.

Together, we walked out the open-air glass doors and watched Derek slam the trunk on my father's Land Rover.

"I don't think there's closure to be had in this situation," Sophia said.

"I can't believe Garrick was here. When could he have had time? He's been working on Katrina's case."

"Let's go home," Sophia said as she put her arm around me. "Garrick will want to know you're there safely."

"Life with my parents is like being thrown in a blender. Same ingredients, but if you get mixed in, it's too late."

"It's not too late. We'll stay away. All of us."

I nodded and let her lead me to the ridiculous sports car that screamed for attention. Sophia got into the driver's seat, and I made no attempt to change her mind. I felt warmed by her presence, grateful that she hadn't even bothered to question our father's strange movements to Napa and back to my mother's lair. I hadn't realized how much I needed someone who didn't question the chaos.

"You see," I said, "my parents . . . Mona . . . they don't want an end to any of this. As long as we're all playing the game, they win. The only way to win is to forfeit and walk away without closure."

"Not before we throw the board and all the pieces. We're done playing this game, Brinn. Our father has walked away from us for the last time. The Wentworth heiresses are your family now. And we are circling the wagons."

CHAPTER 18

*W*e had a silent drive back to the city. Sophia didn't prod me about our father and for that, I was grateful. If there was one thing Bradley Wentworth was consistent on, it was his inconsistency. Sophia pulled up in front of Garrick's security office in the financial district.

"What are we doing here?"

"Garrick asked me to drop you off here."

"Do you know why he was at our father's place?"

She shook her head. "He didn't tell me that, only that he needed the address."

"Why?"

"Brinn, I don't know. He's a private eye in security. I imagine knowing where people are is his specialty. But here's the thing, you can go in there right now and ask him. You don't need me to interfere. That's the thing about your family. You never talk directly. It's time to start speaking directly."

"I'm not ready to see Garrick. What if my father told him all the reasons I'm unworthy of his time?"

"You faced our father today, you can face Garrick. He wouldn't have had me bring you here if it wasn't important.

Brinn, I really think your family, minus Quinn, is incapable of love. If you want to have a real relationship, you need to let that wall down and risk getting hurt. Now get in there."

"Risk getting hurt? That's all relationships are."

"Not with us. Not anymore. Man up and go. I can't park in this red zone forever—even with this fancy car."

"He's probably going to fire me as a client," I said.

"Do you want me to wait?"

"No, I'll get home fine."

"Brinn?"

"Yeah," I answered.

"If you're waiting to be worthy of love . . . you already are," Sophia said.

"Okay." I was confused as I exited the car in the loading zone. I rode the elevator to Garrick's office. It was dark when I entered, and the door was locked. I pressed the doorbell at the edge of the bulletproof glass. Everyone in the desks that spotted the main cubicles was gone for the day and one lonely light lit up the office from his room.

Garrick's handsome face came up on the screen. "Brinn, are you all right?"

"Can I come in?"

"Of course." He buzzed me through, and I shut the glass door behind me. My heart was in my throat as I approached his office. Something about this man made my body react in such an extreme way. It defied rational explanation. I reminded myself that flirting came naturally to men who looked like Garrick. A few moments of weakness did not make a relationship. Still, I craved his presence. His calming nature gave me tranquility.

As I approached his door, I rapped lightly on the doorframe and his gaze met mine. My stomach churned with anxiety that I hadn't felt since I'd been on stage.

This is it, I told myself. *Don't blow it. Try to sound like a profes-*

sional and forget how he makes you feel. He's being paid for his time, so I have every right to be here. Every right to know why he's visiting my father.

"Hi," I said coolly.

His expression didn't change, nor did he look at me like I was female—at least not a female he found attractive. Whereas all I could think of when I saw that sturdy jaw of his was the kiss he planted on me unexpectedly at the ballet opening. The fleeting moments I spent in his arms, and then our chaste night together where I felt safe. Thank goodness he couldn't read my mind and know I'd planned our wedding and saw our future child in my overactive imagination.

The kiss was a necessary operation to protect his client, Katrina, and nothing more. The night in his arms nothing more than too long of a workday. Something told me if he could have written off that kiss on his taxes, he probably would have.

"Thanks for coming," he said while he swept his hand across his body. "Have a seat, please."

"Sophia and I were on our way back from Napa. We saw my father."

He raised a brow as if deciding how this information could possibly interest him.

"Did you need the house I rented again tonight?" I asked. "Katrina hasn't checked in yet."

"No, thank you for that. Jane saw to it that your credit card wasn't charged, and we canceled the house for tonight." He shoved a file in an overflowing cabinet. "She's safe."

"Thank you." I wanted to ask him why I was here, but he busied himself with more files and didn't appear to want to talk. "Is there something . . ." I drew in a deep breath as if ready to perform a speedy *petit allegro* rather than have a simple conversation with a man I found irresistible. "Is there a reason I'm here? I feel as if I'm intruding."

He leaned over his desk and finally looked me in the eye. "Yes."

"And that reason is?"

He stood and slammed the file cabinet shut. "In all my years in this business, I haven't felt this powerless before. I don't know that I can protect her from him without sending her running illegally."

"Katrina?" I asked. Though who else would he be talking about?

"We're playing chess in a sense, and Matt is always one step in front of me."

"It's always darkest before the dawn," I said, trying to sound hopeful.

"I can get Katrina out. That's not a problem." He hung his face low. "But I don't know how to get the kids out legally. Katrina won't leave him without them. These courts assume both parents want what's best for their kids. That's not the case with a man like Donley. He wants to win, no matter who pays. If he had to hurt the kids to hurt her, I have no doubt he'd do it."

As serious as this conversation was, my mind wandered to a place where Garrick Kane was this concerned about my safety. Not that I'd switch places with Katrina, but if one needed a hero, why shouldn't he look like rugged, five o'clock shadowed, sexy Garrick at the end of a long workday?

Garrick shrugged. "I don't know, I felt like you might have answers."

"Me?"

"You think outside the box, Brinn. You seem to be a step ahead of your father. Maybe even your mother, I don't know, but—"

"Why did you go see my father?"

He scratched at the back of his head. "You heard about that?"

"That's a two-hour drive," I said. "You must've had something you wanted to talk about pretty desperately."

"I needed to look him in the eye. I wanted to know how dangerous he was." He paced the length of his office, and his brow was darkened when he turned back toward me.

"What did you decide?"

"He's not dangerous," Garrick said, to my relief. "Misguided and egocentric, but not dangerous. Clueless where your mother is concerned, but safe."

"Why would you think my father was dangerous?"

"You told me he and your mom had a choreographed dance together. After meeting him, I'd say he's more trauma bonded to her than attached."

I'd need to process that comment later. It was too massive to grasp in the moment.

"For now, your father isn't dangerous. Unless your mother grips him again."

I felt a shiver run up my spine knowing my father was headed to the penthouse.

"I shouldn't have called Sophia to bring you here, but I had an idea, which now in light of you standing in front of me seems ludicrous."

"I won't look at you then," I said as I watched my hands in my lap. "Even Batman needs a Robin sometimes." My eyelids withered shut. *I just friend-zoned myself trying to be cute.*

"Donley has the law on his side. I knew that, of course, but I didn't know how long he'd been plotting this, how deep his schemes went to control Katrina. He knows all her weak spots. The children being her weakest link, naturally. She's so strong and yet he manages to find new ways to debilitate her. She's changed her mind about leaving."

"No, Garrick, she can't!" I thought about Katrina's trembling voice when she spoke of her husband. The way she paced that small room as if looking for an answer. "Tell me what I can do."

He moved to the extra chair beside me rather than his rolling office chair. When I met the steely green of his eyes in such close range, I completely forgot what we were discussing, how someone's life relied on him getting this right.

"First off, you should know I lied," he said flatly.

"Whatever you lied about, I'm sure you had a reason," I told him, and I believed it.

"When I kissed you that night at the ballet—"

I held my breath. "You do remember."

"Do you think I always go to soirees and kiss the most eligible bachelorette there?" He laughed.

"Most eligible?" I shook my head. "Have you met my sisters?"

"I could have whisked you away that evening and never looked back. I kissed you because I wanted to kiss you." He took my hands in his. "If you'd been a man, do you think I would've let Katrina be in danger?"

"Katrina again," I blurted. *Go back to the part where you wanted to kiss me.*

"Donley has been selling the narrative for years that Katrina has a drinking problem." He spoke through clenched teeth. "She doesn't have a drug problem, nor alcohol, but he's been building up that lie for nearly a decade so he could use it when he needed it."

My mind snapped back to Katrina, the sweet blonde mother with the perfect smile that hid a treasure trove of trauma. "Where is Katrina now?" I asked him.

"She's in jail," Garrick said matter-of-factly.

"She's . . . what?"

"She's been in jail since early this afternoon. Her kids are with *him*."

"No!" I gasped. "Can we get Sophia involved? Maybe she could—"

"Take it easy. The process is ugly, Brinn. Even if Sophia was still licensed, CPS won't get involved because the children's father is an upstanding member of society. He's considered the supposed victim to her instability and violence."

"Her what?"

"It's crazy, right? Even with all that's been done to Katrina, I've never seen her lash out or even get ticked off, if I'm honest."

That I understand. "You can't show anger in front of my mother either. I understand why Katrina stays so calm. The minute you raise your voice with my mother, she tells everyone how incorrigible you are and how sacrificial and cruel it's been raising ungrateful children. A thankless job, she calls it. Mother can turn me into a raging lunatic while she smirks and tells everyone, 'You see what I deal with? Life with a prima ballerina is not easy.'"

Garrick stared at me as if I'd said something forbidden.

"I'm sorry, now I really do sound like my mother, making this situation all about me. Tell me what's happened to Katrina and how I can help."

"Matt came home in the middle of the day today. Something tipped him off—I knew he had the place wired—and he thought she might be escaping today. When he got home she was in the kitchen making dinner, not packing."

"Did they fight?"

"He threatened her, and she reassured him that she wasn't going anywhere. It was all his imagination, she told him, which only made him angrier that she thought he could be so stupid."

"Is Katrina all right?"

"Physically, yes. She was cutting up vegetables for a roast and Matt grabbed the knife from her hand—"

I gasped.

"He grabbed the knife and he slowly sliced open his own forearm, right above where he could have done any real damage. The man, even in the throes of a controlling rage, is very systematic and scheming. Like I said, this sinister creep is always one step ahead of law enforcement."

"The cops believed him?"

"They had no choice. He was the one hurt. The kids were

crying, and Katrina tried to defend herself, but she was emotionally distraught about how upset the kids were. She tried to calm them down and get them out of the kitchen rather than help Matt, so they turned that against her."

I felt sick to my stomach.

"The cops took that as an admission of guilt and took her down to the station."

"This world is so full of injustice!" I hit my fist on the desk. "I can't hardly stand it some days." Standing, I paced the small office and turned back toward him. "You don't think he would hurt the kids, do you?"

Garrick shook his head. "I don't think so. It would harm his image. I'm clinging to that. She pleaded guilty in her statement to ensure the kids were safe."

"She didn't! Tell me what to do. Why are we just standing here?"

He smiled warmly. "Now you know why I do what I do. The injustice when someone is well-connected . . . it's staggering."

I knew that well enough.

"What if Katrina hadn't come to you before this, Garrick? She might have rotted in jail." I thought about my own situation. I couldn't help it. "When someone sees themselves as the main character in life, everyone else is simply a supporting player."

"The trouble comes when those supporting characters start veering off-script," Garrick said.

"You have to fix this," I told him. "I know you can fix this."

"I love that you have so much faith in me, but let's not forget, she's in jail right now and he's at home with the children. That puts us behind the eight ball, you might say."

My heart squeezed tightly at his resolve. "I do have complete faith in you." I sat at the edge of his desk and looked deeply into his eyes. "You'll get her out. You'll fix this."

"I knew I needed your support because I wish I had that kind of faith."

"I can see it in your eyes. You're not going to leave anyone behind. It's a righteous anger and this hateful man cannot prosper over that kind of goodness."

He scoffed, "You're so innocent, Brinn. This is why you need protection. The court system is no longer set up for justice. He who buys the best lawyer buys justice in California."

I took his hand and put it against my cheek. "We're going to change that, remember?" I said softly.

"He sliced his own arm and said she did it." Garrick stood and walked the short length of his office, the heels of his shoes clicking on the wood. His long legs forced him to pivot after two steps. "Any cop worth his salt should have looked at the trajectory of the wound, but she was hysterical when the police arrived, and they took her off in handcuffs." He repeated the facts in more detail, and he wasn't himself. "Maybe they did it to deescalate the situation and get her to safety, but I don't know how much I can take." He lifted his hand to the sky. "How much does God expect us to take down here?"

I know exactly how he feels.

"Garrick." I forced him to sit by pushing him gently to the seat. I came behind him and put my chin on his left shoulder. "Tell me your idea," I whispered. "We're wasting time."

He seemed calmer not looking at me, while I was close enough to graze against the scratchiness of his five o'clock shadow. "I want you to bail Katrina out of jail. Normally, my office would scurry her directly to a shelter, but that's too dangerous in this case. Donley will find out where she is before the night is through and that puts an entire house in jeopardy."

"Okay," I said calmly. "Bail Katrina out. What else?"

"I'll be with you in the car, but you have to go in the station by yourself."

"That's fine." I lifted my chin from his shoulder and flipped around to sit on the corner of his desk again.

"Donley knows she's getting ready to leave so he's on high

alert. His ego won't allow him to let her go peacefully. This is the most dangerous time. I need her to be in jail for the day so he doesn't suspect she has friends to get her out. We'll go after a late dinner when the coast is clear."

I nodded. I tried not to think of my own mother, but the parallels were overwhelming. If something didn't benefit her, revenge ensued. She couldn't let things go and then became obsessed. She complained about Grandfather not dying fast enough—how they had vacations and soirees planned, but they were home playing nursemaid. It all added up now. *Quinn was right.*

Chelsea Wentworth hated to be out of control and knowing how desperate Matt Donley was to gain authority over his wife, it no longer seemed like a stretch that my mother hastened Wyatt Wentworth into the next life. If I were honest, it was never about the money. My mother simply decided Wyatt Wentworth had lived long enough. These thoughts terrified me for Katrina.

Garrick's forehead creased in concern. "Is this too much for you? If this is too up close and personal, tell me now."

"No," I said honestly. "It's the first thing I've done that has meaning to me since I lost ballet."

He squeezed my hand. "I've got assistance at the station to take Katrina out of jail the back way. We'll hide the fact that bail has been posted until she's safely where she needs to be."

"Which is where?"

"I was thinking maybe Wentworth Manor?"

"I—uh—"

"That's okay, isn't it? Joel is there and there's enough drama with your own family that no one is going to be looking for Katrina in plain sight. There's camera surveillance and it's too crowded for Matt to make a move there."

"How does Katrina feel about that?"

"She's trusting me for now. I gave her a relay number to call, thank goodness she had it on her. We'll have our eyes on her ex to make sure he's not allowed to hurt the kids, and then I have to figure out something long-term. He is smart enough not to do anything illegal, and taking those kids is illegal."

"He sliced himself and blamed her," I reminded him. "That's illegal."

"He's smart enough not to get caught. I've had clients get emotionally tortured while their exes were in jail. Websites started to slander their name, accusing them of things like child pornography and abuse. Evil always finds a way. Matt probably has no less than ten people on the outside ready to do his dirty work for him."

My body was paralyzed by the reality of that statement. My mother's hold over my father gripped him in a way that could only be described as supernatural.

"The truth always comes out. Eventually. My job is to get my clients through the darkness safely, until the light finally shines."

"Garrick, I know this is a bad time, but Sophia was right about you. If this is the only case I ever work on for this foundation, you gave me back my hope in humanity."

"Then let this be the only case you do work on, or it will quickly die again. There's one more thing you should know." Garrick rubbed the back of his neck gruffly. "I feel like I'm at a high school dance with this one."

"Just ask," I told him. "I've already confessed I think my mother may be a murderer. What secrets could there be between us now?"

"Matt Donley thinks I'm having an affair with Katrina."

"Wait, what?"

"That's why I kissed you the other night." He dropped his head. "No, that was the excuse I used, but I kissed you the other night because I wanted to, and it felt like a solid excuse. Two birds with one stone, you might say."

"You could have just asked." I looked up at his eyes and

nibbled on my lip, but then I remembered the severity of the situation. "Then who did Donley think your date was?"

"Someone to build a cover for Katrina and me. Here's the thing," Garrick faced me and took my hands in his again, "I'm not the settling down kind. Donley knows that, but maybe if a certain eligible bachelorette, who is the talk of San Francisco because of the billions she's set to inherit . . . maybe if she starts to see me into a few public events, Donley's obsession will turn elsewhere until we can get the kids out and build a cyber case against him."

"You're asking me to pretend to be in a relationship with you?" I didn't know if I should be flattered or offended.

"Just until we get the kids out and can prove his systematic abuse."

"That could be a long time," I said.

"I know I'm not the socialite type, but—"

"What do you think the socialite type is, Garrick? Who would you set me up with?"

"I don't know. One of those pretty boys in the pastel golf shirts, I guess. He probably drives a Mercedes, lives in a penthouse condo with a view. . . ."

"You've literally just described my father. And gross. I left Wentworth Manor to get away from pretty boys. I want a man who isn't afraid to stand up against injustice." I looked him up and down in his wrinkled shirt with his tie askew and I thought how ruffled he appeared after a day of saving damsels in distress. *It is sexy.*

I wanted to ask him if we should practice a little, maybe get the kiss down to something more proprietary and less heated, but then I worried that might happen.

"So, a ruse. Like Joel had to do with Quinn."

"Garrick, why would a confirmed bachelor such as yourself date someone like me? Just so we can get our story straight."

He stepped backwards and for the first time, let his eyes

drink me in as a woman and not someone he felt sorry for because I wasn't even loved by my own parents. His careful mask fell in pieces around his feet.

"I think what you meant to ask is why would a woman like yourself date a man like me? That's what we need to make this believable. I suppose we can let the press run with the story that your family trauma has contributed to your bad choice in men," he chuckled.

If I'm going to make a bad decision, let him look and act like Garrick Kane.

His forehead wrinkled again. "Brinn, I run a security company for the rich and vapid. I know what I am. I make money on people's fears and misery. You've got a rich hedge fund manager in your future."

"God forbid," I argued. "I can manage my own hedge funds. You put your life on the line for women like Katrina. You're not making money on that, are you? Nor do you need to get involved in that kind of mess. You could leave her in jail tonight and no one would be the wiser. I see you for who you are, Garrick Kane."

He scoffed. "You really haven't Googled me yet." He shook his head. "The one time I want someone to Google my history so I don't have to repeat it, and you can't be bothered."

"I told you, Google has had me married off several times, called me an alleged murderess-for-hire and said I'd have never made prima ballerina without my surname, so why on earth would I trust them to tell me about you? Your kiss told me all I need to know."

"Brinn," he rubbed the back of his neck, "I'm no hero. I'm in this business because . . ." He paused for a moment. "Because the one woman I should've saved died on my watch."

CHAPTER 19

Garrick wouldn't look at me. "I shouldn't have said anything. We've got enough on our plates without going back in time and focusing on me."

"I want to know." I moved his chin so that he faced me. The pain in his eyes was palpable and I felt tortured inside by his expression. This was a man who understood pain on a personal level, not simply by watching his clients. I leaned into him, and his arms came around me. Time stood still while I let go and embraced him without fear. In return, he clung to me as though I really mattered.

"I'd rather you'd have Googled it," he said with a chuckle in my ear.

"I don't want to hear it from Google. I want the truth."

He pulled back and stroked my jaw with a gentle hand. "I'll tell you everything, but not here. We have hours to kill before we can get Katrina. Let's go to dinner."

"Somewhere fancy," I said. "Where we might be seen by the press."

He grinned. "Fair enough. Look at you wanting to be seen by the press."

"If we're going public, we may as well start now."

"You sound eager for this relationship to hit the presses."

"Do I?" I put my fingertips to my heart. "I can't imagine what you mean, good sir."

"You're a troublemaker, Brinn Wentworth, but I wouldn't have it any other way."

We gathered our belongings. Garrick locked up the office and we headed into the elevator down to the garage. We drove to a small restaurant near the country club. The wind whipped through us, and the brisk, salty sea air stung my nose as we made our way inside. The restaurant was on the Pacific Ocean side of San Francisco and boasted stunning views during the day, but in the evening, it was just a vast expanse of black beyond the window. It seemed appropriate for whatever painful secret Garrick held in his heart.

We were seated right away. The restaurant was practically empty with little chance to be recognized or photographed beside Garrick.

"You look disappointed," he said. "Do you want to go somewhere else?"

"It's usually so busy."

"It's a Tuesday."

I sighed.

I wasn't hungry. My stomach was tied in knots from the instability. I craved the routine monotony of dance. Garrick pretending to be my love interest was the one bright star in the dark sky of reality. He'd said outright he wasn't the marrying kind, as had I. But something about this faux romance felt like a warm cocoon of safety that belonged only to us. Once he told me about the woman he couldn't save, part of the veil that shielded me from reality would be torn, so I was in no hurry to get there.

Garrick ordered a bone-in ribeye steak and an ale. I asked for a salad with prawns and a Diet Coke. The waiter took the wine list away as if we'd failed some kind of test and once again, we were alone in the quiet corner of the restaurant.

"You seem sidetracked," he said.

I rubbed my hands together and blew on them as if I were freezing. "I'm nervous."

"That you don't think you can pull off the charade of dating me?"

Dating him, no. The charade of dating, absolutely. I've been living on my own in a beach town pretending to be a student. Showing up for a relationship? I'm not sure I'm capable.

"Garrick, I know you understand you're a sought-after bachelor in San Francisco. Don't patronize me."

"A sought-after bachelor and someone to go the distance are two different things. I can get a date." He leaned across the table and my breath caught under his gaze. "You make me want to be the kind of man who goes the distance."

He said everything I wanted to hear. *Is that part of a plot?* "What if neither one of us is the type to go the distance? I haven't exactly seen a fairy tale played out before me in my parents. That's why I always said I'd never get married. What's your excuse?" I asked playfully.

"My father shot my mother in front of me. I hid in a kitchen cabinet."

I choked on the short breath I inhaled. My hand flinched and the tall glass of water in front of me flew across the table and doused both the linens and Garrick. He stood abruptly and shook off the napkin on his lap. Two waiters rushed over to us and gave Garrick a towel, but he didn't need it. The table received most of the damage.

"Let me reseat you," the waiter said. We left the mess behind and followed him to a new table. I was shell-shocked. I knew I had to hear the rest of the story, but I wanted to escape. I didn't want to know more than I already did. *It really did happen.* If his father was capable, that meant my mother was too.

"I'm my father's son. That scares me. I ignored what happened and we all went about our business while my mother recovered, which made me just as guilty."

I tried to keep the shock and horror from my expression, but I was gutted. I thought he was going to tell me about some frat prank gone awry.

"You were a child! You had to be if you hid in a cabinet."

"I was eight, but I was old enough to tell the police the truth. Instead, I parroted what my dad told me to say. He was cleaning the gun. It went off. She got in the way."

We were two dented cans on the back of the restaurant shelves. No one wanted us, damaged and abused by the people who were supposed to love us. No one else could fix that damage and we both knew it deep down.

"I need a minute," I told him. "Excuse me." I scurried to the ladies' room and opened the long-shuttered door to a stall. I took my phone out of my handbag and called Sophia as I struggled to breathe.

"Brinn, you okay?" she answered.

"Sophia, you knew what Garrick's father did?"

"Of course."

"You didn't think it was necessary to tell me?"

"I figured if you wanted to know, you would have Googled him. You do tend to live in a fantasy world sometimes. I didn't want to hurt you. Garrick gave you hope we hadn't seen in you."

"I told him I'd pretend we're dating for a client. Sophia, I don't know if I can do it."

"Why on earth not?"

"The press will skewer us. They'll say we're both the children of murderers. It will ruin us to be associated with this. Like we think it's okay."

"His dad only shot his mother. She died later of complications. Probably from a very difficult life with that man," Sophia said, as if that wasn't splitting hairs.

"I need to get out of here. I'm going to call a car."

"Brinn, this is just an excuse for you to run. It's a trauma response. You're still letting the masses decide what you should do."

"We both have murder in our DNA." It was the first time I'd admitted it fully. I knew who my mother was and yet I still had this need to keep her secret.

"Garrick has spent his life trying to make up for his father's sin. He's never done anything but rescue people from their abusers. It's ludicrous to think either one of you are responsible for your parents."

"No, he's right. I was right to start with. We're not the marrying kind. I could be a traveling spinster, you know, take along a young female companion to take in the sights."

"Before you pack your steamer trunk and depart for the South of France, I suggest you go hear the whole story." Sophia clicked her tongue. "Touch up your makeup and listen to the man whose kiss made you forget any promise you ever made about remaining single your whole life. You owe him that much."

"I owe you all more. The Wentworths need to separate from this kind of scandal. This is an easy choice before my heart is too involved."

"Hear him out." Sophia hung up on me.

I did as she suggested and straightened my blouse, ran crimson lipstick over my lips and vowed to be strong as I heard Garrick's horrible tale before I made my excuses.

He rose as I came to the table. There were new water glasses, his ale and my Diet Coke alongside a warm plate of San Francisco sourdough.

"I'm sorry," I told him honestly as I fluffed the new napkin over my lap. "I needed to freshen up."

"It's shocking. I realize that. It was unfair to ask you to pretend to be my girlfriend without giving you this knowledge.

I'll find another way to protect Katrina, and I'll refer Mary to a new bodyguard service for you."

I nodded. "That may be for the best. I want to hear the whole story though. You owe me that much."

"I've never told this story to anyone except the police officers. I've been quoted from court records, but other than that . . ."

I grabbed the loaf of bread and ripped off a piece to avoid his gaze.

"I was eight."

I took in a slow breath while I buttered my bread.

"My parents were fighting. They were always fighting. If he said it was black, she said it was white, if he said the grass was green, she'd find some way to tell him he was wrong."

"My parents never fought," I said, trying to separate our situations. "They were painfully pleasant to one another, but then they'd do something to humiliate the other one without ever getting any dirt on them."

"This time was different," he said. "I felt it. The air was off, if you can imagine."

I know exactly what he means, and I hate that.

"There was that look in my father's eye. I can't fully describe it, but I knew it well and nothing good ever came of it. His eyes went black, as if his soul had left him, and my mother stiffened and shut up. She started to beg. Say that she was sorry."

My heart beat rapidly. I nodded because I understood this completely. The dark shadow over the eyes, the person you knew as your parent suddenly gone from what felt like an empty shell of skin.

"He yelled in that way where he believed no one was allowed to question his authority. I prayed to God my mother wouldn't say anything, and she'd been quiet for the longest time during the tension. But then she came back into herself and told him she was done. Done making his dinner, done listening to his threats, done. I think she thought if she showed weakness, he'd hurt her."

The threats. I shook with how much I understood Garrick. *It isn't the same.*

"Dad told her to shut up. He reminded her she couldn't leave. She'd made a vow in front of God."

I ventured a glance at Garrick, and he stared at the candle, transfixed by the flickering light.

"I felt a crippling fear. Usually I'd get in between them or at least run, but I couldn't. As their voices escalated, I bolted from the room and hid in the china cabinet. I'll never understand why I didn't run to the neighbor's house. Instead, I counted. When the gunshots rang out, I counted faster."

I inhaled sharply, still wanting desperately to believe Garrick's situation was so far from my own, but I couldn't deny the similarities. As much as I wanted to. I reached for him and squeezed his hand. "I'm so sorry." I approached the next question carefully. "She didn't die then?" I asked, wondering if Sophia's account was accurate.

"No. The ambulance and police came. My dad pulled me out of that cabinet with one yank and told me he'd been cleaning his gun and Mom got in the way. Did I understand?"

I was suddenly thankful my mother had such a huge audience. This might have been our lives if she hadn't.

"Mom came back to us a few weeks later with a scar on both cheeks where the bullet entered and exited through her jaw." He made a hand motion to show me the trajectory.

His large hand was in front of me, but I was too afraid to take it. Too afraid to offer him more comfort for fear his touch would move me again.

"She was never the same after that. Her fight was gone. Her spirit was like that of a wounded animal. She cared for me. She made dinner and made sure I was clothed, but the mother I knew was gone. She died less than two years later. They said it was an infection from a bullet fragment, but you'll never convince me it wasn't the betrayal. I betrayed her. She could deal with my father's betrayal, but mine? It was too dangerous to be her son. I chose to be my father's."

"You're not broken, Garrick. You have a history, a past that isn't even your fault, but your mother wouldn't want you to live like this."

He scoffed. "Then why don't you want to get married, Brinn?"

"You've seen my parents. They're reason enough for anyone who had a front row seat to stay single."

Garrick chuckled, and in the midst of the heaviness that hung in the air, the laughter sounded like the flutter of an angel's wings. "My parents stayed together after this. Like nothing happened. When my mom died, I was ten and sent to live with my paternal grandmother. I thought I was being primed to be just like him."

"It's not possible." But I felt the same way. Relationships were a landmine. Better to think you're innocent of being like your parents than to test the theory. "We should get to the jail."

"Not yet. We need the station completely empty."

I couldn't wait to escape and searched the restaurant anxiously. I didn't want to be seen in Garrick's presence. It could only add fuel to the press's fire.

"I think we should go," I said. I didn't want to play this game any longer. It felt dangerous. *Garrick feels dangerous.*

"Brinn, if you're not comfortable—"

The waiter came and removed our plates and I searched for something to say. Rather than tell Garrick I didn't feel up to pretending, I lied.

"It's fine. I'll be fine."

"Brinn—"

I weakened. I loved when he said my name. It was as if his voice gave me a warm caress. I needed to avoid direct eye contact. *And to forget about that kiss.* So he was a good kisser? Maybe he wasn't. Maybe it was simply my lack of experience and my sick desire to be special.

Together, we were committed to Katrina Donley's rescue from her monstrous husband—and if pretending to have a relationship with Garrick Kane was the price? Well, I'd have to find a way to spin it. And to shut down any real feelings I had developed for him.

CHAPTER 20

arrick and I arrived at the police station at 12:03 a.m. He said it would be the perfect timing. The evening's DUIs wouldn't be processed yet and the day's arrests would mostly be cleared out. But Garrick was wrong.

"What do you mean she's gone?" I asked the supervising officer behind the glass.

"Gone. Bailed out."

"By whom? You didn't send her home with her abuser. Tell me you didn't send her home with that monster!"

The officer licked his top lip, which forced me to focus on his mustache and the crumbs it harbored. "She posted bail. We sent her home. That's how it works."

"Katrina Donley," I said her name again. "She was falsely arrested today for domestic violence. Who posted her bail?"

As I gave the officer the further details, it was public record —which meant she hadn't used a bail bondsman.

The officer lifted a file and opened it. "Matt Donley. Picked up by Matt Donley tonight at 9:37 p.m."

Nearly three hours ago. The air rushed from me. "Thank you,"

I said as I pushed through the glass door and ran toward Garrick's idling vehicle.

I threw open the door and hopped into his Jeep. "Go! Matt bailed her out. He probably took her home." I felt sick how we'd lingered over dessert, how we'd shared our harrowing pasts not realizing. . . . We were sitting idly while someone else was in danger.

Garrick stepped on the gas and weaved in and out of traffic in the city as we flew across town to Katrina's home, which was behind an iron gate.

"Now what?"

"That friend of yours—"

"Casey," I said. "He's her next-door neighbor."

"Right. Go press the button and see if he'll let you in the house. That might give us some kind of vantage point."

I stepped out of the car and pressed the button to Casey's house. *Please answer, please answer . . .*

"Hello?"

"Casey, is that you? It's me, Brinn Wentworth."

"I see that," he said from the speaker.

"Please let Garrick and me in, it's a matter of life and death."

He buzzed the neighborhood gate without another word, and it opened slowly. I climbed into the Jeep again and showed Garrick which house was Casey's. We drove slowly past an enormous house.

"That's where Katrina lives. The lights are on," Garrick said.

"Everything looks normal," I answered hopefully.

We parked in Casey's driveway and exited the car quietly. We scrambled up the steps to Casey's home and pressed the doorbell frantically. He opened the door before I could knock too.

Casey wore a silk robe like he was an aging porn star and looked at me as if I had two heads. "Brinn, what's going on?"

"We think Katrina might be in trouble."

"Did you hear anything tonight?" Garrick asked.

"Nothing unusual." Casey shrugged and opened the door wider. "Though I have to admit, when a blonde bombshell knocks on my door in the middle of the night, this is not what I had in mind."

Garrick silently shut the door behind him. "Have you heard *anything* from next door tonight?"

"Not a thing." Casey looked out the glass front of his double doors into the darkness. "Is everything okay?"

"Garrick Kane." Garrick reached out his hand to Casey. "Private security."

"Does this have something to do with that note Katrina gave me to give to you?" Casey asked me.

I nodded. "Yes, you can't let Matt know we were here."

"Matt Donley? I don't talk to that guy. He's an ambulance chasing, womanizing loser," Casey said. "Every time he speaks to me, he tries to get me to sponsor him at the club. Otherwise, he doesn't say boo to me. As it is, I don't know how long I'll be able to pay the membership myself."

Casey's house didn't exactly scream poverty. It was stately from the outside and offered a wide open floor plan with tastefully decorated furnishings. Everything was placed around the room's focal point, a large, elaborate white French fireplace, the opening of which was taller than Garrick.

"Have you ever heard them fighting?" I asked Casey. "We think he's been abusing Katrina. And the boys."

"Brinn," Garrick chastised. "Discretion, please."

"Garrick," I said plainly, "we're at Casey's house in the middle of the night trying to spy on his neighbor. I think he has a right to know why we're here. You won't say anything, will you Casey?"

"Never," Casey said.

Garrick stood in front of the bank of glass doors at the rear of the main room. "Is there access to their yard from here?"

"You can climb the fence out back. The back of their house is all sliding glass, so I imagine if the lights are on, you'd be able to see what was happening. Does that help?"

"Immensely," Garrick said. "Brinn, stay here."

Casey opened the back door onto the terrace to his backyard and we watched Garrick disappear into the darkness.

"Is it as serious as all that?" Casey asked me. "This is a completely different side of you, Brinn. I'm impressed."

"I believe it is serious."

"Should I call the police?" Casey asked.

"I'd rather you didn't. Listen, Casey, while I'm here, I feel like I owe you an apology."

"Me?"

"Yeah. I didn't realize that you and your father had lost most of your money with your mother's illness. I'm afraid I judged you as a bit of a spendthrift."

Casey laughed. "Oh, I do spend a lot of money, Brinn. You're not wrong there. It's a strange thing to have money and treat everyone to drinks, vacations, a round of golf or two. Then to not have that ability? It changes who you are. Very humbling."

"Sort of like having a stellar reputation and then, not," I said.

"It shows you who your friends are, which is eye-opening and slightly soul-crushing."

"But now we know who the authentic friends are."

"Listen to you with your silver lining," Casey laughed.

"I pride myself on money not mattering to me," I told him. "But you made me see that's a lie. I'd hate not being able to help people and you've always been so generous. Anyway, I'm sorry I wasn't more understanding."

"It's harder on my dad," Casey said. "First he lost my mother, then his prestige. Starting over at his age hasn't been easy." Casey looked down at his getup. "Listen, make yourself at home, I'm going to get some clothes on."

I heard him moving around in his room, so I called after him while I played with the photos on the mantle. "No one handles change easily, Casey. I snubbed my grandfather's money and all the rules of his will, but in the end, it's comfortable to have money. I gave in. I said it was for my sisters, but that's a lie. It's what I know, so I'm dancing to Grandfather's decrees like a puppet on a string." I took Casey's hand as he came back into the living room. "You won't get any judgment from me."

He wore a pair of ironed dark-washed jeans and a Calloway collared shirt. "Come sit down." He sat on the overly plump white sofa—clearly a remnant of his mother's house—and stared at the fireplace. "I shouldn't have spent a minute feeling sorry for myself. I should have gotten busy."

"This place is beautiful. I've only been to this new place once, do you remember?"

He nodded. "After the Steeple Chase race with your sister. My mother loved this house."

I patted Casey's hand and squeezed again. "She was an incredible woman. I wanted to be like her when I was little."

"Me too," Casey said. "My mom would have never let my dad spend that money on her health had she known what it would cost. That's the kind of woman she was. She would have rather given her life than let us live in this way." He shrugged. "We have enough," he said plainly. "If we have to move, it is what it is."

"Your mother always thought of others like that. I can't imagine." And I couldn't.

Casey's mother was exactly who she portrayed for the press. *Caring. Loving. Generous to a fault.* Just like Katrina Donley seemed to be. *The world simply Isn't fair.* I stood up and paced in front of the fireplace nervously.

"Your friend will be fine," Casey said. "He looks like he could take on a row of assailants by himself."

I smiled.

"You like him."

I nodded. "He's married to his work. And I'm not marriage

material, so we're perfect for each other. We can appreciate each other from afar."

Casey looked at his watch. "If you say so, but I also noticed the way he looked at you. He wouldn't let you follow him."

"He's in security. He's paid to keep me safe."

"Sure," Casey said.

"Doesn't your father live here with you?"

"He does," Casey said. "He's out with the twins' mother. Mary, is it?"

"At this hour?"

"They're usually in by ten, so I imagine Dad fell asleep on Mary's sofa again. It's been hard for him dating a woman who still lives with her deeply Catholic parents. It's like he's sixteen again." Casey chuckled.

At that moment, the back door opened quickly and two boys in pajamas were pushed inside, the blue whales on their pj's in stark contrast to the all-white room. The boys' deep blue eyes were wide with fear as they stared at us while blinking rapidly.

Before we could respond, Katrina, dressed in a pair of black leggings and an oversized Stanford sweatshirt, bounded in behind them, her body trembling. She scanned the room quickly and pressed her boys closer to the fireplace.

To my relief, Garrick came in behind the small family and shut and locked the glass doors. "Turn off the lights," he said to Casey. Casey pressed a button on a remote control and all of the lights dimmed except for the small red light on a fire alarm and an electric candle on the mantle.

"Now what?" Katrina asked Garrick.

Garrick flicked on a flashlight. "We're going to Wentworth Manor tonight. We'll figure out our next step tomorrow." He gathered the small family together. "Casey, do you have a garage?"

"Yeah, it's on the alley in the back of the house."

"Can we get to it from the house?"

"Sure," he said. "Right through the hallway and down the stairs. I'll get another flashlight."

"No," Garrick said. "Meet me in the garage. All of you. Don't open the garage door until I text Brinn."

"Mommy, I want to go home," a young voice said.

"I know, sweetheart."

Under the dark of night, we made our way down several steps into the musty garage that showed the true age of the home and waited for Garrick's message. My heart pounded but I kept my voice calm for Katrina's sake. "Everything will be fine. Garrick knows what he's doing and soon we will be at Wentworth Manor. We have lots of security."

"Mommy, I want to go home," the small voice said again into the darkness.

"We will go home as soon as we can, honey."

"When Daddy isn't so mad?"

"Right. We'll let him calm down and we'll all get a good night's sleep. We're going to a really big house tonight. It's like a hotel!" Katrina's voice was upbeat and animated like they were going on the Dumbo ride at Disneyland.

"Does it have a pool like that hotel we went to in Tahoe?"

"It does," Katrina answered. "At least I think it does."

"It does have a pool," I answered. "A giant pool with waterfalls and a big blow-up swan you can float on like a boat. You can even go behind the waterfall or right through it if you'd like."

There was no answer. A small sob pierced the silence.

My phone chirped. "All right, Casey. Open the door."

Slowly—loudly—the garage door raised, and Garrick's car was under the streetlight. His headlights were turned off. He rushed out of the car and ushered us all into the vehicle. "Katrina, give me your phone."

She handed it to him without question.

"Do you have a Fitbit or a smart watch on?"

"Yes."

"Give it to me."

Katrina did as she was told, and Garrick handed the phone and watch to Casey. "I owe you, man. Will you turn them off and throw these over the fence into her backyard? Preferably in the pool if you can hit it."

"Sure thing." Casey gathered up the electronics, waved at us and then shut the noisy garage door.

Katrina huddled down in the car over her boys, and I felt like retching. To know someone has taken abuse was one thing. To witness a woman covering her children to protect them from their own father—that was another circumstance entirely.

The evil done in the false name of love broke me. The contrast between Casey's love for his mother and Katrina's fear of her husband took me to a dark place.

CHAPTER 21

*T*he car ride was eerily quiet. Garrick drove slowly because the younger boy didn't have a booster seat and the elder was tiny for his age. I put my address into his phone and led him to the manor's underground garage, where he parked beside the BMW. He turned to me as he stopped the car.

"It's okay to eat the food in the house. I have someone on duty in the kitchen at all times, so one less worry."

"Thank you, Garrick. You've been busy," I said breathlessly. Even with all the cameras in the house and security detail, I worried that I couldn't protect Katrina and the boys without Garrick present. The responsibility of the small family weighed heavily on me.

Garrick seemed to sense my fear and while Katrina unlatched the boys from their seatbelts, he stood in front of me. He sensed my trepidation toward him and stepped back.

"This is not your responsibility," he assured me. "I have the place covered. They're working with your security detail, and I'll have Katrina and the kids out of the house by morning. It's just a few hours."

"I won't sleep," I said.

"I've got eyes on Matt Donley, and he won't leave the house without being followed."

I nodded as I nibbled on my lower lip. "Why can't people just do the right thing, Garrick?"

"I ask myself that every day." He helped Katrina with the boys by ushering them into the house.

I led them across the torn-up marble floors toward the mahogany staircase. "Watch your step." I led them to my parents' old bedroom where they could all stay together. "This bed is a double king, so I think you'll all feel safer together here tonight. Can I get you anything?"

"Do you happen to have a pair of sweats or something I could sleep in? These are the only clothes I have," Katrina said.

"Of course." Though as I looked at her tiny frame, I realized that anything I had she'd swim in like a gunnysack. "Let me go gather some things and I'll be right back. I can leave them by the door if you don't want to be disturbed."

Katrina grasped my wrist desperately. "No, come back. Please."

"I'll be right back." I excused myself and passed Garrick in the wide hallway. I grabbed him by the hand and led him down to my bedroom where I could get the real story of what happened. I opened the door, suddenly embarrassed by my opulent mirrored pink room with a layered tulle tutu hanging from my ceiling—as if I were some kind of thirteen-year-old princess.

He cocked a brow.

"Don't say it," I snapped. "I was living in Southern California, remember? This room was designed a long time ago when ballet was my life."

He put up his palms. "Far be it from me to comment on interior design, but I do have one question."

"What's that?" I asked him.

"Can I see your My Little Pony collection before I leave?"

"You!" I slapped him playfully and he enveloped me in a hug before we both remembered ourselves. The heat that his body radiated proved he wasn't as calm as he appeared.

"Why does this case scare you?" I whispered in his ear before kissing it softly. He groaned and pulled away. All of my fears about Garrick and his history were moot next to my desire to be in his arms.

He sat on the side of my bed and pulled me onto his lap. I felt so at home in his arms and the intensity of our situation rendered us both in a weakened state. I wanted nothing more than to curl up beside him and sleep soundly in his arms. To wake up to his warm kisses and be reminded that I wasn't immune to temptation. I was still human and weak, and other people weren't repulsed by me as my mother was. When Garrick was around, I felt as if nothing could harm me, and that was a very dangerous thought. The press would have a field day with us, but for now, we were alone.

"Donley has the courts on his side, and he's obsessed with Katrina." He drew in a deep breath. "Obsessed people are different."

"Different how?"

"Obsessed people are so dangerous because their obsession rules their logical side, and they don't usually have a record until they act on their obsession, so there's very little that can be done to protect their victims in advance of violence. You can't arrest someone for a crime they might commit."

"He's made it look like she committed the crime," I said despondently.

"All they see is the goal of what they want. It doesn't matter who is standing in the way. What matters is that they reach that goal. Most of the time, that just plays out in a relationship that's full of drama, but sometimes it can get pathological."

"And you think that's the case here?"

"Donley is destructive and dangerous. I'd stake my reputation on it."

"I need to get back to Katrina," I said. "I promised her some clothes to sleep in."

"Donley is probably the most dangerous mastermind I've dealt with in ages. He reminds me of my father."

I let out a long, labored breath as I rifled through my dresser and looked for something for Katrina to wear. "She's why you want to change the court system."

"Donley won't rest until he takes those kids from her—and if the courts won't give him the power, he might take it himself. Something inside him needs to destroy her to be at peace. Or so he thinks."

"What if you're wrong?"

"Obsessed people are just that. *Obsessed*. Matt Donley won't even be on the police radar until it's too late."

I shuddered. My mind raced at what I could do to help. I couldn't let Matt Donley win this. Something in me had to make it right before Katrina ended up like my grandfather. "If we have to break the rules, we have to break the rules," I told him.

"Don't go all Wild West on me, Brinn. I can tell you that domestics is a security detail no one wants."

"I'm not going to let him win and neither are you. If I have to send Katrina and the boys away, that's exactly what I'm going to do. I can't think of a better use of my money than to take an abuser down."

"And if she gets caught for kidnapping her children, he could end up with the kids and she could be in jail."

"Then we'd have to make sure they never get found," I said.

Garrick smiled and cupped my face in his large, gentle hands. "Everything about you gives me hope, Brinn. You are, in a word, magnificent."

"And you, Garrick Kane, are not broken," I told him. "Not any more broken than I am anyway."

His eyes slid shut and he kissed me softly. All pretense of acting romantic for the press gave way to genuine passion, and the intensity of it made me want to run again. I couldn't control this, and it scared the life out of me. I wasn't going to be another notch on Garrick's seduction belt while he avoided the discomfort of commitment and I lived under the pretense I was capable of a successful relationship.

"There's a guest room upstairs on the third floor. Go upstairs, turn left, second door on the right. You should find everything you need there."

"We're not going to talk about this?"

"It's just practice for the press, right?" *How cunning I'm acting.*

He said nothing and I exited my room as if it were on fire. I ran down the hallway to my parents' old bedroom and knocked quietly on the door in case Katrina had dozed off. But she answered immediately. "The boys are asleep. They'll never get over what they witnessed today."

"They're safe now. Get some rest." I said, watching them both in the bed with their steady, tranquil breaths. "Why don't you take a bath? There's an antique clawfoot in the ensuite. The bubble bath is in the cabinet. It's my favorite from Italy."

Katrina smiled.

"I'm sorry we didn't get you earlier from the police station. I feel so terribly guilty. Tonight might have been avoided."

Katrina shook her head. "Matt's a smart man. Cunning, you'd say. He'll get his way eventually; I just need to make sure my boys don't forget me before he turns them against me."

"Don't say that! You can't give up now."

"I'm not giving up, Brinn, I'm being realistic."

I handed Katrina a set of yoga gear from when I was actively dancing. "These should fit you and you're welcome to them. My ballet figure has left the building."

Her face scrunched up. "Brinn, you do know you're tinier than me, right?"

I looked down at my body and to hers. "Um, I don't think so."

Katrina shook her head. "If you doubt me, just watch Garrick. He can't take his eyes off of you."

I loved how comfortable Katrina felt around me because I felt the same way about her. "Enough about me, will you keep the boys out of school tomorrow?"

"I think it's necessary. Until we formulate a plan. I hope this has scared Matt enough so he'll behave himself when we go home."

She may as well have slapped me. "Katrina, you can't do that. You got lucky this time."

"If I leave him, he'll get custody. If by some strange miracle he didn't, he'd make sure I never had them. *One way or another.*"

It was hard to decipher a man who didn't put his own children ahead of his hatred, but I'd seen it to a lesser degree in my own mother. All I knew was Katrina's acquiescing to the situation created a desperation in me. "My grandmother lives in Italy, Katrina. She had a terrible flight here, so I know she'll be taking a private jet back home. You and the boys can go with her on the plane. It would be our secret. Garrick doesn't even have to know."

Katrina laughed. "I appreciate your help more than I can say, but I'm not running. I'm going home for my boys. If I leave, he'll see that as a direct attack. The boys are safer this way." Katrina wasn't afraid and I understood her decision. *One just gets weary of fighting.*

"What did the police say when you were brought in tonight?"

"The police," she scoffed. "They treated me like a delusional, insane, hysterical criminal who wouldn't cooperate."

"And when Matt came to bail you out?"

"I begged the police not to let me go home. I confessed to

everything so I could spend the night in jail until Garrick could come and get me. I knew the kids were safe with me being in jail so I might have gotten a full night's sleep. But Matt Donley, ever ready, plied them with his version. He told them I was high-strung and made a drinking motion while he winked. Then he laughed and said he had no choice but to take me home. No one else wanted me. They had a good laugh over that."

My hands curled into fists. "Matt is going to have to learn what it's like to lose because we are going to win this war." If I accomplished nothing else in this world, defeating this one monster was *my* new obsession.

CHAPTER 22

I awoke to find my mother's trial date had finally been set. My phone had blown up during the night with texts, news links and naturally, my mother and father in search of their emotional support. I tried to stay calm at the implications while I rushed to get ready.

I exited my room and once in the hallway, a large man stood outside my door. I jumped back as he nearly gave me a heart attack. "Dude!" It was the first thing out of my mouth. Yes, it made me sound like a '90s teen, but it was my first reaction.

"I'm Denver Keaton, assigned to you by Garrick Kane & Associates."

"Denver, dude, you gotta warn a girl. It's like opening my door and running smack-dab into Half Dome. How tall are you?"

"Six-foot-six, miss."

"You should really be guarding the door down there. That's Mrs. Donley and her boys."

"They're already down at breakfast with their guards," he said. "Mr. Kane had them covered."

"Of course he did. Where is Mr. Kane?"

"I'm unable to provide that information."

"I'm going to see my mother this morning. I take it you'll be accompanying me?"

He gave one nod. "Everywhere until I get word, miss. Though it is not advised that you have contact with your mother at this point in time."

"Mr. Denver Keaton, it's never advised for anyone to have contact with my mother, but that doesn't change the fact that I'm going to see her this morning."

"Very well, Miss Wentworth."

"All right, well, it's going to be a busy press day. Are you familiar with keeping the paparazzi at bay?"

"I generally work in Hollywood," he said with all the inflection of a boulder. He took out a piece of paper from his jacket. "Again, I don't see your mother as an approved destination."

I clenched my teeth. "I'm going to see my mother. You can come along if you must."

"You won't eat or drink anything inside?"

"If you knew how my mother cooked, you wouldn't even be asking that question."

"Noted, miss."

"My name is Brinn. Please call me Brinn."

"Yes, miss."

I sighed and we went down to the dining room where Mrs. Chen had laid out the normal morning spread. There were eggs and bacon, pancakes and today, waffles in the shape of Mickey Mouse for the children. All of my sisters except for Sophia were around the table with Katrina and her boys.

"Katrina, I see you've met my sisters."

"I have, and everyone has been so wonderful. I do hope to be out of everyone's hair this morning."

"Nonsense," Quinn said. "There's no sense in you leaving anytime soon. You're safe here and the boys can play in the ballroom. It isn't being renovated. I'll see if we can rustle up some bikes or scooters."

The younger son stood by his mother's chair. "When can we go home?"

"Soon," Katrina said.

"I'll be out for a bit," I told Katrina. "If you need anything, tell one of my sisters or Mrs. Chen." I turned to Quinn. "I'm going to see Mother. Any messages?"

"Brinn, what are you thinking?" Quinn snapped. "First you're out all hours of the night . . ." She pulled me out of the room and shut the pocket doors behind us. Denver Keaton was still trapped on the other side. I could only hope he warded off danger better than he did my sister. "Why?"

"I don't know. I need to see her. I found out about Garrick's parents yesterday and I just need to go."

"You want to believe her and she's going to convince you. That's what Chelsea does. You can still honor our parents with that strict moral code you're running but do it from afar." Quinn shook her head in exasperation. "Didn't going up to Napa teach you anything? It's not you, Brinn. It's them. Dad is stuck in her web. I'm afraid if you go over there, I'll lose my entire family."

"Grandmother is so cruel to her own daughter. Her loyalties lie with our dad. Doesn't that make you wonder if Mother could receive love, things could be different? No one deserves to be abandoned in their time of need."

"You can't fix her. It's too late. I love Mom and Dad but being around them makes me question reality. I can't take worrying if I'm going to say the wrong thing. It has killed my sense of safety. I can't let Grandfather's death go unnoticed and telling the truth should never be wrong."

I knew she was right. But I felt compelled to go. "I'm strong enough. I need to see her before the trial."

"Brinn, how many times are you going to let her set you up?"

Quinn changed her tactics. "You can call her and give her your support from here."

"I want her to know the world isn't against her."

"And what if it is? What if she deserves for it to be?"

"No matter what she's done, everyone deserves a second chance."

"Do they deserve a thousandth chance? Isn't that why Katrina wants to go home? Do you believe she can save that man?"

Sophia flew down the stairs and landed on the paper covering the floor. "Shhh, you two. There are workers everywhere even if you can't see them."

"I'm done talking about this. I need to do this. Is the press out front?"

"What do you think?" Quinn asked. "I haven't seen my horse since the day before yesterday. They're like gnats out there."

"Any special instructions about Katrina before Garrick gets back?" Sophia asked.

I felt the weight of that responsibility crush down on me. "He said to keep her here. Just let the guards do their job. She shouldn't be any trouble."

"They need clothes," Quinn said.

"I'll take care of it," I said.

"I'll take care of it," Sophia offered in her social work way. "Just go see your mother and get it over with." She approached me and looked me straight in the eye. "You're not her, Brinn, and you never will be. No more than Garrick is his father."

* * *

MY SISTERS' disapproval only propelled me further into my convictions. I wouldn't have been a ballerina if it weren't for my mother. I owed her the respect regardless of other people's opinions. I exited the mansion through the service gate with Denver and drove the short distance up Nob Hill.

I pulled up to the curb. "I'm going to go up to my mother's penthouse alone," I told him.

He shook his head. "No, ma'am. Garrick said not to leave your side and I have no plans to do so. You'll cost me my job."

"My mother will treat you like a dog," I said. "Not the cute, fluffy kind that women carry in their purses either. The kind that terrorizes the streets of third-world countries looking for scraps."

"It doesn't make any difference to me," he said. "When I worked in Hollywood, forget the dog, they treated me like something the dog left behind."

"Funny," I said, but the truth was, I didn't want anyone being in the room when I talked to my mother. "Denver, my mom's not going to talk in front of you and I need to hear what she has to say. I didn't press her hard enough for the truth last time. This time I need to."

He sighed. "I'll wait in the hallway outside. But you need me, you scream, and I'll bust in. Please don't eat or drink anything, you got it?"

"Fair enough."

As we got off the elevator, Denver looked like he was questioning everything he'd just agreed to and unlike Garrick, I did not find Denver's hovering cute.

"I'm on the fortieth floor. I can't go anywhere," I reassured him.

"Make sure the door is left unlocked."

"She's my mother."

He pursed his lips. "I think you know that explanation doesn't hold a lot of water with me."

I knocked and stared back at him. "Move over there where she can't see you."

He did as he was told. I waited and felt the heavy glare of my mother through the peephole. "Who is that?"

"My security guard," I said plainly.

"That's right. I guess you have our money now. It must be nice to afford such luxuries."

I ignored her comment and walked in past her as she opened the door. "Your court date is set."

"How does this concern you?"

"Mom, I want the truth. Did you do this to grandfather or not? Because I've gone on record supporting you, but the reality is, I don't know the truth. When I hear my father has blue lips and he's been here, I'm going to question things, you know? That's a lot of people with supposed poisoning near you."

"I have a tumor. Have you heard?"

"Where are Father and Grandmother?"

She ignored me. "Essentially, you're not only accusing me of murdering your grandfather, but now you think I've done something to your victimhood father. *Please.* That man is such a drama queen. He would be willing to die if it got him attention."

She isn't wrong.

"Stop changing the subject. No more circular conversations. Tell me what happened to Grandfather."

"He died. He was one hundred years old, and he died. That's what happens to old people, Brinn. It's what will happen to me and eventually you someday. People die. I could die from this tumor I have."

"Are you sorry he died?"

She glared at me, and it dawned on me how even in the penthouse alone—with no audience anywhere—my mother was ready for a photo shoot. How I'd wanted to be glamorous like her and float into a room like an angel who didn't touch the floor. The older I got, the more I realized that grounded people—people who were the same regardless of who was watching—encapsulated what I truly desired. They knew who they were, and they didn't need others to validate them. Mary Campelli knew who she was whether alone or with Casey's handsome father.

"I'm not going to lie to you, Brinn. Your grandfather was a menace to me. Always commenting on my looks and making me feel uncomfortable. He put his wife in the grave early and probably drove her to have an affair because she may as well have been a piece of furniture to him. I didn't like the man."

"Did you give him an extra vial of morphine?"

"Nothing I say is going to make a bit of difference to you. All I've sacrificed for you two to have this life and what do you do? You leave me here to rot alone in this penthouse. To face judge and jury without the support of my own family. What did I ever do to make you hate me so?"

"Tell me you didn't do it!" I demanded. As my voice rose, Denver stuck his head in the door.

"Everything okay in here?"

"It's fine," I told him. "I'll be out shortly." Then I turned back to my mother. "Why isn't Mona here? Where's your mother?"

"You tell me! She always did have a sick relationship with Bradley. Always flirting with your father like she was his wife and not me."

I stood quietly. I couldn't defend my father. He was a different sort of person. The kind no one could really get close to.

"Do you really think anyone would care that Wyatt Wentworth was dead if it weren't for his money?"

"I cared."

"He spoiled you rotten. He knew you'd gotten the Wentworth genes and he felt sorry for you. He knew you'd have to use your brain and not get by on your looks like Quinn. It's probably why he left you the money in the hopes you'd run the business. Your father never did have much of a mind for it."

My eyes pooled with tears, but I didn't let her break me. "He left us the money because he wanted to make sure you never got a dime of it!" As soon as I said this awful thing, my body filled with shame. Had all my deep-seeded hatred sowed the tumor my mother now fought? Had the ugliness I tried so hard to hide manifested in her as resentment for Grandfather?

She lifted her hand to slap me, but I stopped her wrist midair.

"You'll never be like me, Brinn. No matter how much money you have. You and your sister weren't even invited to fashion week."

I felt my bottom lip trembling. "You really don't get it, Mother. I never wanted to be you," I lied. Then I sought to destroy her with words the way she'd done my whole life. "I wanted to be Mary Campelli."

I heard her scream, but I hightailed it out the front door. "Push the elevator button!" I called out to Denver.

Mother came after me and her ankle bracelet started to beep like a screeching fire alarm. In the hallway, she was stopped by Garrick, who had somehow taken Denver's place. He looked down on my tiny mother with venom in his eyes.

"I don't think you want to do that, Mrs. Wentworth."

He stood between the two of us while she raged at him and tried to get to me. Garrick kept her at bay with ease while the elevator door opened. He told me to get inside, and I did.

My mother still had fire in her eyes, and she scratched and clawed at Garrick until I saw a trickle of blood appear on his cheek. He kept her at arm's length until we were both in the elevator, then he pushed the button. "Expect a call from the police. This is all on camera." He pointed to the cameras in the corners.

When the doors shut, he engulfed me in his arms and I held on tightly while I listened to the steady beat of his heart.

"What were you thinking?" He kissed me on the top of my head while his arms held me solidly. I fell into his strength, so grateful that it was him and not Denver who met me after the run-in with my mother.

"She did it," I told him. "She'll never admit it, and she'll probably get away with it, but she did it." I pulled away from him to gauge his expression, and he nodded.

He knew. Everyone knew except for me because they weren't flirting with reality.

"I heard you wield a weapon of your own in there."

"What?"

"Mary Campelli's name." He grinned. "You've learned a thing or two from your mother after all. When she went low, you didn't shirk away from throwing your own grenade." He offered a wicked smile. "I'm proud of you."

"You heard what she said about me?" Shame washed over me like a rogue wave at the beach.

"She's a liar, Brinn. A cold, calculating liar. She takes the awful lies she's told you your whole life and goes for the jugular. I can't imagine saying those words to my worst enemy, much less my daughter."

"I just wanted her to love me."

He wrapped his arms around me tighter. "No one is more beautiful than you, Brinn, and she knows it. She is jealous, pure and simple."

The elevator opened to the cavernous lobby, and we stepped out together. Mr. Bennedetti, the doorman, waved at us when I noticed Garrick had stopped and gotten down on one knee.

"What are you doing?" I asked him while I tried to yank him up.

"I'd abandon my fears of marriage for you in a second. I'd marry you without a cent to your name, Brinn Wentworth. I don't think you know how many men would do exactly that if you'd only give them the chance."

"Garrick, get up!" I yanked on his arm. "I get it, you think I need a self-esteem course, but let's not get carried away with the drama. We've both had enough of that in this lifetime."

"The last thing I want to do is add to drama. You should know that about me by now."

I clenched my teeth, venturing a look at Mr. Bennedetti, who was grinning like he was guilty. "Can we go? Because even if you are serious, which I don't believe for a minute, we are standing in a public lobby with an audience. You know how I love an audience, right?"

"That's sarcasm." He nodded his head and grinned. "The devil's speech."

I couldn't help it, I started giggling. "Would you stop? Don't you think we might date a few times before we get engaged?"

"Fair question. I hear where you're coming from and maybe I'm jumping the gun, but I just wanted to get my sales pitch in before you friend-zoned me as your personal bodyguard. I saw how you looked at me when I told you the truth at the restaurant. I needed you to see *me* again, not my past."

"I'm not going to lie. I'm afraid of our pasts, but if I ever decided on marriage, you would never be in the friend zone."

"I've had lots of people avoid me after they learned the truth, but I couldn't take it with you."

"If we were ever to decide we were up to this ugly marriage thing, then I deserve better, don't you think? With a ring and I don't know, a more romantic setting. Maybe the Golden Gate Bridge?"

"Suicide capital? Maybe not."

"The Palace of Fine Arts?"

"A reasonable suggestion, but so basic," he said.

"How about, if you and I get over the trauma of marriage and decide we like each other long-term, you come up with a place. And a ring."

"I don't know that I can afford a ring that would impress a billionaire."

"You don't need a ring to impress me."

"Wow," he pressed his palm to his heart, "that was genuine. You meant that."

It shocked me too. I *had* meant it. Something about Garrick left me unafraid to be vulnerable, and the idea of wearing his ring didn't scare me as much as it should have.

He stood up and met my gaze, his eyes wide with sincerity. "This was ill-planned, and I've made a mockery of something serious, but I knew the first time I laid eyes on you that my protests against marriage were useless. When I heard your mother say those terrible things, all I wanted to tell you is how you deserve all the love. I wanted to make up for every ugly word she's ever spoken to you. I just figured it would take a lifetime."

Tears welled up in my eyes because as much as I wanted to believe him, something inside me overrode his words and I doubted his sincerity. Garrick sensed my hesitation and cupped my jaw with his hands. I leaned into his touch and the world around us evaporated like a mist.

He whispered in my ear, "Any man you let behind that wall and into your heart would feel the same. I pray it's me."

I shook my head and pulled away. "Let's not get carried away."

"I may not be the man for you, but any man in the world would be lucky to have you as a wife. I realized that keeping anyone from hurting you overrides my fear of marriage."

So it was just about his job and protecting me? I felt my wall go back up.

He smiled at Mr. Bennedetti. "She turned me down."

"Keep asking," he said. "She'll come to her senses."

I shot the old doorman a look. "You don't think I deserve a better proposal than that?"

"I know you do, and you'll get one," he said knowingly.

"Garrick," I pulled him aside against the wall, "I don't need you to feel sorry for me."

He shrugged. "No matter how we feel about marriage, I think we both know it's pointless to fight this."

"That's exactly what a con artist would say," I said brusquely. "You sound like a teenage boy on prom night."

Garrick laughed out loud, which was so unlike him. "You did not just say that to me."

I gazed into the depths of his gray-green eyes. In them, I saw a magical world; an impractical, fairy-tale future where I woke up beside Garrick Kane and we left our parents' scurrilous world behind us.

"It's pointless to fight fate," the doorman called after us.

When we got outside on the busy street, the sounds of the city cured any awkward silence. Denver was there to meet us.

"Denver," Garrick said in his old stoic voice, "can you get Brinn home? I have some loose ends to tie up with Mrs. Donley."

I was so confused. And jealous at the sound of Katrina's name. "You're going to help Mrs. Donley now?"

"Just got a text. Mr. Donley is in jail. I need to make sure I keep him there. Denver has you covered."

"Covered from what?"

At that point, the paparazzi came out of nowhere and started taking my picture while shouting at me. "Did you see your mother?" "Is Chelsea in good spirits?" "Do you think your mother is guilty?"

The questions came fast and furious as I heard the constant clicks of their digital intrusions over the roar of the traffic and passing cable car. I ignored them all as I watched Garrick disappear around the corner.

"What the heck is wrong with him?" I asked Denver.

"Garrick's my boss, so you'd be better off asking me what *isn't* wrong with him."

CHAPTER 23

*T*he construction workers pounded away in the mansion as if their lives depended solely on how much sound they created. I stole away into the floral room with Denver a few steps behind me.

Katrina was without her boys on the sofa. She was deep in conversation with a stunning young woman who wore an oversized Disneyland sweatshirt.

"Am I interrupting?" I asked, even though I clearly was. My curiosity got the better of me. *How did she find her at Wentworth Manor?* The striking stranger didn't wear a stitch of makeup and her luminous skin was as supple as a fresh apricot.

Katrina looked up at me with tear-stained troughs through her own makeup.

I kneeled in front of her. "Where are the boys?" I asked urgently.

She shook her head. "The boys are fine. Mrs. Chen has them out in the back yard."

She must love that. I rose from in front of the sofa and focused on the beautiful young woman who'd obviously brought bad news with her.

"Brinn," Katrina said through a sniffle, "this is Harper Emmons. Harper, Brinn Wentworth."

The slender redhead stood up and stuck her hand out. "It's a true pleasure. I feel as if I've grown up watching you in the newspaper. You're even more beautiful in person."

I shook her hand coldly. "I can see you're discussing something important. I'll make my exit."

"Feel free to stay," Katrina said, wiping her tears with the back of her hand. "Harper is apparently my husband's mistress. Or one of them, anyway."

Harper smiled sheepishly. "To be fair, I didn't know he was married before I fell in love. He told me he was a widower."

"That's the oldest line in the book, Harper. Do better," Katrina said, then muzzled herself. "I'm sorry. I know better than anyone how Matt's words feel like the truth."

"Look, it was not easy to come here. I wouldn't be here at all if Garrick Kane hadn't strong-armed me."

"Garrick?" I said out loud, while I felt my fists tighten at the thought of him with this model. Now I really understood what Katrina must have felt. "Garrick sent you here? How do you know Garrick?" I sounded like a jealous shrew, but I was blinded by the fact that I *was* a jealous shrew.

"Let's just all calm down and speak rationally. I'll explain everything," Harper said. "All I ask for is the chance."

It almost seemed supernatural how Garrick managed to be everywhere. At my mother's townhome to greet me, and he somehow found this random home-wrecker and brought her to Wentworth Manor. Maybe my first impression of Garrick as a player was exactly who he was.

"Harper, you wanted the floor. Here it is. What brings you here?"

I'd never seen a mistress up close before and I couldn't have told her from any other woman on the street. That surprised me. It made me wonder how many of my dad's mistresses had been paraded in front of us over the years. Of course, Alisa's mom met my criteria for a mistress. Jennifer Alton appeared troubled, kind of cheap-looking with too much makeup and badly dyed, ratty blondish-orange hair. But what should she have looked like, being left homeless by my father's antics?

In contrast to Jennifer, Harper was fresh-faced innocence. If I had to give her a profession, I'd have guessed kindergarten teacher. She clutched a small Louis Vuitton bag, and I wondered if Matt paid for it. By her gaze, I could tell Katrina wondered the same thing.

After the awkward silence, Harper spoke. "I decided to face you, Katrina. It seemed stupid to hide in the shadows any longer after the truth came out. I was in love with your husband."

Katrina visibly winced.

"First, he told me he was a widower. Then, after that story fell apart because of his campaign, he kept telling me how he wanted to leave you and the kids. He said he was never in love with you, and he'd felt pressured to get married by his firm."

"He wasn't at that firm when we married," Katrina offered, deadpan.

"Look, I know you hate me. You have every right. I know what you must think of me, but your husband is in jail because of me. That's what I came to tell you."

"Matt's in jail?" Katrina looked stricken, as if she'd pay for that later.

"I did the right thing in the end. While I don't want any praise for that, I want you to know that I'm sorry. Really and truly sorry. I didn't know who he was, and I still wouldn't believe it if I hadn't seen it with my own eyes. I thought I knew the real Matt and the disingenuous one lived with you."

"Ha!" Katrina laughed.

"I should leave you two alone," I said. Where I came from, conversations like this were never had, they were swept under the rug and promptly ignored. The air was thick with gritty tension, oscillating between age and jealousy based on a lie.

"No," they both said in unison. "Stay."

"I'll just state my piece and leave—" Harper said. "Matt had some kind of system set up to watch both of us. Apparently, the cameras are very small. They were in a pen. They found two at my place and sixteen at yours."

"They saw him cut himself," Katrina said.

"And make the false police report, yes," Harper confirmed.

Katrina stood up and paced. "It doesn't matter. Video may make it hard to deny the truth, but I know him. Matt will talk his way out of this."

"Not if Garrick has anything to say about it," I said. Even though I was angry at him for having contact with this little minx before me. The jealousy was such a foreign feeling that I vowed to unpack it later after everyone had gone home.

"How did you meet my husband?" Katrina asked.

"On a dating app. He said he was looking for something serious and ready to settle down. He'd had enough of the single life, and it was hard for him to meet women because he was always working."

"If only that were true," Katrina scoffed.

I sat next to Katrina and took her hand. I felt her squeeze me like a stress ball.

"I didn't know he was married," she repeated.

"Until you did," Katrina stated.

"It was too late by then. I loved him. He told me he was young when he married you and that you'd grown apart. That you wanted the divorce and he'd done everything to try and keep it together, but it was clear that it was over. He was done fighting the inevitable."

Katrina sat silently, but her eyes were awash in pools of tears.

"Why are you here? Why not let Garrick tell us about Matt?"

I asked Harper. "I can pretty much guarantee if you want Matt Donley, you're welcome to him."

"Matt lied to me," Harper cried.

"You think?" I asked her. "Where is Garrick?" I asked Katrina again. If he wasn't with her or me, what is it he was being paid for? I felt the betrayal sharply.

Harper interrupted my thoughts. "Obviously, I'm not here to make friends, Miss Wentworth. I don't expect you to understand me, Katrina. Miss Wentworth, you've lived your whole privileged life behind these fancy walls, you definitely wouldn't understand."

"I understand betrayal," I told her.

"Again, I'm not here to justify my actions. I'm here to tell you what happened from my mouth, so Matt doesn't pit us against each other and get away with what he's done."

"He'll get away with it," Katrina whispered, and I knew exactly how she felt. Matt, like my mother, had a supernatural sway with people that denied reason.

"You probably know that Matt is very tight with his phone. Doesn't let it go often," Harper said.

Katrina nodded.

"He was telling me how you were leaving him, but you were guilting him about the children and threatening that he'd never see them again unless he stayed."

"Which as a lawyer, he'd know I didn't have the power to do," Katrina said.

"I know that now. But that's when I realized he was tracking you and I had to do my own research. It was clear he was obsessed with you, not the other way around. He had no intention of ever marrying me. It's the oldest scam in the book, but I fell for it. He told me what I wanted to hear, and thinking I was in love, I believed him." Harper exhaled deeply and then inhaled sharply. "The cameras are set up all over your house. These spy pens. They look like a normal pen, but they record everything and send it to a cloud website."

Katrina's grip on my wrist grew excruciating. "He filmed me?"

"Everything," she said. "At first, I told myself it was just him gathering information for the divorce, but the truth was I meant nothing to him."

"Well, you were the mistress so I think *that* would be obvious," I said.

"Miss Wentworth." Harper glared at me. "I'm not here to defend my honor. I'm here to tell you that Matt cutting himself and blaming Katrina is on film and that's why he's in jail now, but I can't guarantee for how long, obviously. He is a slippery lawyer with a tongue like a silver snake."

"Aren't they all?" Katrina said flippantly.

"H-how did you get the footage?" I asked with my eyes narrowed. "I mean, if Katrina didn't even know there was a camera, how would you?"

"Chalk it up to a sixth sense that I acted on. He wasn't acting right."

"He must have let his guard down with you. He certainly never let me near any of his electronics," Katrina said bitterly.

"Matt was careful with his phone," Harper said. "He never put it down when he was in my apartment, but he forgot about his Apple watch. I'd taken it from the bedside table when he was asleep and stuffed it in a drawer."

"He didn't notice?" Katrina asked. "That seems highly unlikely."

"He noticed. He was in a hurry, and I told him I'd find it before he came back. He'd have to count his steps on his phone until that afternoon."

"That seems sketchy. He bought that?" Katrina asked, her hands visibly trembling.

"He trusted me," Harper said, and I saw that painful, emotional barb land on Katrina. "Anyway, he left the watch. I opened the cloud on the computer with it. He had the clip where he cut himself saved. Almost like he was watching it over and over again for enjoyment. I didn't open anything else. I called the police."

"He may be in jail now, but for how long?" Katrina asked. "Anyway, I appreciate you doing the right thing. But next time, maybe Google who you're dating."

"I did Google him," Harper snapped. "He said you were separated and keeping it secret because he wanted to run for office."

Katrina rolled her eyes. "Give me a break. Reagan was divorced back in the '80s."

"Matt was arrested right away because Miss Wentworth's bodyguard had a tail on him."

I tried to hide my smile at the satisfaction this gave me. I loved the ownership of Garrick in my mind and the fact that once again, he was the hero in the situation. If we went forward, I'd have to give him the benefit of the doubt. Which went against everything in my nature.

There was a knock at the pocket doors and Mrs. Chen slid them open. "Miss Brinn, there is a police officer to see you." Behind her stood one of San Francisco's finest in his black uniform. Tall, blonde, broad-chested, he looked more like a television lifeguard than a cop.

"Can I help you?"

"Brinn Wentworth?" he asked.

"Yes."

"Are you under the influence of drugs or alcohol, Miss Wentworth?"

"What? It's eleven a.m."

"I'm going to have to ask you to come with me."

"Come with you, where?"

"The hospital. It's been reported that you're in imminent

danger of self-harm. We'll have you checked by an evaluating physician, and then we'll see where we go from there."

I shook my head vehemently. "I'm not going anywhere. I'm not going to harm myself or anyone else. You can't just tell me I'm in danger of harming myself when I'm standing right here telling you there is no such danger. I have rights."

"Officer," Katrina addressed the cop, "can you give me a minute with my client? I'm Brinn's lawyer."

He shrugged, put his thumbs on each side of his belt, and stepped back. "Be my guest."

Katrina pulled me to the elevator foyer, where we had some privacy. "Stay calm," she told me. "Any officer across the United States can enforce involuntary detainment, but my guess is your visit to your mother started this. She must be worried you're going to testify against her. This might be her way of ensuring your testimony is not trustworthy."

"Quinn is going to kill me. She told me not to go."

"The officer has to have a medical evaluation. Go in the kitchen and down a few beers."

"What?"

"Wine, beer, champagne. Anything you can get your hands on. If you've been drinking, they have to let you sober up before any doctor can make an evaluation. I'll get Garrick on it before they let you out of the hospital." Katrina pushed me into the kitchen. "Drink up."

I went to the fridge and found an open bottle of my father's wine from the Napa house. I chugged it like it was grape juice and knew I'd pay the price. I wasn't much of a drinker, but if what Katrina said was true, I needed to buy some time. How Garrick had any time for his real job baffled me. This week had been an utter disaster show.

Katrina took the bottle from me and looked inside. "That's enough. You just need it in your system to register as impaired. I'll call Garrick and we'll meet you."

I hugged Katrina tightly. "We're going to win the war."

"We are."

"At least Harper did the right thing," I told her.

"Was it even the right thing?" Katrina asked. "For all I know, Harper might have been worried he'd pick me and rid the world of her."

The police officer came into the kitchen behind Mrs. Chen. He still had his thumbs in his belt like that was his normal stance, his hand near his firearm. "Are you ready?"

I lifted up the bottle from the kitchen island. "I am. Just needed a little liquid courage."

The officer's expression darkened, and I knew Katrina had been correct. I put my wrists out. "Are you going to handcuff me?"

"Of course not," he said. "I want to get you any help you might need."

How I wanted to believe that, but I knew he'd been paid off. I gave him my best withering glance so he'd know I was onto him. "I don't know if you're working directly for my mother or there's a middleman, but if you could get her a message, I'd appreciate it."

"Shoot your shot," he said.

"I wasn't going to testify, but *this* changed my mind. I'm done being manipulated by Chelsea Wentworth. What is it they say? The only thing necessary for the triumph of evil is for good men to do nothing. Tell my mother I'm done doing nothing."

I may have slurred my words a bit, but I pressed my shoulders back, did my best to maintain my dignity and followed the policeman out the door.

* * *

THE HOSPITAL WAS A ZOO. They put me in a room to "dry out" and said they'd be back. I didn't ruminate on why I was there or even that my own mother did this on purpose. Instead, I thought about all the times I'd believed in her.

Sitting in this cold, stark hospital room with everything stealable locked down, I knew Quinn had been right all along. She'd tried to protect me, so I'd know my mother's heart wasn't capable of change. The great Mrs. Chelsea Wentworth had to want to change, and she didn't. She only wanted to win, no matter what the cost.

My grandfather was dead. *Is that what it's going to take for me?*

Katrina burst into the room with an orderly and Sophia. "Let's go," she said.

"The police," I said.

"It was only one. He's taken care of. Get your things. This ruse is over. That woman has played her last hand."

"Did Garrick come?" I asked Sophia as I searched the corridors for his devilishly handsome face.

"He got stuck on something," Sophia said. "Sorry, Brinn. I know you two are getting close."

"It's nothing like that," I lied. "Garrick's a rolling stone and a little harmless romance with me isn't going to change that."

"Since we can't go far with all this going on," Sophia said, "we're leaving for Lake Tahoe for the week. As a family. We need to regroup and plan our strategy."

"Strategy?"

"As the new and improved Wentworth family. Gia planned everything. Quinn already packed your things. It's not up for discussion. We're leaving now before the trial starts. Before your mother can pull another one of her stunts."

I didn't want Garrick to think I'd just up and left him after his ruse of a proposal. I needed to tell him I knew he wasn't serious. "Wha—where—is—"

"Garrick has business," Katrina said, as though she'd read my mind. "He'll see you when we get home and explain."

I nodded. Reluctantly, I packed up my things in the plastic

bag they'd given me and followed Sophia and Katrina out the doors.

I was better off before I'd entertained the idea of marriage. When I was focused on escaping San Francisco and Wentworth family responsibilities, just staying away gave me a purpose after ballet. *If only you hadn't brought me back, Grandpa.*

Single life suited me. I didn't worry about where Garrick was nor when I'd see him again. Now it seemed to fill my every waking thought. I realized how ingrained the rejection of my mother was and how I'd never truly be free of it, no matter how far away I went. The real prison was in my mind and until I escaped hearing her criticism before and after every decision, I was trapped no matter where I was. Garrick couldn't change that. No one could.

CHAPTER 24

Our commuter van stopped on the way to Lake Tahoe in Truckee to drop Alisa off with her mother. It was very dark when the van curved down a long driveway through a well-lit forested path. Metal sculptures of eagles, bears and mountain lions, each with their own spotlight, dotted the route through the heavy brush of pine needles. The effect created its own magical world that I couldn't wait to enter.

We were all exhausted after the drive and anxious to exit what now felt like a dilapidated school bus compared to the luxurious van we'd started out in. The boys were the first off and they took off into the trees with Katrina following behind them shouting that there were bears in the forest. Only black bears, but it had the desired effect and the boys halted.

"You're on the top floor," Gia told me as we stepped out of the van. "Your room has a fireplace, floor-to-ceiling windows and it's going to feel like you're on a cruise ship. Lake Tahoe at your feet. Well, not tonight. Tonight it will just feel like there's a vast black wilderness in front of you. But tomorrow . . . tomorrow when you wake up, you'll be in paradise."

"You sound like a brochure," I told her.

She handed me one. "Casey told me I'd be overwhelmed by the size of the place, but I had no idea. The land juts out over the lake and the house is shaped like a horseshoe. So cool."

"This really is one of the nicest things anyone has ever done for me, Gia. I never know when it's time to rest until it's too late."

"Never mind. We all needed a break. I called Casey and he said we could have this place tonight if we wanted. I guess friends of his own it. Then all I had to do was get the transportation planned and bring the staff back in. Like I said, it was nothing." Gia shrugged under the porch light. "It's not like I had to worry about all you deadbeats and your lack of work schedules."

I laughed. "True enough." I looked up at the massive log cabin which nearly reached the top of the pines. "I'll tell you one thing. Casey will never be poor."

After benefiting from Casey's kindness, I understood how he and his father deserved every gift life offered them. I'd completely misjudged him, and I wondered how many people I'd done that to over the years.

"Casey could marry for money if he wanted to," Gia says. "He'll never do that."

I loved how Gia was able to trust people until they proved unworthy of it, that was a gift.

"You seem to know a lot about what Casey thinks."

Gia giggled at the sound of his name. "He's a good man. Not bad on the eyes either."

"On that note . . ."

Katrina's boys tore into the mansion past us and checked out every nook and cranny, shouting their discoveries while their mother helplessly yelled instructions. Who could blame them? The house was magnificent. According to the brochure, it had "a soaring A-frame window which offered a full view of the aqua blue waters of Crystal Cove, the most sought-after location in

South Lake Tahoe. Snow-capped Sierras across the lake meet the bluest skies." Currently, it offered a large wall of complete blackness, but I still felt myself exhale.

Joel and Sophia came in with some of the bags, dropped them in the grand foyer and went toward the sky-high windows as if drawn by an invisible force. Sophia leaned up against Joel, who was now fairly solid on his cast. "I can't wait for this view. Tomorrow we'll wake up and say, have you ever seen anything so beautiful?"

"And I will say yes," Joel said as he wrapped her in his arms from behind. He stared at the invisible view over her shoulder. "She's about to be my wife."

They stood beside a bear sculpture which had its own indoor rocky river that ran the length of the living room and trickled through the house like a forest creek.

"Not so fast, you two. We still have eight months left on the will." I wasn't ready for my sisters to all run off and get married. We'd only just become a family.

Joel put his cheek to Sophia's and moaned like a wounded animal. "Your grandfather is getting on my last nerve from beyond the grave."

"Get a room already!"

"Gia!" Mary Campelli came into the foyer brushing off the snow from her boots. She was alongside Casey's father, Grant. It shocked me to see her with a man, much less one I knew. I suppose in my mind I'd made her out to be the Virgin Mary.

"Hello, Mary . . . Grant," I said. "I didn't know you'd be here."

"I hope that's okay," Mary said while Grant helped her out of her jacket. "Gia said there were plenty of bedrooms, so we followed you up in Grant's car. Well, we went Highway 50. We didn't have to stop in Truckee. A neighbor is staying with my parents."

"We're happy to have you. It's such a relief to be out from

under all that construction. I didn't realize how the pounding was getting to me until I heard this absolute quiet."

"I'll bet."

"I'll take these to your room," Grant said as he kissed her chastely on the forehead.

"She's on level two. First door to your left," Gia said, reading off a clipboard. "You're directly across from her. No lake view, sorry."

Grant saluted and took the stone stairs two at a time, like a man half his age. Currently, this expansive home felt like the luxury log-cabin ark. Everyone coming in two-by-two and my singleness greatly highlighted, but I didn't care. We'd left our threats behind.

Casey crossed paths with his dad on the stairs and lifted both his arms in enthusiasm. "Great, everyone is here!" he said while looking so intently at Gia, I worried he'd miss a step.

"Did you get everyone's welcome gift put away?" Gia asked him.

He nodded. "I'm so ready for that beach walk you promised me."

"It's covered in snow," Gia said.

"You brought boots. Let's get out there for the sunrise at 6:52 a.m. There's a tram down to the water, so we'll have to be on it by say, 6:30?"

Gia looked at her watch. "It's already eleven."

He gave her a pout.

"Oh, all right," Gia conceded. "Everyone, breakfast is here in the main dining room at 8 a.m. Tomorrow is a free day, and we'll meet back here at 6 p.m. for dinner. The shuttle is here to take you to the slopes or into town if anyone wants to shop. No dressing for dinner. We're on vacation so we're going to act like it."

I climbed the two levels to my bedroom. There was indeed a massive fireplace in the room and two French doors that led to a lit jacuzzi in the granite outcrop. If there was ever a place to get my head together, this was it.

Quinn walked in behind me and handed me my ballet bag. "I brought this for you. There's a dance studio downstairs."

I stepped back and shook my head. "My ankle."

"You have one good ankle, and the dance is in your head, not your one bad ankle."

"Dance is over," I said, but at the same time, I unzipped the bag and my heart leapt at the sight of my toe shoes. I knew every wrinkle in them and I brought them to my cheeks. "I missed you."

"Brinn, now you can dance because you love it. For the sheer joy of it. No one will be watching so now you no longer have to be the best."

"Then what's the point?"

"Fun. To do something simply for the love of it."

"So, a hobby."

"What's wrong with a hobby? Do you think I'd leave horses behind if Avery threw me in a jump?"

"That would never happen to you. You live a charmed life."

"I'll just say this. Dancing as a hobby is better than escaping me and pretending you care about getting a master's in finance."

I snapped my head up. "What?"

"I know you dropped out of school a long time ago and spend your days pretending to be average. You've been beach-hopping and spending the days at Disneyland. Is wearing mouse ears as an adult more worthwhile than dance? Worth leaving me to wrestle with Mom and Dad on my own?"

I was speechless.

"The school called looking for you. Luckily, Mother and Dad were already at the penthouse."

"And Mrs. Chen?" I asked about the manor's resident spy.

"She knows better than to cross me. That's why she picks on you. You're afraid of her. I threatened to fire her bum and now we understand each other." Quinn dropped the bag at my feet. "Lace up for me. You're not meant to be average, even in a hobby. You're extraordinary and yet you seem to be the only one who doesn't know it."

I picked up the bag. "I suppose it's better than getting dragged on a hike tomorrow or worse yet, skiing."

Quinn laughed. "For such an athlete, you sure are an outdoors wuss. I put your leotards in there, too."

"I doubt they'll fit any longer."

"They'll fit. Flood that studio with your favorite tunes and see what your metal ankle is capable of. You can always have a brace made for your weak ankle." She hugged me awkwardly and I realized the twins were rubbing off on us. "Don't forget how much joy your dancing brought to others. Maybe it's your turn."

"I—I . . . went to Santa Monica so I could think," I told her. "When Mother is around, I lose my thoughts and so Grandfather told me to go. He said 'go and find out what you want.' I've been told my whole life what to want. I had to figure it out."

"Did you?" Quinn asked.

"I did. But I had to come back home again to figure it out."

"Get some rest. I want to hear everything in the morning." Quinn left me alone. I'd underestimated how well she read me.

* * *

THE BALLET STUDIO'S bank of windows overlooked the expanse of the sparkling, pristine turquoise waters of Crystal Bay in Lake Tahoe. The granite rocks dotted the bottom of the aqua cove until it darkened to the deep sapphire it was known for.

On the opposite wall, there were floor-to-ceiling mirrors, which echoed back the heavenly view. I felt one with nature without ever stepping foot outside. I sat on a carved granite bench and laced up my toe shoes. My heart leapt at the possibilities, but I drew in a deep breath, careful not to be overcome by exhilaration of my former days when I could fly. Chances were, I wouldn't be able to perform a simple *pas de chat*. The cat's step was so basic, but it required both feet.

I played Rachmaninoff's "Rhapsody On a Theme of Paganini". The romance of the music swept over me like a trance, and I took off across the polished oak floor like I did as a child, when I'd dance for my grandfather. I attempted an *assemblé* so I could land on two feet, but I felt my ankle crumble underneath me.

I was transported back to the stage . . . to the horrified looks on the first few rows of patrons who knew something was wrong. But unlike that day, I drew myself up to a standing position and tried again.

This time I stayed on the toe longer. Just a few seconds, but enough to know with a brace and time, I could dance all I liked, just not professionally.

"I told you not to step foot on stage that night," my mother's critical voice cackled, only this time I spoke up.

"No, Mother," I said to the mirror. "You told me to get out there and dance despite my hairline fracture. It was all about you. It was *always* about you. The willfully ignorant Chelsea Whitman Wentworth in her greatest role as the nurturing and caring mother."

"I beg your pardon!"

I stood horrified as I saw my mother appear by the windows. I hadn't imagined her at all. She stood by the windows, illuminated by the sun behind her as if she was a ghost. My worst nightmare came to pass in her presence. She'd found us. I'd never get away. Believing so was nothing more than one of my fantasies.

"This isn't happening," I said to the wood floor. "Mother is on house arrest." I peeked through my fingers and noted her naked ankle and her trademark Chanel pencil skirt, always altered three inches above the knee. Even nearing sixty, Mother's legs were her greatest asset, and she knew it.

"Casey's outdone himself with this place."

"Where's your ankle monitor? You're not supposed to leave the penthouse. Or San Francisco. How did you know where we were?"

She laughed in her callous, above-it-all way. "It seems my girls are quite anxious to put me in prison. When one considers my innocence, that's terribly disturbing, don't you think?"

"My entire life I've listened to you proclaim the most outlandish things as truth. The police, however, will actually confirm your story. If you're innocent, you'll be acquitted."

"Perhaps it's your own guilt that makes you both so accusatory toward me. Did you ever think of that?" She folded her spindly arms across her chest in the haughty manner she'd perfected. "After all, didn't you disappear to university to avoid caring for your *beloved grandfather?*" She spit the word grandfather, as if it left a horrible taste in her mouth.

I began to back away but quickly hit the wall of mirrors. "I want you to leave."

"I bet you do."

"We've said all we have to say to one another."

"If that were true, I wouldn't be here. Since my own children won't take my call, it seems I have to track them down. Stellar time for a vacation, I might add."

"Where's Dad?" I knew my father wouldn't let her hurt me. He may not have ever championed my cause, but he wasn't cruel either. Just clueless because the world outside his head didn't seem to exist for him.

"Your father is probably upstairs asking the entire family why they thought to go on vacation when my trial starts this week. Anyway, we're here to tell you that all charges have been dropped. I'm a free woman, so there is no trial. Your father and I thought it was a lovely time for a ski vacation. It's been so long since we were in Switzerland."

I never thought my mother was capable of doing her own dirty work, but the hatred in her eyes told me otherwise.

"I'll scream if you come any closer. You're not welcome here, and you need to leave. I'm done with this ruse that you're my mother. You've never been a mother to us."

"Brinn." She shook her head, showing her eternal disappointment in me. "You're always the victim, scared of your own shadow and determined to continue with this irrational narrative that I'm some kind of monster."

"You killed my grandfather." I'd said it. I felt such satisfaction in finally speaking out my truth. The fear left me. "What are you going to do, kill me too?"

"Just because I didn't mother you the way you thought you should be mothered doesn't make me a criminal. Do you think you'd be where you are without me pushing you? If it weren't for me forcing you in ballet, you never would have left the house. Always moping about your sister being prettier, whining she had better horsemanship or that she was skinnier, loved more . . . it was pathetic. . . ."

I started to question my own memories. I had believed those things, but I didn't remember ever voicing them to my mother.

Her tone changed to a lighthearted, casual song, as if I should be captivated by her words. "I saw you growing in ballet. I used your own jealousy against your sister to motivate you to compete and wonder of wonders, you rose to the occasion. This is the thanks I'm given that now because I was tough on you, you think I'm capable of murder." She walked closer to me but stopped abruptly when I backed into the mirrored wall. "Even if I had done it, a little morphine in a dying old man isn't criminal."

"Actually, it is," I told her.

"Doctors do it all the time."

"You're not a doctor. You had no right to play God. Say what you want to say and go. Fine, you're free and everyone was wrong about you. Is that what you need to hear?" I wanted her out of the house, especially before she discovered Mary was upstairs. That wasn't a scene I wanted to witness.

"One day, Brinn, you'll have your own daughter. Then you'll understand how you must treat each child individually. Separate personalities require it. I treated you the way you needed to be treated to excel. If that makes me your enemy, so be it. One day you'll understand, and you'll forgive me. Know that I already forgive you."

I started to feel dizzy . . . confused. But I fought the swirl of emotions in my head and focused on putting an end to Mother's words. She never communicated, she manipulated. Which meant she was here for a reason, and I couldn't let her wear me down.

"Who let you in the house?" I demanded.

"Your father and I thought a getaway might be what we needed to celebrate these ridiculous charges being dropped. He booked the private plane and here we are. If we ever hope to put this family back together, we need to have these hard conversations. We need to be together."

My truth bubbled up from the pit of my stomach, where I'd stored all the rage I'd kept hidden tightly bound within my person. "You never answered my phone calls as a child. You never replied to a text. Now you suddenly want us to—what? Pretend that we are a close-knit family? The only thing we've ever coordinated is our outfits for the press."

"Oh," she tossed her manicured hands, aptly shaped like a vampire's claws, "you exaggerate constantly, Brinn. You always were such a drama queen. If I didn't answer the phone, I was busy. Your needs were always attended to. Mrs. Chen was always there."

"No." I shook my head. "I'm not a drama queen and I never

have been. Please refrain from making sweeping statements about who I am . . . when you clearly have no idea." I struggled to find my breath.

"That's simply not true, darling. Shouldn't I love you enough to tell you the truth about your flaws? Maybe one time I didn't answer a call and you'll hold it against me? I held the framework of San Francisco society in my hand."

"No. Every single time I called, you didn't answer. It was on purpose. I know that now."

I watched the color drain from her face and looked out over the lake to avoid bursting into tears. It *was* true. I'd hit a nerve. "You really sound paranoid, Brinn. Maybe you should talk to someone about that."

"You answered the phone for Father, for Quinn, for anyone in San Francisco society . . . probably even the renewal on your car warranty. *Everyone* but me."

"You're imagining that. You always were overly sensitive."

"I've got your message loud and clear. I'm not worthy of love. Mission accomplished."

"What rubbish. Do you hear yourself? You sound positively deranged."

"Do I?"

Bright splotches of red brought color back to her cheeks as a seething rage took hold within her. The mask was off. *That's the mother I recognize.*

"You really don't understand how impossible you are," she said. "You couldn't stay upright on a horse, so we put you in ballet. Your grandfather paid anyone who would take you in as a pupil, but I'm the villain of your story. All right, then."

"I was a prima ballerina!"

She scoffed. "Because your father paid the head of the arts council. It never occurred to you how the offices were named Wentworth?"

"Brinn is a prima ballerina because she worked like a dog to get there and no one in San Francisco danced better than her!" Quinn entered the studio and I'd never been so glad to see her. She came beside me. "Brinn, she's lying. She wants you to second-guess yourself. Somehow she gets a thrill out of it."

I grabbed Quinn's hand.

"Mother, I'd like you to leave and if you don't, I'll have security escort you out. You weren't welcome here and you may as well let Mrs. Chen know she's fired the minute I get home. I've had enough of her treason."

"Fine, tell Brinn what she wants to hear, but look at how she's turned out without my guidance. She was caught in a clutch at the ballet opening—with a notorious San Francisco lothario, no less. How I suffered being stuck in the penthouse for the opening, only to open the newspaper and see my daughter kissing some second-rate Casanova."

"Actually," Quinn said, "I thought making out with Garrick upped Brinn's stock quite a bit. Her phone rang off the hook after that."

"Don't encourage her," my mother said. "Who do you think she'd be if I hadn't kept tabs on her? Oh, she's too good for Casey Sutton, but she can't control herself around some two-bit cop wannabe at the ballet of all places. I couldn't show my face there after that."

"You couldn't show your face because you were on house arrest. Let's not blame Brinn for that."

"That kiss, by the way, was part of my charity work. I kissed that man to protect a client."

A shuffle from the door by the staircase caught my attention and I turned to see Garrick Kane's boot hit the bottom step, then exit the way he came in.

"You invited him here?" Mother said, dropping her head. "He's trash, Brinn. He comes from trash, and he will always be trash. The apple doesn't fall far from the tree. Do you know his father shot his mother?"

I walked toward my mother. "Was it worth it to be the prettiest, most admired woman in all of San Francisco at the expense of your own family? Did those people give you whatever it was you needed?"

"A child is called to respect their parents."

"A parent is called on to not exasperate their children." I untied my toe shoes and slipped into my slides. "Maybe it was worth it for you, but I choose differently. I want the people closest to me to believe in me. This apple is going to fall as far from the Wentworth tree as I can get." I headed toward the staircase.

"I suppose you've seen the women that man dates?" Mother called after me. "You think he's with you, why?"

The stairwell was empty. I climbed back down the steps and looked at my mother. She was so incredibly stunning, she had everything. Why was she filled with so much venom? An outer work of beauty devoid of a conscience.

I posed with my hand to my hip and tossed my hair back. "He's with me because I am freaking Brinn Wentworth, prima ballerina, finance major and heiress!"

I heard Quinn giggle as I chased after Garrick, praying he'd hear me out.

CHAPTER 25

J entered the massive living room to find the rest of the family alongside several uniformed policemen with Officer Kendall asking me to remain quiet by holding his forefinger in front of his mouth.

"What's going on?" I asked Gia.

Mary came up beside me and put her arm around my shoulder tightly, as if holding me in place. "This will be over soon."

Quinn came up from the studio, followed by our mother, who assessed the situation and pivoted back to the staircase. Officer Kendall took to a run, followed by two officers. The chase was over before it began and all four of them emerged from the steps.

Two more officers guarded the entry doors as I tried to process what was going on. *All charges were dropped. She's gotten away with it, just like I predicted. What now?*

Officer Kendall spoke loudly. "Chelsea Wentworth, you're under arrest for the murder of Wyatt Wentworth the first, felony insurance fraud and the solicitation to commit the murder of an elected official." He placed Mother in handcuffs while he read her the rest of her Miranda rights.

Mother's cool demeanor and natural composure disappeared behind a terrified expression, until her natural need for vengeance reappeared and she scrutinized my father to assess his guilt. He looked away and Mother's face ushered a chill down my spine. Officer Kendall paused, as if allowing us all to revel in his prize capture for the sheer pleasure of making her suffer longer in the humiliation.

Even the kitchen staff froze. Everyone stood silent with mouths agape, only the trickling sounds of the manmade stream were heard. We were all present: Casey, his father Grant, Mary, Gia, Sophia, Joel, Katrina, her boys . . . even my bodyguard Denver Keaton had reappeared. After he'd allowed the police to trot me off to the hospital yesterday, I didn't know how he could show his face. A lot of good he was.

Everyone is here except Garrick.

Mother appeared so small and fragile with a wide-eyed, pathetic blinking, as if to tell us how wrong the officers were. My first instinct was still to rescue her. To pound on Officer Kendall's back and tell him this was all a mistake, that charges had been dropped . . . Mother was innocent. But I didn't. Like the rest, I stood transfixed by the spectacle and let it happen.

Mother wriggled free of the officer's grip and faced my father with her hands tightly clasped behind her back. "Twenty-six years and two beautiful children." She narrowed her icy blue eyes that incited terror in us all. "This is how you treat me? It wasn't bad enough you betrayed me throughout our marriage, you couldn't let it lie. I should have let you marry your high school whore," she spat as she walked toward Mary.

Grant stepped between them. "Don't say anything you'll regret, Chelsea."

"The only thing I regret is that this tramp didn't marry my husband. The agony I could have saved myself if I'd married a man who wasn't an embarrassment in society. I should have known he wasn't really a Wentworth. Rather, a loose street dog in heat the entire time I was married to him."

"Mother." I ran in front of her, but she offered me a look of disgust. She didn't want my pity.

"If you're smart, you'll learn from me. Find a man of noble birth, not a dog who can't stay on his own porch."

With that, Officer Kendall and the other policemen left the house with her being pushed in front of them. We all looked at my father for an explanation, but it was clear he wanted to escape questions like he always did when times got tough.

"You owe us an explanation," I said, surprised by my boldness. "Why'd you bring her here?"

When it was clear that no one was going to let him leave the room, he cleared his throat and started. "The district attorney dropped the charges to take her off her guard. They didn't know if they could prove first-degree murder beyond a reasonable doubt with her legal team. They wanted a confession."

"It still doesn't answer why you brought her here," Quinn said.

"They let her go and gave her enough rope to hang herself." Dad went toward the cowhide sofa. He dropped his head in his hands.

"You got a confession out of her?" I kneeled under him on the floor.

"I did. The police had the private plane bugged. The pilot was an undercover officer." He rubbed his head roughly. "Why did she make me do that? Why didn't she just tell the truth?"

"The truth made her look bad," I told him. "The brain tumor?"

"Another lie," my dad said sadly.

"She really confessed?"

"She said she did what needed to be done and threatened . . . well, never mind," Dad said. "You should know that your grandmother has been arrested too."

"Mona?" Quinn exclaimed. Since she was our only living grandmother, there wasn't really a need for the question.

"Mona took out a rather large insurance policy on my father. She claimed they were entitled to it. This was nearly a decade ago. I guess they got tired of waiting for my father to go. They didn't need that money. I'm still on the board of directors of Wentworth Industries. Mona and your mother were the sole beneficiaries."

"I'm sorry, Dad."

"The love of money. The root of all evil," Mary said. "How much money does any one person need?"

Dad looked up at Mary in regret. Tears filled his eyes as he stared at her. A lifetime seemed to pass in front of him. "If only I'd known how you loved me back then. I was a fool, but be sure of this, Mary, you were lucky to have escaped me."

Mary came toward him and took his hand. "You were a good man when I fell in love with you, and I believe you'll be that man again. Turning Chelsea in was a good first step. It couldn't have been easy."

He rose and drew her into an embrace. "I never deserved your forgiveness."

"You have it regardless. Things are just as they should be." She walked back to Grant's arms and the two of them went to the dining room toward the breakfast buffet.

My father looked broken, but it remained to be seen who he'd be without my mother. Only time would tell. Quinn sat down alongside him and consoled him.

Katrina came toward me with oversized Denver Keaton. "Brinn, I guess this is goodbye. I owe you more than I can say."

"You owe me nothing, Katrina. Your strength inspired me to stand up to my mother. Do you have to leave? We've only just started vacation."

"My lawyers stood up for me in court yesterday to get a restraining order. Garrick testified in a statement."

"Good," I sighed.

She shook her head. "The judge denied it. He said that Matt had only hurt himself. He hadn't proven to be a threat to the children and me."

I felt sick. The wheels of justice often turned so slowly, they failed to help victims.

"We're going on the run until the trial. Deacon is coming with us, and my lawyers will be able to reach me if you need anything." She leaned in and we clung to each other like we'd never see each other again. *How I pray we will.*

"Please be careful, Katrina."

"I wish there was another way."

I nodded. "Me too."

"Garrick thinks Matt is too dangerous at this point. His political career is over, his mistress has left him, and he won't ever blame himself. The mess he's made of his life will be my fault in his head."

"He'll use your running away against you."

She nodded. "He will. He'll say I kidnapped his kids and he'll convince plenty of people he's the real victim. But he won't get the chance to hurt us thanks to your help."

"Whatever you need. I'll make sure you get it. Just ask."

She shook her head. "We're on our own now. This escape is illegal, and I won't have you or Garrick involved. I've squirreled away enough for now, but I will always love you for being there."

I clutched her again tightly. "Please let me know when you're back."

"You know I will." Katrina's boys hurled themselves down the stair rail and landed with two thumps on the stone floors. "Let's go, kids. Grab your suitcases by the door."

The boys did as they were told for once and filed out behind Denver. The house became eerily quiet again.

"Has anyone seen Garrick?" I asked, my voice echoing throughout the living room/kitchen.

"In all the excitement, I forgot," Casey said from the dining table. "He's here. He wanted you to meet him down at the beach landing. There's a tram outside that door." He pointed to a glass door by the studio staircase.

Relief flooded my system. In my haste, I couldn't take the time to change, so in my pale pink leotard and tights, I climbed into the tiny glass gondola that reminded me of Willy Wonka and pressed the "down" button. Periwinkle-blue tracks angled sharply downward over the granite cliffs, leading the way toward the water. I fogged up the glass, hyperventilating until the ride finished with a harsh jolt and the glass door opened to a small concrete deck at the lake.

Garrick greeted me in a forest-green flannel and a pair of dark-washed jeans. He wore a five o'clock shadow and blended in so well as a mountain man, it almost made me forget how incredible he looked in a tuxedo on opening night.

"I worried I wouldn't see you for a while."

"I drove four hours to see you." He took my hands.

"You had to send Katrina away."

He nodded. "Illegally. I had to trust my gut. This is the part of the charity you need to keep away from. I have no doubt Matt will litigate if he finds out that I'm involved."

"She has enough money to keep her and the kids safely hidden, so I'll stay out of it for now." I stretched my arms back to take in his tall frame. "I like this rugged frontier look." I used my most seductive tone. Which wasn't saying much. "Is there a tree you need to chop down or do you have time to talk?"

He rubbed the back of his neck. "Not you, dressed as a ballerina, making fun of my outdoor-appropriate clothes. You must be freezing."

"I didn't want to give you the chance to leave."

"I'm not complaining about the view, mind you. Why you choose to hide this incredible figure, I'll never understand."

"I don't hide it. My mom just taught me how to cover up my flaws."

Garrick let go of my hands and circled me. "I'm missing any so-called flaws."

I placed my hands over my bum. "Garrick!"

"The flaw was in your mother's eyesight." He put his hand on the cart door. "It's cold out here. Let's go back to the house."

"No," I said, shutting the door, which caused the tram to hike itself back up the long, steep track. "My lumberjack already has the fire pit going. Let's sit down. I don't want to share you with anyone."

"It's not like I rubbed two sticks together," he laughed. "I flipped that switch over there and that fire started right up."

"Please, can we stay down here? It's chaos up there and I want to explain what I said in the studio."

"You don't owe me any explanation, Brinn."

"When I said that I only kissed you to protect Katrina—"

"You *did* kiss me to protect Katrina."

"Maybe I did, but that was only because I hadn't kissed you before. Now that I know what I was missing, I want to kiss you every minute of every day."

He chuckled and led me to the fire pit. I sat in an Adirondack and Garrick laid his jacket over my legs. He leaned in and kissed me softly on the lips. "Your mother is right about me though. I'm not marriage material. I am trash."

"We've already ascertained that neither one of us is marriage material. Besides, I'm not holding you to that fake proposal, if that's what you're worried about. I just want to be with you."

"I'm a man of my word, Brinn. When I say something, I mean it. But you deserve so much more. A genuine proposal with a diamond the size of that huge crystal in the living room upstairs. You deserve a man who isn't broken and can love you without trepidation."

My stomach twisted. "You heard that? Garrick, I'm sorry. My mother is no one to call anyone names."

"It's not the first time I've heard it and I'm sure it won't be the last. Most mothers wouldn't allow their kids to play with me. People are weird about it when your father shoots your mother. Go figure," he laughed.

"Or when your mother poisons your grandfather." We smiled at the absurdity of our connection.

"I came to the Gala that night at the request of Joel. He was worried your mother would show up and intimidate Sophia. He asked me there as backup so Sophia wouldn't be intimidated in case Chelsea snuck in." He stared down at his boots briefly, then met my eyes. "Then I saw you on the other side of that door and I knew I had to see you again. Imagine my shock when Sophia brought you into my office. It was a sign."

It is a sign.

My body started to shiver. This sign felt bigger than the ED billboard across from Mary's terrace. Garrick had known my mother was bad before I'd ever stepped foot in his office. No wonder he'd been cautious about me. His apparent rejection had nothing to do with me. How many times had I put my mother's lens over people's actions?

I looked up and my breath caught at the view and a new world appeared for me. "Look at the sun coming up over the lake. Those petite turquoise waves lapping against the granite." I paused to take it all in and marveled at the wonders around me. "The beauty all around us is sheer perfection. This is why I left for Southern California."

Garrick's brow furrowed. "Lake Tahoe is in *Northern California*. Well, actually, we're not even in California. We're on the Nevada side."

I laughed. "Thanks for the geography lesson. I meant

metaphorically; the beauty is all around us. But I didn't need to go to LA to find it."

"Metaphorically? Big word. Did I mention I'm in security?"

"I went down south to get away from people that seemed annoyed by my presence. I wanted to be around people who were nice to me. People who didn't care what was in my bank account or what kind of handbag I carried. I found friends who enjoyed being with me because I was a good time. I needed to figure out what I wanted."

"Are you a good time?" He nudged me with his shoulder.

"Apparently not as good of a time as you," I teased.

"Don't believe everything you read, Brinn Wentworth. You should know that better than anyone. Besides, being a *bro* helps my cover with the charity."

"A *bro*? What are you, sixteen?"

"When I'm with you, I am. I get butterflies in my stomach like I did when I first saw Shari Henderson in sixth grade."

"What happened to this great first love of yours?"

"She broke my heart. She asked Dean Williams to the Sadie Hawkins dance." He shook his head with the memory. "Right in front of me, too. Cold-hearted, that Shari."

"The harlot! How dare she!"

Our gaze intensified and he turned toward the water again. "I'm sorry you were your mother's target. You don't deserve that. No one deserves that."

I sighed. "Quinn had it as bad as I did, I just didn't realize it. Being the favorite, Mother had higher expectations for her."

"That's one good thing about being the son of the criminally insane. Expectations are extremely low."

I squeezed his hand tightly. "While I was in Santa Monica, I hung out with tattooed artist types. Musicians who do it for the love of the art, that kind of crowd. I'm sure they had no idea what Chanel is."

"I can't really picture you banging out a beat at a poetry reading."

"That never happened, I can promise you. After a while, it became as empty as San Francisco. When I was forced back, I knew my grandfather did right by me bringing me home."

"Your grandpa did right by me, anyway. I can't imagine not having met you."

I leaned my head on his shoulder. "I always saw Wentworth Manor as such a dark place, but it turns out, I was always surrounded by love and family. Even there. I just chose to focus on the people who made me work for it."

"I promise never to make you work for it." He looked deeply into my eyes while he took both of my hands. "There's no pressure, Brinn. We can take as long as we need to work up to an engagement, but I'm here. I'm not going anywhere unless you ask me to."

I ran my hand down his jaw taking in his sincerity. I couldn't imagine asking Garrick to go somewhere, but I had run before.

He stood up and put his hand out to help me up. I took it and felt that familiar spark as I pressed up against him. He made my heart quicken at the mere sight of him. Garrick would always be the dangerous kind of attraction; the kind that forced me to walk toward him no matter how risky it felt.

"I know you're not the marrying type," I reminded him.

"And I know marriages are cursed in your family," he repeated my words. "It sounds like we're both going to have to roll the dice to make this work."

"I can't think of anyone I'd rather gamble my life with."

As we were about to seal our future with a kiss, the gondola returned to the landing and my father emerged from the glass capsule. Garrick and I quickly separated.

"Brinn." My father came toward me and wrapped me in the tightest hug I'd ever received from him. My body instinctively became rigid, but he held on until it became stifling.

"Thanks for getting the truth out of her, Dad," I said into his shoulder before I pulled away from him. "I know it wasn't easy."

He sniffled while he nodded. I hadn't been that close to my father in ages. I noticed his skin puckered near his ears where his facelift hadn't quite healed properly. I recognized that from the women in my life. Once again, I vowed to age gracefully.

"You weren't upstairs with the rest of the girls. I thought you should know that I've dropped the lawsuit against my father's will."

"Truly?"

He gave one curt nod and for me, erased his hug. "I'm sorry I put you all through that nonsense. Your mother and my lawyers talked me into it." He turned to Garrick. "I'm very susceptible to suggestion."

"I think that may run in your family." Garrick smiled down at me, and my heart fluttered at the warmth that swelled within me.

"This man saved my life," Dad said, as he slapped Garrick on the back. "He recognized the telltale signs of arsenic poisoning when the doctors didn't."

"You did that?" I asked Garrick, who shrugged as an answer.

"He did. In return, when he came to Napa, he asked that I leave you girls alone. I dropped the lawsuit the next day."

"I'm glad, Daddy. Now you can get to know your daughters. All of them."

"I look forward to that. Garrick here, along with your sister's boyfriend Joel, are going to help me find my real father."

"You are?"

Garrick nodded. And I wondered if I'd ever know all this man did for others.

"Who knows? Maybe we'll inherit more from that guy." My dad genuinely laughed. I couldn't remember the last time I'd heard that sound. "I'm going up to the house now. Casey's going to play me in a round of pool."

"You spoke to Grant?" I asked tentatively since he'd embarrassed himself following Mary all around the gala.

He stared out across the lake. "I saw him. Some part of me will always love Mary. I'll always love your mother and on a different scale, Alisa's mother."

"Jennifer," I said.

"Right, Jennifer. That's it. I think it's time for a fresh start."

I hope that doesn't mean a new twenty-year-old stepmother.

My father closed himself in the gondola and left us alone.

Together Garrick and I pondered the future over the gentle waves below us. I smiled at the irony that brought us together. The rage and anger we witnessed as children now moved us toward a life of love. What was meant for evil, God used for good. Maybe the entire world viewed Garrick and me as broken vessels, but the view from above was different. The view from above took what was meant for evil and turned it into good.

ABOUT THE AUTHOR

Kristin Billerbeck is a bestselling, award-winning author of over forty published novels. Her work has been featured in The New York Times and on "The Today Show." When not writing, she enjoys good handbags, bad reality television and annoying her adult children on social media.

Visit her at:
www.KristinBillerbeck.com

ALSO BY KRISTIN BILLERBECK

Kristin Billerbeck Author Page

Swimming to the Surface

PACIFIC AVENUE SERIES

Room at the Top

The View from Above

ASHLEY STOCKINGDALE SERIES

What a Girl Wants

She's Out of Control

With this Ring, I'm Confused

What a Girl Needs

SPA GIRLS SERIES

She's All That

A Girl's Best Friend

Calm, Cool & Adjusted

STAND-ALONE TITLES

A Billion Reasons Why

The Scent of Rain

Split Ends

The Theory of Happily Ever After

CPSIA information can be obtained
at www.ICGtesting.com
Printed in the USA
LVHW021549070922
727709LV00003B/270